"Quite the Little Philosopher, Aren't You?"

he said derisively. "You dragged out your soapbox and let go with all the 'intelligent woman' clichés you could think of. It only proves my point. You're only half a woman—the outside half. The packaging is superb, the brain topnotch, but as for the rest . . . I have my doubts."

She was seething. "The old 'If you love me you'll prove it' line? That's hardly worthy of you, Sloan. Talk about being full of colossal ego . . . You certainly can't be beaten."

He moved in on her, gathering her to him. His breath was warm against her skin, his lips soft, demanding in their expertise. She lost all logic in her whirling response.

OLIVIA FERRELL

has always wanted to be a writer. While raising a family and working she began her first novel, *Love Has Its Reasons*, which we now proudly present to you.

Dear Reader,

Silhouette Special Editions are an exciting new line of contemporary romances from Silhouette Books. Special Editions are written specifically for our readers who want a story with heightened romantic tension.

Special Editions have all the elements you've enjoyed in Silhouette Romances and *more*. These stories concentrate on romance in a longer, more realistic and sophisticated way, and they feature greater sensual detail.

I hope you enjoy this book and all the wonderful romances from Silhouette. We welcome any suggestions or comments and invite you to write to us at the address below.

Karen Solem
Editor-in-Chief
Silhouette Books
P.O. Box 769
New York, N. Y. 10019

OLIVIA FERRELL
Love Has Its Reasons

Silhouette Special Edition
Published by Silhouette Books New York
America's Publisher of Contemporary Romance

SILHOUETTE BOOKS, a Simon & Schuster Division of
GULF & WESTERN CORPORATION
1230 Avenue of the Americas, New York, N.Y. 10020

ISBN: 0-671-53548-X

First Silhouette Books printing September, 1982

10 9 8 7 6 5 4 3 2 1

Map by Tony Ferrara

*To B. and J. D. for all their
help and encouragement, and
Tom, who dreamed*

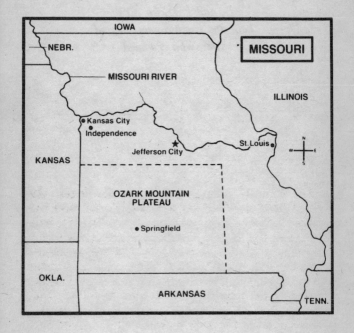

Chapter One

$\mathcal{T}$he normally composed Cara was not herself. An errant alarm clock and too many long days at work had caused her to oversleep, and now she was forced to rush more than she liked to arrive at the Complex on time.

Hurrying down the back stairs of her apartment building, Cara mentally ticked off the tasks awaiting her at the office. When she reached the tenant garages, she hurriedly slid into her small Triumph, then saw with dismay that the gas gauge registered nearly empty. Arriving home late after another of the dawn-to-dusk days since Mr. Quinn's departure, she had failed to notice.

"Darn," she muttered under her breath. That meant another delay.

Resigned now to arriving late, she shot confidently out into the stream of traffic on the two-lane highway, skillfully merging with the fast-moving commuters.

The young woman in the small red Triumph had

become a familiar and arresting sight as she flashed along the suburban avenues of Springfield each day. She often drew second glances from her fellow commuters as she traversed the residential areas into the heavy traffic of the industrial section on her way to the Triad complex, where she was executive assistant to the President.

For Cara Lang, normally very conservative in nature, the purchase of the bright red sports car had been an extravagance, and an atypical choice for her, but she loved driving it. She rarely noticed the impact the bright red of the auto, which contrasted so sharply with her flashing dark looks, made on the men she passed. The blue-black shine of her shoulder-length hair was in itself unusual enough, but Cara also possessed a creamy ivory complexion to complement it. Her large black eyes, which could flash a signal of anger or glint with impish humor, were fringed with naturally long black lashes that gave her a perpetual look of wide-eyed innocence, belying the intense purposefulness of her nature.

At this hour Cara should have been more than halfway to Triad Industries. Her office, in a modern marvel of concrete and steel, was part of a complex of several buildings housing the various businesses under its corporate umbrella.

Triad Industries, a medium-sized electronics manufacturing firm, had been the brainchild of a man in his middle years who hoped to pass on something of value to his children and grandchildren. That had been before his only son was killed in a boating accident, leaving no family of his own. For several years Mr. Quinn, the President and founder, kept the company thriving, but most people felt that in the last few years the effect of the tragedy and other discouraging circumstances had caused a slow downfall of the company which had begun with such great promise and potential.

Reaching the fringe of the business district, Cara glanced anxiously at her gas gauge as she watched for a station. Naturally, she noted irritably, the nearest one was busy, and while she waited in line, her mind turned back to Triad.

The Complex, as it was called locally, housed some three hundred employees during the hours from eight to five. Most had a long working history there; some had been ready for retirement when the downward trend developed. In its twenty-five-year history Triad had suffered the usual pangs of rapid growth—the lulls between spurts of economic good fortune, and the leveling-off periods that naturally occur in business. But more recently Triad had entered a long period of stagnation and had seemed destined for dissolution.

Then rescue had come. Rescue in the guise of an offer from a large conglomerate to include Triad among its possessions. At least, Cara had mused, considering the possibilities, Triad would provide an immediate tax write-off for the corporation. And Cara was in a position to know.

Independent and bright, Cara had not risen to executive assistant to the President by luck alone. She had applied for the position of typist upon graduation from business school. Her climb through the ranks from clerk-typist to secretarial pool to her current status had come as the result of hard work and natural skill. And she was proud of that fact, though well aware of the "sugar daddy" label with which her relationship to the head of Triad, Mr. Quinn, had been tagged.

Since Mr. Quinn was more than forty years older than she was, she supposed the gossip was inevitable, though no less disturbing. She also understood that petty jealousy accounted for a lot of the talk. As a way of countering it, she had striven to overachieve, while playing down her flashing good looks and keeping to herself a great deal.

True, she and Mr. Quinn had always been close, but only as friends and coworkers. Cara had valued that friendship, regardless of the gossip. Her naturally independent nature could allow the meanness of such envy to flow over her, ignored as an exhibition of ignorance and insensitivity. As a result, people attributed to her a certain haughtiness, which she admitted was probably deserved.

With the gas tank filled, she headed toward the Complex, forcing her mind to the day ahead and away from its inauspicious beginning.

As she negotiated the thinning traffic, Cara's mind began to wander back to all the trouble that Triad had just been through and the resulting takeover. In retrospect, Cara realized that the move and the subsequent publicity had generated some desperately needed new business for the firm, allowing most of the employees to return to work on a part-time basis that would soon become full-time once again.

Looking at the arrangement from a strictly economic point of view, Cara realized that the economy of Springfield had received a real boost when the news was released that Sloan Montgomery himself planned to personally supervise Triad and get it back on its financial feet. The name Montgomery Industries alone had been magic, but the man himself was an added bonus.

Sloan Montgomery's record of financial wizardry was unparalleled. An added plus, at least in some quarters, was his immense masculine appeal, which the society sections of the newspapers discussed endlessly, making him an instant celebrity in the city, as well as in the corporation itself.

Many a feminine heart had fluttered in anticipation of

this new personality entering the social picture, not to speak of the local financiers, who were lining up to pick his brain to determine how he had attained his considerable financial success in so short a time. But all this advance publicity did little to impress Cara. In fact, she cared very little about the man and was only concerned that her job was secure.

Cara felt that her position had always been generally safe unless, of course, the plant closed completely. Though she had only met Sloan Montgomery briefly, when his advisors accomplished the actual takeover, she was aware that he rarely stayed with a company he acquired longer than it took to get it running in a financially secure and efficient manner. That is, when he involved himself at all. Unless the company challenged him in some way, he generally sent one of his many underlings.

Though uncertain of Sloan Montgomery's method of operation, Cara remained fairly secure because, with Mr. Quinn retired and enjoying a much needed vacation abroad, she was the only person with full knowledge of the company's various aspects. As a result, she felt certain that Montgomery couldn't afford to replace her with one of his own men until Triad was operating efficiently again. The thought of a demotion left her cold and she refused to consider it.

She smiled confidently to herself as she drove. Nothing very important would change. Her position was secure, she was certain. And security was very important to her.

After reaching the Complex and whipping into her marked parking space, Cara hurried through the upper floors to her office. As usual, her desk was overloaded with correspondence, status reports and month-end balance sheets. She set to work immediately to clear her desk before going to the Accounting Department, where she had been lending a hand the last couple of days. With a smaller staff and no functioning President, she had pitched in where help was needed.

A quick cup of coffee at her desk while she double-checked figures did nothing to fill the empty space left by a minuscule breakfast of a slice of toast. By the time noon approached, Cara had completed the major portion of her work and was more than ready for lunch.

The employee lunchroom was not her usual choice for a noon break, but with the heavy workload of the past months eating there had become a habit. Today Cara welcomed the sterile atmosphere as she moved down the line, choosing the various dishes that appealed to her. Glancing around the large room as she paid her bill, she was pleased to see a vacant table for two near the wall. Only one large table, marked with a reserved sign, stood nearby.

As she set out her dishes and sat down, she became aware of a commotion among the diners when a small group of men entered the hall. She recognized the tall man in the center as the new owner of Triad and supposed that those with him were his attorneys and advisors. She knew that they had been scheduled to tour the Complex, though she had not been invited to join them, a fact which she mildly resented since she was, at least officially, the man's assistant. He seemed to insist on doing everything his own way, in his own time, leaving her in the dark. It was a practice she hoped would not continue now that his office would be moved to Triad from wherever he had last conducted his many corporate interests.

Sloan Montgomery was a man unto himself. He made headlines no matter what he did, or where he did it, caring little for public opinion. Quite a man for the ladies, as well as for the dollar, was the general consensus, and many a heart had been broken when he failed to follow through to the altar. Cara found herself wondering if it had been an urge to escape from some such situation that had now brought him to Triad.

Deep in her own musings, Cara jumped at the low voice near her ear. "The newspaper photos didn't do him justice, did they?"

"Wh . . . Susan! What a start you gave me." Cara gestured somewhat reluctantly to the chair opposite her, for most tables were now filled. "What did you say?"

The statuesque blonde settled into her chair before speaking again. "I said the newspaper photos don't do him justice. The whole group toured our department this morning and he's mighty impressive."

Susan Stafford managed the secretarial pool and she wasn't terribly well liked for her condescending attitude toward the girls under her. Their own relationship had been rocky, especially after Cara had been promoted out of the pool and become, technically, Susan's superior. But Cara never pushed the point and Susan never acknowledged it. Cara smiled ruefully as she replied, "But you're easily impressed, Susan."

Pulling a face, the young woman answered in kind, "Yes, I'll admit I can go for anything that looks good and gives me a good time. But he's the ultra-dominant, ultra-aggressive type I could easily become seriously interested in." Munching her crisp salad, Susan glanced speculatively at Cara, who was intent upon her own plate. "How about you?"

Cara's fork halted in midair. "What about me?"

A slightly smug smile flickered across Susan's face. "Don't play Miss Cool with me. What kind of man do you prefer? Someone you can mold to your specifications like that Larry you've been seeing? Or are the rumors really true? Do you have a father fixation? Mr. Quinn's retirement must have put a crimp in your style. Sloan Montgomery's certainly not what I would consider a father figure."

Cara laughed lightly to cover the anger she felt rising inside her. Susan Stafford was an intelligent, highly motivated woman who fully believed in being a free-thinking, liberated woman of the 80s—in her own interpretation. The two of them had little in common: Susan considered Cara basically old-fashioned in spite of the rumors concerning Mr. Quinn, rumors which she knew quite well were unfounded; Cara, on the other hand, considered that Susan worked overly hard at becoming what she believed a liberated woman should be. It was there that their differences began. Their whole personalities simply clashed.

Because of these differences and the bad feeling on Susan's part about Cara's advancement, their relationship was more a speaking acquaintance than anything else. But Cara could appreciate Susan's complete openness and honesty, if nothing else, and so they were able to maintain a sort of truce.

After several seconds in which she gained control of her temper, Cara answered Susan's question. "Well, first of all, I don't see Larry that way; we have a close friendship, nothing else. As for the rumors concerning Mr. Quinn and myself, you know me well enough to guess my feelings on that point. It's no one's business."

She waited a moment before continuing. "But I certainly don't envisage myself involved with someone as aggressive and domineering as your Mr. Montgomery. I'd feel like braining him half the time, I'm afraid." She sipped her coffee before going on. "No. I prefer someone in between, I think. Assured, but sensitive. A definite personality, but able to bend when necessary."

With a sneer, Susan began to stack her empty dishes. "A dishrag is what you want. Someone to control. Nope, not for me. I want someone strong enough to make me feel like a woman. And I think our new boss is just the man for that."

For some reason Cara let Susan's speech needle her. "Better a dishrag than a piece of sandpaper. I can do without it—and without him."

An amused but speculative look crossed Susan's face, sharpening her well-defined features slightly. "Good, because I can't. And since I felt you would be my only competition, that leaves me a clear field."

In spite of herself, Cara was slightly taken aback. "How do you mean?"

With an almost sly expression Susan stood to leave. "Why, Sloan Montgomery is quite a hunk of man from what I've read and seen today. Besides being the best-looking brute I've ever seen, he's wealthy, unmarried and, I hear, very good in bed. I couldn't ask for a better combination."

Cara realized then that Susan was entirely serious. Though not totally naïve, she had nonetheless been a little dismayed by the obviousness of Susan's general attitude toward the opposite sex, but this was a new aggressiveness.

Smiling slightly to cover her obvious aversion to the topic, Cara stood to gather her dishes. "Then more power to you. I wouldn't get within ten miles of a man who fit those specifications so perfectly. The battle wouldn't be worth the prize."

Shrugging, Susan smiled slightly. "Just as long as we understand each other. Besides, you should feel flattered I even considered you as an opponent. Blondes do have more fun, you know." Susan laughed sharply at her own words. "I noticed him watching you in here yesterday."

She held up a hand to forestall Cara's protest. "No, I know you didn't see him, but from the attention he gave you he certainly might consider trying you out. And you *will* be working together. Curiosity is the key, I've found, and right now Montgomery is curious about you." Smiling smugly at Cara's tight face, Susan stepped away from the table. "But I can handle that. See you."

Cara refused to answer Susan's small salute as she turned away. Inwardly fuming at the audacity of the other woman, Cara turned to pick up her purse, noticing for the first time that the subject of their conversation sat with his group of men at the adjacent table. As she glanced over, one man's eyes caught her look and held it for a moment. Sloan Montgomery himself.

She should have known. Susan had been louder and more baiting than usual. Montgomery's proximity had to be the reason. Cara felt a shiver of apprehension. What if he had heard any, or all, of their conversation? Embarrassment momentarily stained her cheeks, then she squared her shoulders and strode from the room with an attitude of self-assurance bordering on arrogance.

She didn't really feel like attacking the heavy workload waiting for her. But, straightening with determination, she decided that she didn't have time to worry over Sloan Montgomery's bruised ego. Besides, he had probably been too busy with his own conversation to really hear anything. She hoped.

Entering the Accounting area, Cara found one of the clerks toiling over a page of figures in a small office. Though the department didn't offer much space, Cara always enjoyed working there when necessary.

This room, which had once been her own office, was pleasant. The windows faced east, letting the warm yellow walls reflect the morning sun. Several plants graced the long windowsill, and the homey atmosphere softened the tedious toil of endless checks and counter-checks of accounting columns.

At Cara's entrance Kate, the clerk, turned to her with an exaggerated sigh, brushing back an errant brown curl which persisted in falling across her forehead.

"Well, was Montgomery in the cafeteria today? He was yesterday, fraternizing with us lowly slaves." She frowned comically. "You know, I wouldn't mind a little fraternizing with our esteemed leader. He travels in some pretty powerful company." Kate leaned back in her secretarial chair. "I wonder if he's half as sexy as his pictures."

Cara smiled wryly at the dreamy look that settled over Kate's expressive face, and she fed a report into her typewriter. The girl was the romantic sort, but Cara wished she would come up with some other subject as an excuse for a break. They were both tired of the endless figures, the extra burden of work instigated by the takeover, but time was of the essence, too. And no one was more aware of that than Cara.

She carefully lined up the report form in the machine before answering Kate's earlier question, her back still turned to the girl as she concentrated on her task. She was tired of discussing Sloan Montgomery, and the prick of Susan's words was still sharp. As a result, her answer was unnaturally curt.

"Yes, Montgomery was there, with his full contingent. Must be quite an ego trip to have people at your beck and call like that, though I doubt his ego needs feeding. It's probably quite large enough on its own with worshiping millions like yourself and Susan to feed it." She grimly started typing as she continued. "As for myself, I see nothing to be impressed about. Making decisions from a distance leaves a great deal to be desired, and that's his usual style. How we got so lucky as to merit his exalted presence I'll never know. Now, let's get back to work. I've had quite enough of the high and mighty Sloan Montgomery for one day.''

A small smothered gasp from behind drew Cara's attention back to Kate. Swinging around in her chair, she saw with a kind of sick horror what had drawn such a sound from the girl.

The object of their discussion was framed in the open doorway, and behind him was the group of men he had lunched with. Sloan Montgomery's tight, angry face glaring at her over his folded arms and determined stance told her without doubt that he had been there long enough to hear her unfortunately timed comments. She swallowed quickly before attempting to apologize and was stopped when his clipped words broke into her jumbled thoughts.

''Miss Lang, you will accompany me to my office.'' It was a demend, not a request, and the low voice brooked no hesitation on her part. Straightening her shoulders, her legs trembling strangely, she reluctantly rose to follow his tall frame from the room, past the men waiting in the hall.

Everything in Sloan Montgomery's manner evidenced his anger, and a more formidable man Cara had never encountered. He indicated to an associate that the others should continue the tour on their own, his glance carefully avoiding Cara as he turned away again. In that brief moment aware of the strong masculinity and dominant personality of the man, Cara felt a stab of anger that she had allowed even that small response. He was the type of man she decried, yet encountering him, even in this fashion, evoked an unwelcome awareness of him.

Thoughts danced crazily through her mind as she followed the swiftly moving man. How could she explain? She could hardly put the blame on Kate, or Susan, when she was guilty of as flip an answer as could have come from either of them. Whatever the provocation, she should have minded her tongue. But she hadn't, and now she would have to pay the price.

What could he do? He could fire her. He would certainly be within his rights. But still, her record should count for something and he needed her knowledge of Triad. Somehow, though, she was unable to convince herself that fairness would overcome his anger.

If she lost her job, could she find another on the same level? She doubted it. But she might soon be facing that necessity. And without any recommendation from Triad she might well be out on the street with a very grim future.

Suddenly realizing that she must look like an errant child meekly following the principal to his office, Cara straightened her shoulders and took a quick step to catch up with the stiff-backed figure striding down the hall before her. A touch of anger at his attitude arose, but she strove to quell it, knowing that now was not the time for a show of temperament, however justified she might feel it to be.

Her heels tapped sharply as she followed Sloan down the hallway leading from the lower management area to the familiar executive offices. The painted walls gave way to mellow wood paneling, the décor subtly distinguishing the second level executive areas from the higher management offices. It appeared that they were headed toward the President's suite of offices, which surprised her, as Montgomery had yet to officially move in.

Shoving open a heavily carved oak door, Sloan strode through, leaving Cara to hurry after him before it swung shut in her face. Without waiting to see if she had followed, Sloan turned toward a matching door marked with a new brass plate, stamped with his name in Roman type. The print burned into her brain. She didn't like the way the situation was developing. She didn't like it at all.

As she walked, thoughts continued to flick through her mind at a rapid pace and she didn't notice that the taut figure had halted before her. She skidded to a stop, almost colliding with the man glowering down at her.

Automatically, she muttered, "I'm sorry."

His low voice cut across her savagely. "I should think so."

The whole thing was getting more ridiculous by the moment. Anger bubbled over in spite of her resolve. "Now look here . . ."

"No. You look here."

She noticed his angry countenance and stopped, almost gritting her teeth in the effort to keep her true feelings from showing.

The anger in his face altered not one bit. "You seem to make a habit of looking foolish, Miss Lang. I'm disappointed, to say the least." He seemed to consider her more closely for a moment, his forbidding look making her even more uncomfortable and stubbornly angry because of it. "I expected . . . well, shall we say, someone a little more discreet, considering everything I've heard about your excellent *reputation*."

The word was clearly emphasized, intentionally cutting. His narrowed eyes and tight mouth matched the coldness of his voice. The brown eyes were dark with anger beneath his straight brow. Suppressed rage flowed from him in waves and she staggered back a little from the impact of it. She had never seen anyone so overpoweringly and unforgivingly angry.

"Mr. Montgomery," she began, her voice tense.

Again he cut off her attempted explanation. "I wouldn't say anything more if I were you. You've done a rather thorough job of talking too much for one day."

She stepped back again, momentarily overwhelmed by the force of his anger and knowing the situation would only worsen if she attempted to explain. She searched frantically for an escape, a way to gain a respite, however brief. Her only thought was of putting space between this volatile man and herself, to give herself some thinking room.

Her searching hand encountered the office door. Fumbling for the handle, mesmerized by his cold gaze, Cara swallowed convulsively. The situation, the anger, were much more than she had bargained for. She needed time to reevaluate her position, to consider more fully the predicament in which she found herself.

She jumped, cringing involuntarily as his words struck her again, halting her escape attempt. "Hold it. You're not going anywhere until I'm finished with you." He allowed his now insolent gaze to travel insinuatingly down the length of her body. She could feel him assessing her trim figure, the neat, close-fitting one-piece beige dress that showed to advantage her slim waist, flowing out over gently curving hips and up over full, well-shaped breasts. His gaze was almost a touch, and she shivered as if he had stroked her trembling body. She felt undressed, exposed, almost violated, as his look traveled back to her now snappingly angry black eyes.

"You don't like being analyzed either, do you? I didn't find it particularly enjoyable and you had a lot less to go on. I, at least, have information on you from reliable sources, not office gossip."

Her heart sank. She knew there was no escape. The man before her seemed almost amused at the frantic look that must have crossed her face. "You might as well settle down and stop trying to get that door open. I'm not finished with you yet." Then his low, cold voice dropped even lower. "And from the look of the packaging, I may not be finished for a while."

Her face blanched at the implication of his words. "I beg your pardon?"

"I think you should, and you will, but let's get on to other things first. Sit down."

In spite of her resentment, she sank obediently onto the nearby couch. Sloan Montgomery paced the floor before her, his leashed anger still evident.

"Now then, Miss Lang. Since you have assessed my methods of operation as those of an ignorant fool, my personality as somewhat less than acceptable to your high standards, and have expressed a desire to experience as little of my presence as possible, I think my proposition will permit us both to reassess our, shall we say, *first impressions* of one another."

Once more Cara struggled to overcome the grip of tension and break in to explain what he had overheard. But, as before, her attempt was cut short. Speaking very carefully, as if to a slow-thinking child, Sloan's voice overrode her own.

"It is my understanding that I have inherited you as my Executive Assistant. That being the case, you will have ample opportunity to become even more familiar with my methods and possibly upgrade them to meet the standards you require—beginning tomorrow. You will report at eight A.M.; my day begins earlier than Mr. Quinn's and probably will end a little later . . . due to my younger age, I imagine. I'm certain you made allowances for his . . . ah . . . limitations."

She could hardly miss the implication of that last remark and was stung by it. She struggled to listen more carefully to what he was saying, trying to fathom the underlying meaning of his words and not liking what she sensed in them. "You will stay, though, until the work is finished or I say you can leave. You will act as my assistant and private secretary, plus perform any other *duties* I deem necessary, without exception. I believe you're accustomed to that. From what I understand you have always been quite willing to accommodate yourself to the 'needs' of your employer."

Though her face burned, she steadfastly refused to dignify his innuendoes with a retort. She clenched her teeth in utter frustration.

"Your friend Kate will no longer require your assistance as she will have another confidant with whom to share her views of her supervisors." The silence was heavy. "Do I make myself clear, Miss Lang? Or must I go on to explain how difficult it is, even for someone of your caliber, to find a good position with no recommendation?"

The hidden threat cut off any protest she might have made. Cold fear gripped her as the knowledge of her total vulnerability made itself abundantly clear. She was trapped. Sloan was exerting a type of blackmail and doing it very effectively. Either she must take the position as outlined, with all its implications, or there was no job at all for her here. But even as she realized what was happening, she understood nothing of the reasoning behind it.

The rough voice broke into her consciousness again. "You will spend tomorrow becoming acquainted with the methods you so loudly decry." Did she imagine the pregnant pause or was she oversensitive? He had alluded several times to things that she could only interpret as connected with the rumors centering around herself and Mr. Quinn, another misunderstanding she would need to clear up immediately. ''From then on, I expect you to be ready to carry out any responsibility with the expertise I demand. And I demand the best.'' Again the significant pause. ''One can always be replaced, can't one?'' The sarcasm was heavy. ''Am I making myself clear?''

His abrasive manner taunted her. She would have liked to scream at him, throw his words back into his face. Instead, her response was reduced to a stiff nod.

During his speech she had refused to face him, preferring instead to concentrate on words rather than the speaker. Unconsciously, she had clenched her hands so tightly that the knuckles were white, her nails making deep half-moons in her palms. If he noticed the extreme to which she went to avoid revealing any reaction to his cutting remarks, he did not reveal it.

His voice was tight when he spoke again. ''Come on. I'm taking you home.''

The prospect of spending more time in his presence startled her out of her numbed state. Her voice was soft but intense. ''No. I'd rather you didn't bother. The afternoon isn't over. . . .'' Cara rose then, forcing her leaden legs to move.

When Sloan moved to stand directly before her, she steeled herself against stepping away. Unable to avoid looking at him, she centered her eyes on his lapel while struggling to quiet the erratic beat of her heart, which was racing at his closeness.

Now his voice was caressing in its suggestiveness. ''No. The afternoon isn't over . . .''

She was mesmerized by the slow movement of his hand rising, by the strength in his long fingers. Tantalized, she swallowed as he seemed to come closer without really moving. She stood as those fingers slid across the collar of her dress, the dryness of her mouth causing her to swallow convulsively.

She trembled as those same fingers lowered to brush lightly across the swell of her breast. She knew he was watching her reactions.

". . . And we could fill it very satisfactorily."

His hand curved against the softness of her breast with an arrogant possessiveness she hated, drawing a smothered gasp from her as she stepped back from him.

"No!" She felt strangled by her own breath even as her body responded involuntarily to the sensual movement of his hand against her. He didn't understand; it was all due to those stupid rumors about her and Mr. Quinn. Could he actually have thought this was what she wanted?

His voice was barely above a whisper, caressing her senses as his hand lay against her. "No?"

She could only shake her head again, still avoiding his gaze. A long silence stretched between them.

"Come on. I'm still taking you home. Tomorrow will be time enough for us to get to know each other."

Recognizing the steel in his words and ignoring the implied meaning of them, Cara acceded.

With no recollection of how she had gotten there, she found herself beside Sloan and approaching a low gray Jaguar parked in his reserved parking space. As he helped her slide into the soft, black leather bucket seat, his touch seemed gentler then she would ever have imagined it could be.

The door closed with a firm click and she stared straight ahead as he rounded the car to his own seat. She felt his gaze slip over her set features briefly before he brought the powerful engine to life. Its low throbbing matched the beat of her heart, somehow personifying the power of the man beside her.

Without a word he drove from the lot and joined the mid-afternoon traffic, apparently in no doubt as to the direction to take. She supposed his research into her life had given him her address. With a slow sigh Cara laid her aching head against the cushioned seat back. She allowed her mind to drift as the man beside her deftly maneuvered the car through traffic without hesitation.

No words were spoken and none were necessary. Cara was as drained of emotion and strength as if they had spent the past hour in a battle of actual physical strength and passion.

Half an hour later Sloan pulled up before the older brick apartment house she had lived in for the past year. Before Cara could move, Sloan was out of the car and had opened her door, extending his hand commandingly. Uncertainly, she surrendered her cold hand to his as he pulled her from the car. Somehow it was indicative of surrender to his power over her and she felt uncomfortable.

She avoided looking at him as she walked stiffly by his side. His hand at her elbow guided her through the apartment entryway and up the single flight of stairs to her door. When she found her key, he forestalled her, taking it and fitting it into the lock in a single practiced move. Stepping through ahead of her, he looked around with a curious eye while he waited for her to follow.

"I'm leaving now, Miss Lang. Just remember what I said. I'll see you tomorrow."

The comment sounded like a threat and she glanced at him involuntarily to find a studying look in his face. How could she forget anything about today?

With a fluid grace unusual for such a large man, Sloan crossed the room. Without further comment he slipped the lock and carefully closed the door behind him, leaving Cara alone to cope with her confused feelings and dread the coming days.

Chapter Two

*C*ara awoke with a feeling of uncertainty, as if from a nightmare. For a moment she couldn't determine the reason for her tenseness, until the traumatic events of the previous day came back to her.

The evening had not been much better than the rest of the day. She had alternately felt ill with apprehension, then dominated by an angry determination. It had been very late when she fell at last into a fitful sleep.

Glancing at her watch, Cara saw that she had a little over an hour before leaving for the Complex. She would have to hurry; she would need to call a cab, since her car was still in the Complex lot. She held back the thought that she would have to deal with Sloan Montgomery again today.

As she ran a hot shower, Cara's mind recaptured the Sloan Montgomery she had met. True, she shouldn't have said those things, but they were nothing more than her own opinion or a repeat of what the newspapers had printed time and time again. Yet she could understand his being angered by them. What the newspaper printed was one thing—hearing it from an employee was another.

Still, the extent of that anger baffled her and kept recalling the episode to her thoughts. A man powerful enough to transform a small family company into a far-reaching conglomerate by the time he was thirty-six was no one to be toyed with. Nevertheless, his anger had gone beyond normal bounds. The sexually sarcastic comments had been designed to hurt, to humiliate, to cheapen. Yet there had been so little to say in her own defense, even if she'd been given the opportunity.

She felt Sloan's retribution had exceeded what was called for, even if his ego was wounded. And besides, she somehow doubted that it really had been. Cara felt Sloan was too self-assured to let a mere employee harm any part of his enormous ego.

From everything she had heard about him, Sloan Montgomery was a man accustomed to having his own way. Yet there was nothing in him to indicate pomposity, the false self-importance that was so often seen in men of his stature in the business community. Opinion was that though he could command people to do his bidding by the sheer power of his position, his people worked hard for him because they genuinely wanted to win his approval. He had the reputation of being uncompromising, a man of discipline, a loner whose liaisons with women were short-lived, but other things were evident, too. He instigated loyalty in his people and they rarely left his organization. He had the knack of making his people feel like a necessary part of the whole corporate picture. None of this indicated a man unable to control his emotional reactions or one who ruled like the tyrant he had seemed to Cara.

Sloan Montgomery was a man of contradictions, then,

an extremely complex man. A man who somehow intrigued her despite her resentment of his actions.

Reaching the end of that train of thought, she abruptly turned off the shower and stepped out into the steamy room to wrap a soft towel around her slim form. Briskly drying herself, she considered her subtly altered position in the company. Certain that Sloan had intended to keep to his plan of having her go on working for him—on his terms—she was still unsure whether it was as a kind of punishment or for some other obscure reason of his own. Somehow she didn't see him as a vindictive person, but neither could she see him making such a decision for strictly personal reasons. His work was too important, the company in too precarious a position financially for him to indulge in such games.

Crossing finally to the long closet at one end of her bedroom, Cara turned her mind to more immediate problems. From the clothing she reserved for office wear she carefully chose a tailored black knit suit. She dressed methodically, working hard to achieve the appearance of confidence. Right now she needed all the confidence she could get.

Her creamy white lingerie nearly matched her smooth skin, which was much paler than her Greek heritage should have dictated. Her flawless complexion, wide black eyes, shining dark hair and flashing smile made her a standout in any crowd. Her attractive appearance afforded her numerous opportunities for dates, though she studiously avoided any lengthy or serious attachments.

In recent months Larry Compton had been her steady companion, but neither of them had ever considered a permanent relationship. Cara enjoyed her free life, at least so far. Now, though, she had questions as to whether she still had control over her life. Sloan Montgomery confused her, left her doubting everything she had once believed about herself. And he certainly was a man accustomed to being in total control of all around him, companies and people.

Slipping into the straight black skirt and a soft off-white blouse trimmed with delicate lace at the collar, Cara picked up the suit jacket as she left the bedroom, dropping it over the couch on her way to the kitchen. She still had mixed feelings about reporting for work, but felt certain Sloan would not allow her to get away with staying home. He would see it as a personal affront and take it out on her accordingly. But neither did she like the idea of submitting to his dominance, as he seemed to expect. A streak of perverse independence kept rearing its head, though realistically she knew she could not allow it to control her actions. Maybe the answer was to compromise, to take each day as it came and cope as best she could.

She gulped a quick glass of orange juice, then returned to the bedroom to finish dressing. Her makeup for the office was simple. A brush of blusher across her high cheekbones, a touch of shadow to bring out the depth of her eyes. A swirl of mascara on her already thick lashes finished her regimen. Running a brush through her heavy shoulder-length hair, she again studied the reflection of her small but distinctive features critically.

The oval of her face was broken by high cheekbones and overshadowed by her large eyes, now faintly smudged with fatigue from her restless night. In her opinion her wide full-lipped mouth was too large for her face, but others considered it sensuous.

Her hair fell smoothly from a middle part to turn under just above her shoulders. Classic, though out of style with the current fashion for curly hair, it suited her and she was astute enough to know what worked well for her in the fashion department. For this reason she stayed away from fads, choosing instead the tailored, always-in-style clothing that suited her best.

Because of her natural reluctance to draw attention to herself, she chose her office outfits to indicate the efficiency she prided herself on. Attractively feminine but subdued styles reflected her attitude, enabling her to feel confident in her appearance and ability. To her mind, one personified the other. Until now, she amended, as she straightened. Until Sloan Montgomery had burst into her life.

With a somewhat unsteady hand Cara smoothed the last hair into place before returning to the kitchen for a quick breakfast. She knew she should call a cab, but she was deliberately delaying.

She jumped when the doorbell chimed. Moving quickly to the door, she unconsciously smoothed back the wings of hair framing her pale face.

She swung the door open and froze when she saw the tall figure lounging against the door frame. His gaze traveled slowly down the full length of her five-foot-six frame and back again. His look made her self-conscious about her slit skirt, which opened in front to give a glimpse of her shapely legs as she walked. She waged a silent war with herself to fight down the mixture of anger and apprehension caused by his sudden appearance.

"What are you doing here!" It was more an exclamation than a question.

Unperturbed by her agitation, Sloan straightened and stepped past her into the room. "Making certain you report to duty." Turning, he intimidated her by his mere presence. "I imagined you might have some second thoughts about it."

Her mouth firmed. She hated to admit that he had been correct in his assumption, but she had contemplated not showing up for work and she felt uncomfortable that he had anticipated that. Her nerves quivered as she again experienced a touch of the total dominance he had exerted over her the previous day.

He stood over her, carrying his height easily. The powerful shoulders tapering to a trim waist and the long-muscled legs spoke of an athlete instead of a desk-bound executive. From his deep tan she judged that he was an outdoor person whenever possible, though she doubted he had much time for recreation. Not of the outdoor variety, she amended wryly, remembering the newspaper accounts of his various and varied female conquests.

Continuing her own assessment of him, she noted crisp brown hair left fairly long and brushed back from a wide brow to frame his strong face. Thick and full, it curled under slightly to just brush the collar of his tan silk shirt. Her eyes shifted and she took in well-shaped brows over deep brown eyes that could turn hard and appraising, as she had already experienced; a straight, autocratic nose, firm mouth and square, determined jaw completed the picture of a man accustomed to leadership and decision. He wore his tobacco-brown suit in a manner that said he accepted as his due the expensive cloth and cut. The way it molded his muscular frame gave ample evidence of his blatant masculinity. The shade of his clothing complemented his coloring and his confident attitude said without words that he knew it, but was not really impressed with the picture he presented. She liked that in him and grudgingly admitted that he was perhaps the most attractive and compelling man she had ever met.

"Well?" His low voice broke into her contemplation of him. At the same time he recognized and accepted her appraisal, while dismissing it with a sudden tightening of his mouth. Glancing at the wide gold watch encircling his thick wrist, he gestured toward her jacket, which was lying across the couch. "Shall we go? There are several things I want to cover on the way to the Complex."

Mentally shaking herself, she straightened her shoulders. "Nearly. One more moment."

"That's about all you have. I have a meeting scheduled for eight-thirty and I won't be late." With that, he crossed his arms before him as if challenging her to exceed his time limit, ignoring the flash of anger in her dark eyes.

Compressing her lips, Cara moved past him to stack the few dishes in the sink, then hurried, without seeming to, to the bathroom to brush her teeth. Though aware of his impatience, she was determined not to be forced into scurrying around like a frightened schoolgirl again. Once had been sufficiently humiliating.

In a few minutes she slipped on her jacket, ignoring his offer of help, picked up her purse and, without a word, stepped out into the hall.

As they left the building, her nerves tightened again on seeing his car at the curb. The gray Jaguar seemed as menacing as the man following close behind her. It seemed to crouch beside the curb, waiting to take her in and carry her off at his will. She blinked hard to rid herself of the absurd thought, but still the image persisted.

After shutting the passenger door firmly, Sloan moved around the car in long strides to slide in beside her. His size brought him too close for comfort in the confines of the sleek Jaguar. She could smell the scent of his woodsy cologne and experience once more his total masculinity assailing her senses. She didn't want to be so aware of him. He made her feel vulnerable and young and she didn't like that feeling.

As he reached for the ignition, his arm brushed against her knee. She moved quickly away and heard his muffled exclamation as the engine roared to life. After deftly swinging the low-slung car away from the curb, he remained silent for several blocks. Carefully ignoring him, Cara watched the buildings they passed with feigned interest.

Lost in her thoughts, Cara sighed softly. As tense as she felt right now, she wanted this drive to go on forever, because she dreaded what would happen when they reached the Complex.

Sloan's rough voice broke into her reverie. "Cara—is that short for anything?"

The suddenness of his words startled her. It was the first time he had spoken her first name, and somehow the way he said it seemed almost a caress, despite the natural roughness of his voice.

Keeping her face averted, she answered. "I'm surprised you don't know. You have my employment folder, haven't you?" Her answer was unnaturally curt as she strove to ignore the attraction she felt pulling her to him, threatening to overcome the control she knew she must maintain to be able to work closely with him.

His voice maintained the flat, almost uninterested tone she had begun to associate with the controlled attitude he always exhibited. "Yes, I have your file. But people often fail to fill in the blanks properly if they're not fond of their full name. Especially women." His profile was stern when she glanced at him, though she thought she detected a touch of humor flickering about his mouth.

She recited her answer carefully. "Cara Anne Lang is my proper name. My grandparents were from Greece; that's where I got my hair color." She glanced quickly in his direction again. "My correct age is on the form, too.'' She couldn't miss a chance to score even a small point in her favor.

Smiling slightly with a somewhat complacent air, she crossed her long legs and settled back to once more watch the passing traffic.

His cool manner remained unruffled. ''If most women looked like you, they wouldn't need to lie about their ages.'' He hesitated a moment and she waited for the next words, familiar now with the pauses he deliberately used to throw her off balance. ''Besides, twenty-four isn't an age to be sensitive about.''

Though she refused to look at him, she felt his gaze linger on her while they waited for a traffic light. Her nerves tightened, as time lengthened, and she jumped as warm fingers touched her thigh. Jerking around with a tight, angry expression, she encountered his still-stern countenance. ''If I'm to successfully negotiate this traffic, you must cover those deliciously shaped legs and that bit of lace you call a slip.''

A flush rose across her cheeks as his tanned fingers smoothed the skirt that had worked its way up her thigh. She hoped he would let her embarrassment pass, but her hope was in vain.

Impatience seemed to tinge his voice a few minutes later as he pulled into the parking lot and spoke. ''You needn't act the Victorian virgin. I'm sure you're not that inexperienced. No one who looks like you could be.'' With expert ease Sloan swung the auto into his parking space before she overcame her anger enough to answer.

''You may be sure of many things, Mr. Montgomery, but of that you're not—and not likely to be.'' She was rewarded by the look of consideration he cast over her. The look spoke volumes.

Turning slightly toward her, he leaned casually back

before speaking. His naturally husky voice filled the car. "I think I *am* sure of that, Cara. At least, for now I'll assume I am." Then his gaze narrowed as it raked over her, again undressing her visually. "I believe I missed a prime opportunity yesterday. And I don't miss many."

It was as if he 'had thrown out a challenge and her mouth tightened with her refusal to take it up. She wasn't certain what he meant, or what his purpose was in baiting her, nor was she sure she really wanted to know. But she recognized the testing tone of his words. He was right. With her dark attractiveness and unusual looks, she had heard just about every line imaginable and fended off many a man confident of his own expertise and appeal to women.

"I'm sure you don't. But I'm not your usual type of woman, so don't think you know all there is to know about me. Not everything is in that little personnel folder you have, Mr. Montgomery."

Her remarks were rewarded with a slight tightening of his lips, and she felt she had scored another point in her favor. As she noted his appraisal of her she couldn't help feeling that this conversation was somehow an extension of yesterday's encounter. Her only question was as to the reason behind it all. Why his sudden interest? She had barely met Sloan Montgomery prior to yesterday. Their main contact had been indirect: memos, short and to the point. He hadn't bothered to speak to her by telephone, leaving all such communication to his subordinates. She hadn't even been able to replace a receptionist/assistant for the executive suite because of his lack of interest in such trivia and she had had to get someone from the pool to help until his arrival.

Sloan spoke again, breaking into her thoughts. "I'm sure that's true. And I'm looking forward to discovering what's behind that face. . . . A real woman may lurk behind those startling black eyes after all.'' He studied her a moment longer. ''Oh, yes. I've checked you out very thoroughly. I always do—with those who are to be, shall we say, confidantes?''

She tried to match his calm attitude, though her temper was fast on the rise and the obscure tone of this conversation made her uncomfortable. ''Apparently not thoroughly enough, judging by the opinions you've expressed about me.''

A faint smile touched his mouth. ''That remains to be seen. But I'm seldom wrong.'' His appraisal of her continued for so long that if he didn't say something she knew she would scream aloud with the tension. ''Another thing, if you plan on continuing to try scoring points off me, don't. You'll lose.'' The arrogance of the man infuriated her. He seemed to read her mind, as well as second-guess her every thought. ''And the name is Sloan. I like to relate to my employees on a more personal basis. Especially my *personal assistant*.''

The way he emphasized the words pricked her anger even more. For a few minutes they faced each other in the close confines of the car, measuring one another for their own purposes. The tension between them changed; it was no longer a tension born of anger but of something more intangible, something she could feel but not define. She was certain that Sloan, too, was aware of it, possibly creating it, definitely using it to his own advantage. She sought to break the hold he seemed to be exerting over her. ''If you plan to be on time for your meeting, you had better hurry.''

As she reached for the door handle, she was caught, his firm grip encircling her arm. Seeing the wide strong hand against the dark material of her suit she carefully drew a deep breath, trying to control her reaction to the contact. "You wanted something else?" She met his gaze directly and the deep brown intentness of his look held her against her will.

"Yes, I want something else." His look was probing, his voice low and somehow intimate. His hesitation hinted at something other than his next words indicated. "I'll be in this meeting until ten-thirty or so, and I'll have some dictation for you early this afternoon. Before then I want brief analyses of some reports on my desk; keep it to one page each, if possible. You'll know what I need." His fingers slid across the material of her sleeve in a caressing movement as they left her arm. "Now we'll go inside."

She felt a surge of obstinacy at his insistence on controlling every situation, but fought it down. At his nod of dismissal she opened the door and slid from the car. Relief at escaping the confinement of the car—and Sloan—flooded over her.

In a minute he had caught up to her and without speaking they crossed the lot together, entered the building and rode the elevator to the executive offices. A new young receptionist was on the telephone. Fleetingly, Cara wondered just when the girl had been hired and when Sloan had moved in, as he apparently had. Somehow the accomplishment of all that without her knowledge made her ill at ease, firing her already aroused anger even more.

Taking note of the determined set of Cara's head, Sloan nodded before turning away. Only the quiet click of the outer door told of his leaving the opulent office suite.

Ignoring the interested receptionist, Cara pushed open the heavy paneled door to her office and let it fall closed behind her. Leaning back against the panels, she waited until her pounding heart settled before glancing around the familiar room.

This was also the inner reception area for Sloan's private office, which lay to the left. Scanning the room as if for the first time, Cara sensed Sloan's stamp, which was already subtly evident, even though the room looked almost the same. The warm paneling, floor-to-ceiling windows framed by pale green draperies, the soft green plush carpet had not changed, yet there *were* changes. Lamps were different and everything looked somehow brighter, snappier, more up to date.

Moving to her desk, Cara frowned when she noticed the name plate turned face down in the center of the walnut top. With trembling fingers she turned up the brass plate; the clear engraving took her breath away when she saw it. CARA LANG. So she had been correct in thinking that there was some method to all of this, something more than had been readily apparent. Her retention as Sloan's assistant had not been decided yesterday but far enough ahead to allow this plaque to be made.

The knowledge that he had included her in his plans, even for a short time, without her being aware of it bothered her more than a little. Again she felt manipulated, forced into something over which she had no control. Knowing Sloan was behind it all made her even more apprehensive. But, she decided, if he had plans for her on a more personal basis, he had another think coming.

With that decision, Cara turned her mind toward work. Sloan's office door stood slightly ajar and she pushed it open tentatively to peer into the dimly lit room. Though she hadn't been aware of it yesterday, he had definitely moved in during the time she had been occupied in Accounting. The feeling of his presence was so strong that she almost expected to see him sitting behind the large antique library table which had replaced Mr. Quinn's standard oak executive desk.

The décor here was the same as in her own office, except that the greens were darker, more masculine. Circling the room as if she had never been in it before, Cara touched the new appointments lightly, noting the subtle changes Sloan had made almost overnight. A handsome gold pen set, a tooled leather case of cigars and a few folders were the only items on the large table top. She found herself wondering if Sloan smoked, but dismissed that possibility as the car had held no tobacco smell, nor did the office. The cigars were apparently for guests, a courtesy gesture, she decided.

There were no family pictures anywhere in the room. The credenza was clear, except for an appointment book and more files. She knew that Sloan wasn't married, though women were greatly attracted to him. She herself had experienced the pull of his masculinity and the sensual quality which was an innate part of his personality. And, as he had stated himself, he was known to take advantage of ''opportunities'' whenever they were presented.

That he went where he chose, took what he wanted, was readily apparent. Because of his family background and his business talent, he could pick and choose at will—companies, material possessions and women. All were at his beck and call. All except herself, she reminded herself again.

Cara left Sloan's office, crossed to her own desk, the folders in hand, and prepared to get down to business. The intercom buzzer interrupted her before she could even begin.

''Yes?''

A light voice responded to her. "Miss Lang, this is Lea Foster. The new receptionist. I just wanted you to know that if there's anything you need, just let me know."

Thrusting away any resentment she held for not being involved in the girl's hiring, Cara just hoped that she could handle the work Cara customarily entrusted to her assistant. "Thank you, Lea; I appreciate that. I'm sorry I haven't had the opportunity to meet you before now."

"That's okay. Today's my first day anyway, and I'm a little nervous. Would you like coffee? Mr. Montgomery requested that coffee be served first thing and be available all morning, unless he has meetings away from the office."

Coffee would be welcome now, Cara thought. She could relax a bit as she went over the reports. "Yes, thanks. I take cream."

"Fine. I'll bring it in to you in a few minutes."

Deeply involved in the first reports, Cara almost missed the light tap that announced Lea's arrival. A blonde curly head popped around the corner, followed by a curvaceous figure bearing a tray with a cup, a coffee carafe and a cinnamon roll. It was Cara's first chance to get a good look at the girl, and she definitely fit her voice.

"Hi. I thought you might like a breakfast roll. I'm always nervous my first day on a job and can't eat a thing. And this is a sort of 'first day' for you, what with the boss here all the time now." Lea was as bubbly and friendly as she looked, her words running over each other in the excitement of getting everything said at once, and her grin was infectious. "Here all right?"

She slipped the tray onto the edge of Cara's desk. Glancing at the name plate, she bubbled on. "Is the plate all right? Mr. Montgomery said he ordered it, but that he wasn't sure if Cara was short for something you would rather use or if you would want 'Ms.' Lang. He said to change it if necessary.''

Lea's good humor and naturally happy disposition were just what Cara needed and she leaned back in her chair. "It's fine. Cara is my real name, my mother's invention, and I don't use Ms. And yes, the roll is exactly what I need. You're a lifesaver.''

A dimple creased the girl's cheek as she smiled. "Good. I'll get back to work, then, and leave you to yours. Mr. Montgomery is a tough taskmaster, I've found out already, but super, too. He's made quite an impression around here. Everyone likes him already from everything I've heard.'' She hesitated for a moment in the flurry of talk. "I've been curious as to who would be assisting him—if you'd stay or if he'd bring in someone. Men like him often do bring their own assistants, I understand. But you certainly come highly recommended.'' Lea hesitated and took an exaggeratedly deep breath, as if realizing she was running on. "Well, if you need anything, Miss—''

Cara interrupted. "Please, just Cara.''

Lea's eyes widened. "But Mr. Montgomery insisted.''

"And so do I—on being just Cara—especially when it's only the two of us.''

Lea was hesitant. "Well, all right. When it's just us. I wouldn't want to cross Mr. Montgomery, though; I understand he's quite a handful when he's angry.''

Cara grimaced slightly. "I imagine so. Thanks again, Lea.''

Apparently, Lea had done her homework or else she had an astute ear tuned to the rumor mill. She was tactful, too. There was no way she could have missed hearing what had happened between herself and Sloan yesterday, but she hadn't mentioned it.

Lea hesitated, as if she were going to ask a question, then flashed a grin instead before crossing to the door. "Good. See you later."

As she watched the door close, Cara wished she had asked if Sloan had mentioned just how long ago he had ordered the name plate. It might give her a clue to the situation in which she found herself. But questions of that sort might cause speculation, which would only get back to Sloan, and somehow she didn't want him to think she was that interested. And so much for his first-name basis with employees. For her he was Sloan; for others he was Mr. Montgomery.

Cara poured a cup of coffee and munched the roll while she concentrated on the reports. In a short time she had several sheets of notes to type. Just as she finished the task, the outer door swung open and Sloan strode confidently into the room. It seemed that he entered rooms in much the same manner as he approached everything else—with total dominance and the expectation that all were awaiting his presence.

Flinging his briefcase onto the couch in his own office, he loosened his tie and approached Cara, who watched somewhat apprehensively. As he walked he sorted through the various messages he'd picked up from Lea's desk on the way in. Placing his hands on her desktop, Sloan leaned toward her, exuding a power and confidence that put her on edge. "Any questions?" His gaze pinned her to the chair.

She licked her lips nervously in spite of herself, facing him squarely. "No, I'm quite familiar with normal procedures."

"Good. I can fully expect things to move smoothly right away then."

Straightening, he touched the coffee carafe lightly. Finding it still hot, he poured some into Cara's cup and sipped it, munching the remains of her cinnamon roll. The unexpected feeling of intimacy the small act created almost unnerved Cara as he watched her over the rim of the cup. She couldn't decide if he had purposely stirred her emotions with the action, but in any event he had done so and was fully aware of it.

He continued to stand before her, legs apart, the cloth of his trousers pulled taut by his muscled thighs. Watching her carefully, he noted the slight flush staining her high cheeks as she tried to marshal her thoughts and emotions. She was sure that he was deliberately baiting her, but there seemed to be nothing she could do about it.

He finally broke the silence. "I meant to mention a few things to you on the way over this morning, but we were, ah, sidetracked." Pausing for a moment, he continued holding her gaze. "I normally arrive before eight, but you need not be here until eight-thirty." So, she thought, he could amend his own instructions. "When you arrive, we'll go over my schedule for the day and make any necessary changes. Then you'll be free to organize your own day. Most of the letters I want you to do can be composed from the notes I'll make in the margins of incoming correspondence and reports. You'll find that I prefer the straight-forward approach in all my communications." Naturally, she thought, as if she hadn't realized that already. "I want you to read any reports that come in; become familiar with the projects and keep me posted via synopses of them. We'll fall into a workable routine, I'm certain. Any questions?"

Cara was feeling a little overwhelmed by the burst of instructions and a little foolish at her earlier thoughts that she might have been retained more as a personal convenience than for her abilities and knowledge of the company. "No, not at present. As you say, we'll work out a satisfactory routine."

He interrupted, abruptly setting the coffee cup back onto the tray. "I'm quite certain I *will* be satisfied. In every way."

Again he inserted that suggestion of a second meaning in his words, but she pointedly ignored the implication. If he intended to get a reaction from her, then she would not allow him to see how much his words and actions rattled her normal self-confidence.

Carefully schooling her smooth features, she rose, folders in hand. "These are the report condensations. I'll leave them on your desk."

She refused to try to interpret the look he gave her and followed him as he abruptly returned to his own office. He flicked on the overhead lights and shrugged out of his suit jacket, the action stretching the fine silk of his shirt across the contours of his muscular chest. Then he slipped the buttons of his cuffs and rolled back the sleeves to reveal tanned forearms heavily covered with light brown hair.

She knew that she wasn't the first woman to be affected by this man's potent masculinity, but she also knew that he was the first to affect her in such a way. She also knew that she must control the extent and result of any such attraction to him. It was not going to be easy, but she refused to be only a single addition to any man's "black book." When she fell in love it would be with a man who loved her for her own unique qualities, not just because she was physically attractive or could temporarily warm his bed.

She frowned suddenly at the direction her thoughts were taking. Sloan was the last man she would have expected to trigger off such thoughts. He was arrogant and abrasive, definitely the last man she would think of in connection with the word "love." Attraction, certainly, that could not be denied. But a deeper emotion? No, definitely not.

The click of the locks on his briefcase brought her back to the reality of the man before her. Removing a legal pad from the case, he tore off several sheets and handed them to her. "I hope you can read my own form of speed writing. In my haste, I tend to lapse somewhat. Just type these into some form. Anything you can't read leave blank for me to fill in. They're just for my reference, so you don't have to be too perfect—just moderately so." His face was unmoved despite the suggestion of humor, and Cara found herself wondering if he ever genuinely smiled.

As he closed the case, Cara watched him, analyzing the many facets of character she had seen in him so far. "I'll have this dictation finished by noon. The next few days may be a bit hectic; I've been making do with temporary help for the past several days while I've been in transition and I've gotten a little behind. There will be several tapes for you to transcribe today and tomorrow." He shuffled papers from a drawer as he spoke. "I trust the shift in employers won't be too disappointing."

So he couldn't resist one last jibe. Suddenly anxious to leave the room, Cara had already moved to the door when he spoke again. "I'm glad you're here, Cara."

Searching his face for a clue to the tone of the moment, she finally spoke. "Thank you." She left the room swiftly and missed the sudden tightening of his mouth at her quick departure.

Her legs were weak as she moved carefully to her desk. What did he want from her? Events were moving entirely out of her control, shifting her thoughts and affecting her life without her consent. It made her uncomfortable, wary, apprehensive of the outcome.

Sloan was a demanding man and she would find it difficult enough to adjust to his accelerated working pace without any sort of personal relationship entering into the picture. And a personal relationship seemed to be what he was considering.

The prospect of an involvement with a man like Sloan threw her even further off balance. He was an arrogant man, absolutely certain of himself and his effect on others. When Sloan Montgomery spoke, things moved. And he expected the same of her. But Cara was determined to be the exception to the rule. She was accustomed to having total control of her own life, both inside and outside office hours. And she would let nothing be changed by Sloan Montgomery, whatever his intentions.

Forcing her thoughts back to the business at hand, Cara began to decipher Sloan's notes. His bold handwriting was easy to read, though it was evident that he had taken notes quickly and without thought as to form. He had his own brand of abbreviation, but the notes were clear and concise and, after making a few clarifying notations of her own, Cara was able to type directly from them. She wished the man himself were as easy to decipher.

As she slid the last page from the typewriter, she heard Sloan's door open. She glanced at her watch, surprised to see that it was well past noon.

Sloan slid his appointment book across her desk. "You'll need to write my appointments in your book in order to schedule around them. You may need to attend some of the meetings with me." At her brief nod he continued, glancing at his watch. "I have a luncheon meeting now; I'll return around two." He saw her glance at the tapes in his left hand and set them on her desk. "The red coded ones are the most important. The green ones can be worked in as you get to them."

With no further comment he strode out the door, straightening his tie as he went. For a few moments Cara continued to stare at the closed door, awed by the amount of work the man had accomplished and the manner in which he had done so. He exuded the calm assurance that there was no problem he couldn't solve if he approached it sanely and logically. She reluctantly admired that in him and realized that she would probably learn quite a number of surprising things about Sloan as the days passed.

Hurriedly dismissing those somewhat disturbing thoughts, she turned back to her work, determined to prove her worth by finishing as much as possible before he returned.

A short time later Cara was interrupted by a brief tap on the outer door, followed by Lea's blonde curls popping around the edge. At Cara's questioning look, Lea explained the tray balanced on her arm. "Mr. Montgomery said you would probably skip lunch and told me to order sandwiches for you." She smiled widely. "He said you wouldn't feel like going to the cafeteria. And he was right. It's one o'clock and you're still slaving away in here."

So he had known she would avoid the cafeteria. It was something she hadn't consciously considered herself, but he had. Somehow this sudden sensitivity to her feelings confused and unnerved her more than the cold mask he usually wore. It totally contradicted her earlier opinion of him.

"That's wonderful, Lea. How thoughtful of you, and of Sloan," she added reluctantly. "I'd lost track of time, but I am hungry, now that I think of it."

"Good. Hope you like tuna salad. There's milk, too, or more coffee if you prefer?"

At Lea's questioning look she shook her head. "No. Milk is fine and I love tuna." She cleared a space for the tray. "I'll just go freshen up first."

"Fine, I'll take any calls." With a small wave the vivacious girl was gone. Cara decided that Lea would make a wonderful receptionist. She was happy and cared about people. Funny, that made her think of Sloan again.

As she walked down the hall, she considered this last action, another unexpected one, evidence that behind Sloan's brusque exterior and cold, calculating words was a man who cared, a little, anyway. Maybe he'd almost forgotten how, but this time he had cared. It was another piece in the puzzle of Sloan Montgomery, a puzzle that was becoming more intriguing by the moment.

As she washed her hands at the sink, Cara became aware of the murmur of words coming from the outer lounge of the ladies' room. The tone of the words arrested her as she recognized the familiar voice of Susan Stafford. She realized that Susan and her companion were speaking about her and Cara wished that there was some way to escape without having to encounter them, but she was trapped.

". . . All I know is that one moment she's saying she wouldn't be interested in him if he were the last man on earth and the next she's retained as his personal assistant. And he usually brings in someone he's worked with before when he moves into a new company. That much I do know. And then that little disappearing act they both pulled . . ." There was a small pause before the voice continued. "You don't have to guess what talents she employed to get that little bonus."

Susan's angry voice carried clearly and Cara's face flamed at the accusation she could not refute. The rumors that must be circulating were humiliating and unjustified, and she was hurt by them even as her mouth set in anger. A softer, calmer voice answered Susan's more dominant tones, but she couldn't make out the words. Then she heard Susan's reply, and her stomach tightened.

"Well, all I can say is, it won't last long. Cara's much too untouchable, too inhibited, to hold a man like that. I suppose she's a temporary challenge to him, but cold fish is still cold fish, any way you cut it. And I can't see Sloan Montgomery putting up with that for very long. He'll change women before he'll change his ways. He must be between women right now, and that leaves an open track for me. You wait . . ."

Cara listened thankfully as the voice trailed away, cut off by the closing of the outer door as the women left the lounge. Her face and hands clammy, Cara leaned sickly against the sink. So she wasn't the only one who suspected that Sloan might have ulterior motives in retaining her. It seemed that everyone was fully aware of the implications of Sloan's actions, and she was condemned beforehand. Pulling her shattered emotions together, she carefully left the lounge after making certain that neither of the speakers was around.

Cara returned to her office and forced down the sandwich while checking the notes she had typed. Keeping her mind carefully occupied, she was able to momentarily put in abeyance the conversation she had overheard and concentrate on the routine of her work.

Turning to Sloan's dictation, she slid a tape into the dictaphone and heard his husky, deep voice. His dictation was easy, clear and concise, as his notes had been, with few hesitations. He seemed to know exactly what to say and did so with economy of words, while thoroughly covering the subject. It was more evidence of the type of man Sloan was: always to the point, practical and logical, but always completely thorough.

By working steadily, Cara had a stack of correspondence awaiting Sloan's signature when he returned. He scanned the letters briefly, signed them, then went directly to his office, closing the door with a decisive click and leaving Cara to muse over his actions.

At four-thirty Cara was stretching cramped muscles and flexing tired arms, having been bent over the typewriter for several more hours. She gathered the newly completed letters and entered Sloan's office, where he had worked steadily all afternoon. The sight of his dark head bent over her letters made her fingers suddenly long to touch the thick hair where it fell to brush his collar. She was startled at the intensity of her feelings.

"Is that the last of the letters?" Her concentration had been so deep that she blinked at his words, momentarily disconcerted, before regaining her normal demeanor.

"Yes, that's the last."

Leaning back, his arms behind his head, Sloan regarded her carefully composed face. She felt again that he was reading her every thought, tracing her every emotion. His gaze was intent but his face was as unreadable as ever.

"You're even more efficient than I was told. It seems I've found a treasure—if you can keep up the pace, that is."

All the warmth of the compliment was wiped out by the inferred slur on her ability. Determination firmed her mouth as she faced him directly, meeting the challenge, her retort edged with indignant anger. "If you can, I can."

Without waiting for further comment, she reached for the signed letters. Involuntarily, her eyes flicked over him as she came within his reach, unavoidably wary.

A corner of his mouth lifted in derision before he spoke. "Don't be so jumpy, Cara. I rarely dispose of valuable personnel. And as long as you're valuable to me, you'll be cared for—jobwise, that is." The man was dangerous in his ability to read her mind. At her incredulous look, he continued. "Oh, yes, I know you. Quite well, I believe. And I also know how rumors fly." He didn't miss the flush that crossed her face. "They've started already, haven't they? And you don't like them."

His direct gaze met her own for a long moment. "I thought so. You weren't quite so on edge earlier today." He hesitated momentarily. "What did you expect? Immunity? I'm afraid that just isn't possible under the circumstances. The hours, the closeness of our working conditions, all those lend themselves to speculation. Speculation which I've made fact upon occasion, I admit. The question now is, will this be one of those occasions?" At her continued silence his deep voice came again. "It will work out . . . given time."

His barbed comments and insinuations were intended to get under her skin, and they did. But she determined again not to give him the satisfaction of knowing it. Without a word she retrieved the signed letters and left him still sitting, his arrogant face smug at her stiff-backed departure. The battle was on and she determined to be the victor, not the prize.

Back at her desk Cara prepared the signed correspondence for mailing, straightened up and was soon on her way out of the building.

As she reached her car, Cara looked up when she heard a call from across the parking lot. She grimaced inwardly when she saw Kate Harris running toward her.

As much as she liked Kate, she didn't want to go over the last two days with anyone. It was too new and she had too much thinking to do about it yet. But there was no way to escape as Kate approached.

Breathless from the run, Kate half-collapsed against the car. "Cara, I've been worried. What happened?"

Cara stalled, not willing to say more than was necessary. "What do you mean?"

Kate frowned, recognizing the evasion. "Now don't you clam up on me. We've worked together too long for that."

That was true, but she was still unwilling to reveal everything that had gone on. "I'd have thought the rumor mill would have filled all that in already. I've been retained as Sloan Montgomery's executive assistant."

Kate grimaced in mock anger. "I know that! And it's quite a feather in your cap. He always chooses the best to work for him, though he normally brings in his own personnel. And I'm glad for you. No one deserves that kind of recognition more. But you're evading the issue. I want to know what happened yesterday when he hauled you out of the office." The brunette settled herself against the car, ready to stay until she got a satisfactory answer.

"He was angry, naturally, but I ended up keeping my position. That's all there is to the story." Mentally, Cara crossed her fingers, hoping that Kate would accept that and leave. She should have known better.

"Sorry, but I don't think so. Mr. Montgomery sent for the things you'd left in Accounting and you disappeared for the afternoon. Besides, Susan Stafford swept through the office this morning asking all sorts of questions and making all kinds of suggestions. So what really went on?"

Kate was too astute by far. Cara searched for something to say that wouldn't hurt the girl's feelings or reveal her own emotional involvement. "Kate, it's been a long day and I'm tired. I just want to go home and relax."

Cara's expressive eyes held a plea Kate could not ignore. "Okay, if you insist. But there's more than what you've said, I'm certain. Susan had a lot to say, none of it complimentary." Receiving no response from Cara, Kate continued. "Word has it that Mr. Montgomery can be fair or he can be an absolute terror if he's crossed. You don't get where he is so quickly without being more than a little ruthless and I was concerned about you after seeing him in action." The girl's look was expressive. "He wasn't satisfied with something John Vernon said during today's meeting, and John was about ready to cut his losses when Sloan was finished with him. But if Sloan Montgomery puts a bad sign on you there's no place to go—at least not in this town. He may not have been here long, but his advance publicity has been very potent. Everyone who's anyone is racing to do favors and gain the inside track with him. It's incredible how they've all fallen in line behind him." Kate's expression changed suddenly. "He does know the circumstances behind what was said yesterday, doesn't he? I mean, you did tell him?" At the look on Cara's face, Kate was immediately contrite. "Oh, Cara, I'm sorry. I should have said something myself."

Cara shook her head. "No, Kate, it wouldn't have made a difference. Besides, everything turned out just fine." She thought of Sloan's threat, but dismissed it.

Kate reluctantly accepted her word. "All right, but I wish you would tell him." With a pat on the arm Kate turned to her own car, giving Cara another quick wave.

Cara watched Kate's car disappear into the line of traffic. For a moment she longed to confide in someone.

She wished she could talk out the uncertainties she felt, the attraction she felt for the tall, dynamic man who was now her boss, analyze the threat he posed to her emotional stability. But it was impossible. She was alone with her uncertainties.

Realizing that she was standing alone in the growing darkness, Cara hurriedly slid into her own car and joined the stream of evening traffic. A little while later, after letting herself into the comfortably familiar apartment, she kicked off her shoes and padded into the bedroom to change. She slid quickly into faded jeans and a long-sleeved jersey top of light orange that lent warmth to her pale cheeks, then pinned her hair atop her head loosely and creamed off her makeup.

She decided to relax for a little while, so she put her feet up and began to flip through a new magazine. The shrilling of the telephone intruded on her moment of quiet. On hearing Cliff Dane's voice she relaxed again. Cliff was a friend who had also been her supervisor in Accounting before her advancement to Mr. Quinn's office.

Though he was divorced and older than Cara by some twenty years, theirs had been a real friendship. A warm man, slightly taller than herself, with the beginning of a paunch and thinning hair, he had always gotten on well with Cara, and his call was less unwelcome than someone else's might have been.

"Cara? I just wanted to see if you're all right."

Somehow Cliff's sincere concern brought the sting of tears to her eyes. "I'm fine, Cliff. I wanted to call you today, but . . ."

Cliff broke in. "No problem. It's not really your responsibility anyway. You were kind enough to lend a hand when I needed it and I appreciate that. Sloan had a temporary there this morning and she'll stay until I find a permanent replacement. Meanwhile, Kate and I and the others can limp along. Besides, I can't fight progress, can I? I'm just sorry you had a bad beginning with Sloan."

The silence was heavy, as Cara hesitated before answering. She wasn't deceived by Cliff's pretense; he really wanted to know if she was happy working with Sloan. Though, she thought grimly, there was little to be done if she wasn't. So instead of voicing her doubts, she reassured Cliff by saying what he wanted to hear.

"No, I guess you can't. And the job is fine. I'm certain Sloan and I will get to work well together." Even Cara had to admit that she sounded convincing.

Cliff's relief was painfully apparent and he dropped the forced jovial attitude. "I'm glad, Cara. When I heard what happened, that Sloan sent down for your things, I was worried. With him, you never know. When he trusts you everything is fine. When he doesn't, well, he's like lit dynamite, all set for the explosion. And heaven help anyone in the way. All sorts of things come apart."

Cara swallowed drily. Things had certainly changed since Sloan's arrival.

Carefully steadying her voice, she reassured Cliff that everything was fine. "Yes, he does tend to make quick decisions and expect an immediate response." And that's not the half of it, she added to herself.

"That's Sloan. Though he doesn't make snap decisions; it just seems that way because he plays his cards so close to the vest, you might say. No one ever really knows what he's been thinking or planning until he does something. Like with you. He asked about those reports you turned in while I was on sick leave a few weeks back. I guess that's what started him thinking about having you continue in your position, instead of bringing in someone as he usually does.'' Cara was getting tired of hearing about Sloan's usual habits.

''It just so happened that he came down to talk to you at a bad time.'' There was another pause. ''He's fair though, Cara. Tough, but fair.''

He seemed convinced, but Cara wasn't so sure. All the department heads had had the advantage of protracted meetings with Sloan after the merger had been set. Naturally, he'd turned on the charm and won them over. But she had not had that advantage. She agreed with Cliff's picture of Sloan as tough, though. It seemed to her that he would apply any pressure he felt was necessary to achieve the results he wished—by fair means or foul.

''Thanks. I appreciate what you're trying to say. Sloan was angry yesterday, and rightly so. None of it should have happened. Thanks for your concern, Cliff. You're still the best.''

His returned laugh reaffirmed the easy camaraderie they'd achieved over the years. ''Well, I'm just glad it's straightened out. He understood, I think, when I told him about what had happened. Susan gave me a few hints about what came before; then Kate filled in the details, so I passed it on to Sloan when he stopped by the department just after noon. He won't hold a grudge, though he *was* upset that you hadn't told him about it yourself.''

Cara clutched the receiver. But before she could say anything, Cliff continued. ''And I know working with Sloan will be good for you careerwise.''

Cara frowned, gathering her scattered thoughts. ''You told Sloan . . .''

Cliff seemed surprised that she hadn't known. ''Sure; I saw him today and we spoke about you. I can't recall how it all came up in conversation, but I thought he ought to be set straight on what happened.'' Cliff seemed genuinely surprised that Sloan hadn't discussed it with her. ''He didn't mention it to you?''

Her voice was low. ''No. He didn't. He was probably too . . . busy.''

''Well, at least he knows the truth. I didn't want him thinking what he'd overheard reflected your normal attitude. Besides, Susan made it quite clear, as usual, what her position was—about you and about Sloan. Now there's an aggressive female for you!''

Cara silently agreed.

''Well, got to run, Cara. Take care, and if there's ever anything I can do, you know where to reach me.''

As she replaced the receiver, Cara felt strangely depressed. So Sloan knew the truth of the situation that had triggered his anger, yet he had said nothing to her about it. But then, considering what she had seen of him, she couldn't imagine Sloan apologizing for anything. He would never open himself up enough to her to admit that he had been wrong. There would be no companionship in working with him, as there had been in her other positions. In fact, Sloan seemed to be constantly holding himself in reserve, seldom changing his facial expression. Even when he taunted her, he was in total control of himself and the situation and showed only the briefest flickers of emotion: amusement, humor, triumph.

Discipline. A key word in her own life seemed to be the basis of Sloan's working personality. And perhaps it was necessary in light of the enormous responsibilities he carried.

She frowned as she began to understand a little of the workload he had. Even her position as his assistant would be more demanding than working for Mr. Quinn, and she determined that whatever happened, however

Sloan acted, she must allow for the enormousness of his responsibilities and how they weighed upon him. Whatever her personal feelings, she would do the best job possible. And Sloan would regret the disparaging remarks he had made about her personally, as well as regarding her working capabilities. She would show him—starting tomorrow.

Moving about the apartment, idly straightening pillows, picking up magazines and newspapers, Cara thought about the conflicting sides of Sloan's personality. She had seen only one side of him; Lea, Kate and Cliff had given her glimpses of others.

She marveled at the change her attitude toward him had undergone during the last few hours. In a way she felt that she had discovered, maybe even understood, a little of Sloan's basic nature. He was a man who insisted on the best—in himself and in others—and was annoyed when people didn't measure up. He seemed almost driven by the desire to do his utmost in everything. That was evidenced by the few years it had taken him to build the large conglomerate he now headed.

His singlemindedness was also evidenced by the manner in which he managed the businesses he controlled and the people he kept around him. In spite of the vast reach of his business interests, and despite what she had said to Kate in anger, he became personally involved in the companies his corporation took over, making certain they were well on their way before he went on to something new and challenging. A certain restlessness seemed to drive him, she thought.

With that Cara collapsed in a chair in front of the television, absently switching it on. As the picture formed, she wondered just what drove her new employer to greater, more challenging ventures. Whatever made him strive for such near-perfection in himself seemed to be a basic part of his makeup. She couldn't fault him for wanting to exact top performance from himself and those around him—most men in management did—but he exhibited a driving power that most of them didn't have. Somehow, thinking of his being driven made Sloan seem more human, almost vulnerable.

Cara had to smile at the thought of the great Sloan Montgomery being vulnerable in any way. She could identify with him more on that level, see him as more approachable.

In some ways she was cut from the same cloth. Not driven, not ruthless, but still striving to achieve, to be the best she could be. She pushed herself to the limits of her ability, whatever the challenge. And it was these similar qualities in herself that made her feel that working with Sloan just might work out after all.

Suddenly she realized how late it had gotten and she switched off the television in the middle of a program she hadn't really been watching anyway. Stretching lazily, she turned off the lights and headed for bed. She was tired, but she felt much better about herself after her evening of self-examination. And she felt better about Sloan, too, believing she might have solved some of the complexities of his character, or at least come to understand him a little, which would let her tolerate him, if nothing else. It might be possible now to work with him naturally, without all the tension that had made this day so long and tiring.

Chapter Three

$\mathscr{A}$s the days passed, Cara began to be more aware of Sloan the business tycoon. She watched as he skillfully handled the complex problems of reorienting the staff to a positive attitude, replacing the almost apologetic one that had become the norm as Mr. Quinn became more and more apathetic in his management of the corporation. Cara realized that she had been surprisingly unaware of how much deterioration had taken place throughout the whole plant in both attitude and performance, but the change of bosses pointed out how much improvement had been needed in all areas.

Readjusting her work habits to Sloan's hyperactive schedule strained Cara's capabilities to the limit. Sloan demanded the most from her skills and time and she strove to match his expectations.

With her knowledge of the personnel and functions of each department, she was able to help in the remotivation process. But besides this and the company's normal activities, Sloan was busy with plans to upgrade each area of the corporation—production retooling to accommodate new lines, research into areas in which to make new inroads, and questions of new programs for marketing and advertising, whether the current personnel could handle the changes. All these were a part of Sloan's everyday activities, additions to the normal schedule of any executive in charge of a good-sized corporation.

Other interests under the Montgomery Industries umbrella added to the daily load, as well. Not a day went by without numerous telephone calls and correspondence between the Triad offices and others in the Montgomery conglomerate. If she had taken time to consider, she might have been overwhelmed by the newly accelerated pace. As it was, she just handled each thing as it came up and didn't take time to worry about all the hundreds of other duties that had claims on her time.

Lea was a godsend, whom Cara grew to depend upon to handle and screen most of the calls, leaving her free to give her attention to other, more pressing business. Most of the routine correspondence became Lea's job, along with many of the corporate letters and reports. But what Cara really appreciated was Lea's inherent good humor, which never seemed to falter. Whenever things were the most hectic, whenever it seemed that there would be no end to the seemingly hundreds of calls upon her time, Lea could be depended upon to come up with just the right touch to lighten the load.

One day she brought in a bouquet of daisies, a simple gesture but one that left Cara feeling brighter all day. Sloan had glanced at the flowers with a raised eyebrow, but made no comment. His attitude piqued Cara a little, but she ignored it, chalking it up to his inability to give in to normal human feelings.

She was constantly amazed by his abilities. His mind seemed to hold the myriad details concerning his business interests like a computer. Ask a question, wait a moment, and out popped the answer. At times she could almost swear she heard wheels turning.

Very quickly, her apprehension at working with Sloan was replaced with awe at the vastness of his interests and excitement at being part of such an organization. The advisors and managers connected with his various corporations became first-name acquaintances within a few days, because they kept in frequent contact with Sloan. In a short time they began to recognize Cara's efficiency, and if Sloan was not available would pass on information through her. Though she sensed a unity of purpose with these men, she was careful never to exhibit anything less than a completely businesslike attitude, knowing that was what they, and Sloan, expected from her.

As Sloan recognized her attention to detail and her acute powers of observation, he began to accept her as a working partner more than as a subordinate. She felt that she had accomplished something monumental the first time she recognized his change in attitude toward her and her work.

But this change did not extend beyond their working relationship. After the first few days he disregarded her completely on a personal level, and that began to intrigue her. Sloan was a man interested in women—if the newspaper accounts of his social activities were any measure. And the comments she occasionally overheard in the halls indicated that his attractive good looks hadn't escaped the members of the female sex who came in contact with him throughout the Complex. But to her knowledge he never received telephone calls at the office from any of the women he dated. Apparently, that was strictly taboo and they adhered to the rules. As to his behavior with her, he had never repeated his remarks about her "duties." And for some perverse reason Cara was curious as to why he had abandoned that initial course of action.

As the workload smoothed out and she became better able to handle her growing responsibilities without having to think out each move, Cara grew more aware of Sloan the man. Her first impression had proved correct. His attractiveness could not be denied, nor could his totally virile masculinity. Secure in her own attractiveness and femininity, still Cara occasionally wondered, in her more pensive moments, just why Sloan hadn't followed up on his suggestive comments of those first two days. Though she would have rejected any overture he might make, she could not help wondering about the situation between them, which had turned into an emotional stalemate, with neither side demonstrating the slightest interest in the other. There was no doubt in her mind that he had meant what he'd said. Sloan was not a man to make idle threats or comments. He never wasted words, whether on a business or personal level. That much she was sure of.

She could almost laugh at her curiosity about his inattention to her. That was what she wanted, wasn't it—for him to leave her alone? She had made that clear from the first. And here she was wondering what was wrong because he had exhibited no interest in her at all during the past weeks. For all the notice he paid her she might as well be another filing cabinet. Just as long as she functioned at top efficiency, she amended. When she failed to do that she had no doubt she would hear plenty from Sloan on the subject.

Still, she couldn't help wondering what kind of man he was inside. She found herself taking small incidents and looking behind them for further clues to Sloan's personality. She began to see a pattern, an utter avoidance of sentiment, of anything even remotely personal.

It was almost as if he had cut off that part of his nature, as if he refused to allow a place in his life for such trivial things. The first time this was brought clearly to her attention was on Lea's birthday.

Lea had mentioned several days earlier that Tom, her fiancé, and his family had planned a small celebration for later in the week and that she hoped she wouldn't have to work late that night. Cara made a mental note of the occasion, knowing how important it was to Lea. For her birthday, and as a way of saying thank-you for all the things Lea had done to smooth the way, the responsibilities she had taken beyond what was normal for her position, Cara planned a small cake-and-coffee party for the clerical staff. Sloan was to be away for a lengthy morning meeting, so Cara planned an extended coffee break and invited the staff to drop by whenever their schedules allowed. All was in order—until Sloan returned early.

The party was in full swing, with everyone having a good time, because Lea was a favorite among the staff. Several of the executives had joined in the celebration, as they all knew Lea and had been won over by her infectious smile. But the party atmosphere was soon dispelled, with a dozen people to witness the scene. Cara's face still flushed at the memory of it.

Several of the office staff, Cara, and two or three of the management personnel, including Susan Stafford, had been laughing at an involved tale of Lea's first encounter with Tom's distinctly conservative parents— embroidering a little on the contrast between their "stuffy" conversation and her bubbling chatter—to the delight of everyone listening. Suddenly, the outer door was pushed open and Sloan came to an abrupt halt just inside to take in the scene with narrowed eyes. Everyone froze. It took no words for Sloan to make his disapproval known and almost silently the crowd melted away. Unfortunately, a number of people, including Susan Stafford, stayed long enough to witness the scene that came next.

Sloan had been quite verbal in his disapproval of the waste of time and energy on a party when there was so much work to be done. Cara's attempt to justify the occasion as a way to loosen up a little and give people a break was futile. Sloan's angry gesture and abrupt departure to his own office left Cara standing, almost literally, with cake on her face. Susan's smug look as she strode languidly from the room spoke volumes. It was not an occasion Cara would soon forget.

After that she began to turn her mind more toward the idiosyncrasies of Sloan's personality. She was intrigued by his apparently total lack of human foibles. He left no margin for error or fatigue. He drove himself beyond the normal working limits of anyone else she had ever encountered. By the end of the day her mind was often so weary it was difficult to decide what to eat for dinner. By contrast, Sloan seemed to be working at the same level of concentration, with the same attention to detail and at the same pace as he had been early that morning.

He was always at the office before she got there and still there when she left. Nothing escaped his attention; no detail went unnoticed, no doubt or hesitation unquestioned. Often she felt that he was the inquisitor, she the defendant, when she turned in a report that was something less than he expected. She stuttered out excuses, which was not her usual behavior. Then she would draw herself up and assume his attitude, refusing to explain or excuse anything. The plan seemed to work, as their working relationship smoothed out after that. He appreciated assurance and determination.

She also discovered, with some irritation, that Sloan was seldom wrong about anything. On the few occasions when he had been incorrect in an assumption, he ignored the incident. She entered this on the minus side of the mental slate she kept on him. He didn't admit defeat, which was good to some extent, but then he never apologized, which she felt to be a flaw. On the whole she had to admire him for his accomplishments, his determination. But she was sure that there was a great deal missing in his personal life. And she often wondered at the reason for those missing pieces.

Each day brought new challenges. Sloan himself was challenging, making her rise above the capabilities she had known she possessed. He expanded her thinking into areas of business heretofore unknown to her, and she gained in confidence because of it. Still, Sloan himself remained a mystery. She never got any closer to understanding him than she had on that night weeks ago, and the insights she had gained then seemed shallow now.

The restlessness she had seen in him early in their acquaintance never abated. It seemed that his energy couldn't be satisfied with the chairmanship only of his own corporation; he needed the continuing challenge that rebuilding and revitalizing Triad gave him. And once he had Triad running smoothly, he would no doubt look for further challenge. In her weaker moments the thought occurred to Cara that this same restlessness, this same need for challenge, would make Sloan unequalled in a personal relationship. He would certainly never be dull. And, when she allowed herself, she wondered just what Sloan might bring to a more intimate relationship.

Three months passed quickly, and with the arrival of

summer Cara was more than ready for a vacation. She was tired. Though the effort to think through each task had lessened and she did her work with more confidence, the strain of the past several months was telling on her energy. The bright sunshine outside her window begged her to come out and enjoy it. There was nothing she would rather have done than sail on a nearby lake, or just sit in the shade of a big maple and let her mind float. She couldn't understand how Sloan maintained the pace he set for himself without some sign of fatigue.

As she gathered the last of the day's correspondence to drop off at the mailroom, she noted that it was just past five-thirty. An early evening for once. Sloan had been away almost all day, which had enabled her to catch up on some detail work she had been putting off. As a result she felt entirely justified in leaving at what could be considered "on time."

When she got home Sloan was on her mind. More and more she had watched to see if he would let up on his schedule as Triad's problems became less involved. But he just filled the hours with more work from his other interests, while keeping a strict eye on the changes he had instigated at Triad.

She was more and more intrigued by the man. In spite of herself she had begun to think of him more as a man than as her employer. His own attitude toward her had not altered; if he had intended his coolness to pique her curiosity he had succeeded.

While undressing, she took a moment to look at herself objectively. She was attractive; Sloan had said so himself. So why, she wondered, was he keeping so carefully away from her? His chilly attitude had been a welcome relief at first, but now she was seeing it as rejection and her feminine pride was pricked by it.

His attitude annoyed her and she had found herself

dressing more for his benefit than for the sake of utility. She had even begun to doubt her own attractiveness, something she'd never done before. And she began to consider herself in relation to Sloan the man, something she had determined not to do.

As she showered, Cara thought about the man who had become almost the total center of her life. He was attractive, intelligent, intriguing; she'd never met his equal before. But his lack of personal disclosure on any level made it difficult to conceive of him on a human level at all. She found herself analyzing him physically in an effort to gain some insight.

His attractiveness was just as compelling, just as strong, as it had been at their first encounter. She tried to put herself in the place of the women she saw pictured with him in the society columns, imagining his solemn face creased in a smile, a teasing light in the somber and occasionally hostile brown eyes. She tried to hear his husky voice whispering the words that women like to hear and failed. She even visualized those wide strong hands touching her intimately, his skin against her own, and her body grew warm with arousal. She knew the feel of his mouth against her own, and knew she wanted to feel it again.

At this point she thrust such thoughts from her mind and reminded herself that Sloan set the pace of his own life and she had no place in it outside the office. He had accomplished what he had intended; he had made sure that he had a knowledgeable executive assistant who could cope with the demands of the job without complaint. He had read her correctly. The insinuation that she might not be equal to the job had ensured that she would do everything in her power to prove him wrong.

Yes, she thought, as she rinsed off the soap lather, Sloan was certainly someone to be reckoned with on any level. As she stepped from the shower to wrap her damp body in a long terry robe, the unexpected sound of the doorbell interrupted her thoughts. Rubbing the dampness from her dark hair, she strode to the door, thinking it must be a neighbor wanting to borrow something. The last person she expected to see was Sloan.

His attractiveness struck her as powerfully as ever. His tall frame was dressed in tan corduroy slacks that molded his muscular thighs; the dark brown cotton shirt open halfway down his chest revealed a thick mat of hair in which a small medallion sparkled.

Questioningly, her eyes rose to meet his direct gaze. "Cara."

Surprise coupled with the effect of his presence prompted her next words. "Sloan? You're not still . . ."

She frowned, a crease forming between her brows. How stupid! Of course he wasn't still at the office.

"Evidently. Are you going to invite me in?"

The low tones worked on her senses, and she unconsciously drew the robe closer about her. "Of course." She gestured vaguely to the room behind her, closing the door after him. "Is something wrong?"

"No, not really." Turning to glance down at her figure, revealed by the drape of the robe along her damp skin, he continued. "If that's your normal 'at home' attire I'll plan to come more often."

Again his words were heavy with implication after so long a time. He was doing it again, using words that made her body tingle with excitement. At her silence he continued in a less provocative tone. "This progress report needs some revising and I'll want it as soon as I get in tomorrow. I'll be late; I have to be out of town by seven-thirty and it may be ten or later before I can get back. You'll need to rearrange my two early appointments."

"Certainly." Silently, she chastised herself for the reaction his voice set up in her and forced her thoughts into a more businesslike vein as she took the folder he offered her. So much for thinking he had a personal reason for coming.

Still, she couldn't help letting her personal feelings and curiosity come to the fore. Absently, she dropped into a chair near where he slouched on the couch, tucking her feet beneath the folds of her robe. "Is there anything else I can do?"

She'd been reluctant to ask, for fear he would misinterpret her concern as prying, but she sensed that something was bothering him and wanted to help if she could.

"No, just that." His voice was flat, emotionless, yet he sat, studying his hands.

Something in his manner nagged at her, something that she couldn't define. "Are you all right?"

He glanced up suddenly, his rough voice grating. "Why shouldn't I be?" The sharpness of his manner made her wince and a silence stretched between them. "I'm just tired; it's been a long day."

She was surprised that he would admit to anything like that, and it encouraged her to try again. "I'm not surprised. Your hours are too long." When there was no reply she continued, watching the tightly controlled face for some flicker of emotion; the opportunity to get closer to him was just too great to ignore. "Sloan?"

Just saying his name aloud felt good to her, and the realization of how good worried her, especially when she knew he wouldn't welcome any suggestion of familiarity.

"I'm all right." He spoke as though his mind was elsewhere.

Suddenly, unbidden, the wish that he would confide

what was on his mind swept over her, sweeping caution away. "Are you sure? I mean, you look worn out. Why not take a day off, relax? During the short time you've been involved with Triad, you've spent long hours with our problems and still contended with your other business interests, too." At his silence, she continued. "And I'm certain the newspapers haven't recorded all the things you've had to handle. You're going to be heading for a breakdown at this pace."

His answer was quick, his look piercing, daring her to question his work schedule or anything else about his life again. "No problem. It all has to be done and there's no one else to do it. Too many things, too many people, depend on this company's survival."

"I realize that the company needs your guidance; I'm one of those people who depend on the success of Triad. But that's just the reason you should take time off. One day away won't cause irreparable damage. Better one day than who knows how long if something should happen to you."

Again there was a significantly long pause as he stared into the distance, his face averted. "Your salary would still be paid, along with everyone else's."

His cynical attitude and coldness made her anger flash, until she remembered her earlier resolve to hold her temper. "I'm not concerned about that. Money has never been that important to me."

"It's not, until you don't have it."

His attitude annoyed her and her annoyance showed in her retort. "But you can't honestly relate to that, can you? You've always had money as well as people at your command." She remembered accounts of the estate where he had grown up, the private schools he'd attended, with top grades, it had been carefully noted.

"The money, anyway. You're right about that."

"And your family? Aren't they more important? Won't they be worried if you force yourself to the breaking point? Haven't they noticed the hours you keep?"

"It's of no interest to them what I do." The coldness was heavy in his voice. It gripped her heart, making her wonder at her own foolishness in voicing concern about a man like Sloan.

But what once she had began she stubbornly continued, determined to break through the shell he kept about himself, to learn something about this closed man. She leaned toward him. "Your parents? Even if you see them infrequently, surely your mother . . . ?" She hadn't heard anything about his parents being dead, so they must be aware that he was working too hard.

"I have no parents."

The sadness she felt at those words was as strong as if it were her own loss. "Then they're both dead?"

"They're alive, for what it matters."

The hard, flat sound of his voice should have been a warning to her to leave well enough alone. But she was driven by a desire to know the man behind the public personality everyone else saw.

Doggedly, she pursued. "But . . . ?"

He broke in, his voice heavy with bitterness as he rose to pace the room restlessly. The very tautness of his body, his restlessness, showed the strain the conversation was putting on him. "My mother, and I use the term loosely, left when I was nine and I haven't seen her since. Nor do I have any wish to."

Tears of compassion stung her eyes. Her own home-life had been so warm, so comforting, so supportive. It was a great part of the reason she was the sort of normal person she was. It hurt her that he had not had the same support.

"That must have been difficult for you, and for your father. Are you close to him?" The silence stretched on so long that she thought he might not answer. "Sloan?"

He stood with his back to her, looking out the window at the night. Again the silence, but she let it stretch, feeling that he was making a decision of some sort. This moment was important and she was willing to wait, knowing he needed the time right now. The story wasn't a pretty one. She could almost see the lonely boy he had been, changing to the solitary man before her. His aloneness tugged at her heart and she found herself wishing she could be a part of his life.

The desire was so strong that it gave her cause to question her own motives. She wanted to fill his life with something warm, with care, possibly a little of the love he had missed. Sloan was not a trusting person; she was. She wanted to teach him some of that trust.

Cara recognized that a struggle was taking place within him. She was on the verge of learning something about Sloan, of getting below the surface to see the inside self he so carefully hid. Why he should even consider trusting her she didn't know, in light of his expressed opinions of her. But she wanted to know him, wanted to see behind the façade he kept up in front of the world, so she didn't question his motives any further.

At last he spoke, the decision apparently made. "My father is who I'm seeing in the morning. He's in a private hospital out in the country. They called me earlier this evening. He's had another stroke and I have to talk to the physician in charge and sign some treatment papers."

Her fingers gripped the chair arm so tightly that her knuckles went white. "Then he's seriously ill?"

The rough voice was again flat, the tones controlled.

"He's an alcoholic; he's committing slow suicide. It will be a good day when it's finally over."

Emotion flooded over her; a combination of sorrow and the sympathy she knew he would reject overwhelmed her. She longed to hold him, comfort him, as she would have comforted anyone else under the same circumstances. But with Sloan it was more. She needed to comfort him, as if by doing so she could also comfort herself. "Oh, Sloan, how awful. You must feel so at odds with yourself about him. He's so very ill, and he is your father. You must love him for that."

" 'Father' is the operative word. There's more to parenting than conceiving a child. Never mind; you don't . . ."

She stood and walked toward him in her effort to make him understand. "But I do, Sloan." She hurried on before her courage failed. "I care. I would like to share this with you, if you'd let me. Sharing helps." She found herself almost pleading with him to let her into his life, something she could hardly believe she was doing.

"It's of no concern to you—or anyone else."

There was almost a threat in his voice and she understood his meaning. No one else must know about his father or anything else he had said. But she wanted him to believe that she cared about what happened to him. Cared about him as a human being, as someone she worked closely with. What she wasn't ready to reveal to him was that she also cared for him because of a growing personal involvement that she was totally at a loss to explain.

Knowing he might reject contact, she stood quietly behind him, within touching distance, but without touching. Her voice was soft in her first tentative steps toward offering something of herself to him. "Yes, it is. It's part

75

of what makes you who you are. And that concerns me. Not just because you're my employer, not just because you pay the bills, but because I care. Can't you understand that people care about each other? Care because we're fellow human beings?" There was no response, but she knew he had heard her. "Does your mother know he's so ill?"

"No." His voice was weary—whether from exhaustion or the emotional strain he was under she couldn't be certain.

"Doesn't she have the right to know? She must have loved him once or she wouldn't have married him."

"Not everyone has the ethical way of thinking you do. She married him for financial security—until something better came along. And as for her knowing about his illness, she has no right. No right at all." As he spoke, an anger seemed to grow in him, bubbling over the normally cool exterior he maintained. She felt the tension in him building to a breaking point. "She was, and is, a glorified prostitute. Selling herself to the highest bidder, asking only a wedding ring and a bank account. A very large bank account." Again the hesitation, as if he were gathering his shell around himself once more. "No, she has no rights." His normally rough voice was even rougher with anger and other emotions he was holding tightly under control.

Cara was shocked, both by what he said and his vehemence in saying it. But she quickly gathered her thoughts and forced her voice to be calmer than she thought possible, in view of all she had just learned. "Then she left you with your father deliberately? With no intention of coming back to you?"

"Of course. Nurses are nearly as good as mothers. At least as good as she was, anyway." The bitterness covered by the sarcasm came through the carefully controlled words, cutting into her. Her hand trembled with her longing to touch him, but she knew she must not.

"What about your father? Is that when he started drinking?" Her voice was soft with unshed tears.

"Yes. His way of forgetting, I suppose."

"And is that why you took over his business interests at such a young age?"

His head jerked up, but still he faced away from her. "You know about that?" He seemed genuinely surprised.

"Certainly. Newspaper journalists are very forthcoming when big business is involved—especially business involving people like you."

"And what kind of 'people' am I?"

Knowing that he wasn't angling for a compliment but really wanted to know her opinion, Cara considered her answer a moment before speaking. "You're a shaker and a mover. A strong, determined, brilliant businessman. A man who expects a lot from people, but even more from himself. One who cares very little for what anyone else thinks of him."

She stopped a moment to form her thoughts carefully, realizing how important her words and his reactions might be. "And now I've begun to understand why you're such a difficult man to know. Why you've built such a wall around yourself." To still her longing to reach out to him, she hugged her own body tightly.

There was almost amusement in his voice when he spoke. "That's a little different from the opinion you expressed not too long ago."

She grimaced to herself. "But that was before I knew anything about you, and unfair, I know. But, you must admit, you are a difficult man to know."

He turned now to face her, only a step separating

them. She could feel the warmth of his body, smell his cologne. A sense of intimacy, a sensuality, played upon the taut strings of her emotions. His rough voice came again, so low it almost seemed that he was speaking to himself. "But if those same newspapers you speak of are correct, there are others who don't find it so difficult to know me."

Visions of the newspaper photos and gossip columns danced in her mind. "I've seen pictures of the beautiful women you've been involved with. But that's not the real person, the inside person, the important part of Sloan Montgomery. You work very hard at keeping him hidden from those around you. And you're as successful at that as with everything else."

"You think those other women haven't known the 'real' Sloan Montgomery?" Though his expression remained unchanged, she sensed his amusement. It aroused her temper, but she realized that it was only another ruse, a way to keep the conversation about himself from becoming too serious.

She faced him squarely. "Oh, I'm sure they know a certain side of you very well. But not the part I'm speaking of. Not the real you, unless you've been a great deal more open with them than I think you have. I don't think you let anyone get close to you."

Again the hint of intimacy rang from the words he spoke, but a certain change of tone was also evident. It was as if he realized that he might be revealing more than he wished by his evasion and was using his blatant sexuality to avoid further revelations. "Ah, but some have gotten very close. Conversation after lovemaking can be very revealing, especially if the feeling is good. And I've had no complaints about my performance." As he spoke again, one hand moved to push her hair back and her nerves clamored at his gentle touch, wanting more.

Behind the smoothly caressing words the cold, cynical Sloan was back in full force. The wall that he had let down a little had been erected again and he was once more trying to throw her off the track. It was a tactic she recognized.

"I'm sure you haven't. But are they looking beyond mere performance?" She took on a tone to match his own, though she felt the conversation quickly sliding away from its initial level of meaning. "I'm beginning to wonder if you've become so accustomed to performing, on one level or another, that you've forgotten how to feel, how to care for anyone outside yourself. I wonder whether you're afraid to let go and just be yourself."

She stopped, appalled at her own audacity. But the words were spoken and she waited for the reaction, her own temerity spurring her to go on when he said nothing. "Are you afraid, Sloan? Afraid to be vulnerable like the rest of us? Afraid to be open to hurt, able to recover, learn, and go on. Are you able to give something of yourself to someone else?"

His answer was quick this time, his words cold and thrusting as a sharp blade, his mask firmly in place. "I bet you take in stray cats, too."

The words hurt but she forced down an angry retort. "Sometimes. At least I can take a chance on loving something outside myself, even if it does hurt. And sometimes it hurts a lot."

He stood arrogantly before her, his arms folded in an aggressive attitude. "Are you setting yourself up as an example of perfect behavior? If so, may I remind you of an incident several weeks ago?"

Now it was here; the opening she had hoped for had

come. It was a chance to clear up more than one misunderstanding, but now that she knew him better, what could she say that wouldn't sound too sympathetic? He wouldn't accept that. But she did have to make an attempt, if not for Sloan, then for her own peace of mind.

"I think you have to understand, at least try to understand, what's behind a situation before you can judge the people involved."

"Are you saying I set myself up as a judge without knowing the facts?"

She recognized the aggression, the censure in his voice, the watchful look in his dark eyes. What could she say that would make the difference? He would bait her, then cut her to ribbons. And while she recognized his plan, there was little she could do to avoid it.

"In a way. By virtue of your position alone you're forced to be a judge in many cases. But I can't believe you'd be so unfair as to take an isolated incident and build a whole case from it; I'd give you the benefit of doubt."

Now you've done it, she thought as the words were spoken. Talk about stepping in where angels fear to tread.

"You don't know all the facts." His voice was flat, with a hint of anger seeping through. She felt the danger but plunged on, knowing that there was no backing down now.

"Neither did you, but you made a judgment all the same." She kept her voice controlled, carefully keeping any hint of accusation from it. It was an effort to face him, but she did it.

There was a sharp sound of derision. "You hit hard, don't you, Cara?"

She drew a deep breath. At least he was still listening;

he hadn't cut her off. "So do you. And I would like to say one more thing, then forget the whole incident. The comments you heard that first day weren't intended as you took them. I realize you know the circumstances now, but I'd like to apologize anyway. I'm sorry you were hurt by something that was spoken in the tension of the moment and not meant in a personal sense."

She plunged on, taking the opportunity offered by his silence. "Lea's birthday party was another incident. She deserved some recognition for her work. She's always willing to do more than her share and she's helped me, and you, tremendously. Her birthday gave me a chance to say thank-you and an opportunity to create a good feeling between members of the staff." She halted in her explanation for a moment, but when he said nothing she continued. "I'm sorry if it seemed unbusinesslike, a waste of time, but I think it accomplished something."

Time ticked by slowly as she watched his carefully controlled expression and waited to hear how he would receive her apologies. At last he spoke. "It's very easy to apologize when you have something to gain by it."

She was mystified. "What do I have to gain? I didn't have to say anything; I could have left well enough alone. It makes no difference to me."

"Everything has a price. And you want to be my permanent assistant, and possibly have a secure position when I bring in my replacement after this adjustment period is past."

She was astounded and so angry that she nearly sputtered in reply. Her hands clenched; she was dying to strike the arrogant look from his handsome face. "In the first place, I wasn't aware that my position wasn't permanent. Secondly, do you think I'd grovel like that? If I can't make it on my own, then I don't deserve the job. You really are everything I've heard about you—

and more." Then she stopped, aware of what she had said, and to whom.

The silence that followed was heavy as she strove to come up with something she could say now. But then he spoke, the insinuation heavy in his growling words. "Quite a little Miss Righteous, aren't you? So untouchable, so aloof, so . . . sterile? I don't think so, but I'd bet you like to see yourself as above all the rest of us and our baser natures." Again he paused before continuing. "But I don't believe any of that is really true. You say one thing and do another. You get all haughty about the kind of man I am, but I'm just like most men, if they would admit it. And just how do you expect a man to know if a woman he cares about is compatible with him unless they prove to each other that they are?" Almost imperceptibly, he moved toward her, still without touching, though he might as well have been for the damage his nearness was doing to her.

Again she had the feeling of being analyzed, as if he was measuring her reaction to his words. She had to wonder whether he really meant them, or was only using them to get a reaction from her.

When she refused to answer, he changed the subject and went on. "As for the other, that was a very nice apology, but if you expect anything so flowery from me . . ."

Gratefully, she redirected her thinking. "As I said before, I expect nothing from you, Sloan. You can only be what you are and I can appreciate and understand that. Anything less and you wouldn't be the man I know you to be."

His short laugh wasn't prompted by humor. "Well, how gracious of you." She burned with the derision in the words. "But if you're being truthful, I should repay you in kind. And I must say, you're different . . . in some ways. Most women expect quite a lot, generally very tangible things, especially when an apology is involved. But I forgot, you may have something tangible in mind." Her mind raced as he spoke. "Your career. And, always keeping in mind that someone will have to manage Triad after I leave, perhaps the 'token female' need not be relegated to the position of executive assistant. Am I right?"

Whether he was being deliberately provoking to cover up his half-apology or to needle her, Cara could not be certain. But again his words had pricked her anger. "I'm not a 'token female' in any sense of the word. I work for what I get and you can't deny that. Look at your little personnel folder if you need proof. It just so happens that I'm good at my job and the facts prove it, if proof is what you're looking for. And that's all I'm going to prove to you, because if your thinking really is that shallow, which I doubt, you're not worth proving anything else to. You get out of a relationship just what you put into it—and a relationship with you must certainly be a one-sided affair for any *real* woman!"

The derision in his words matched her own. "Quite the philosopher, aren't you? Dragged out your little soapbox and let go with all the clichés you could think of. It only proves my point. You're only half a woman— the outside half. The packaging is superb, the brain topnotch, but as for the rest . . . I have my doubts."

She was seething now, her black eyes flashing like coals of fire. "The old 'If you love me you'll prove it' line? That's hardly worthy of you, Sloan. I would have thought you could come up with something better than that. The great Sloan 'Love 'em and Leave 'em' Montgomery, setting the standards for everyone around him. Talk about being righteous and full of colossal ego . . . For that you certainly can't be beaten."

She was so thoroughly angry that she didn't care what retribution Sloan might exact. At this moment she hated the restrictions being a woman placed upon her. There was nothing she would have liked better than to beat some sense into him.

She could almost see the wheels turn in his mind, see the enjoyment he derived from the anger he awoke in her, the shot of adrenaline he got from the repartée. Though he put down her intelligence as well as her womanhood, he certainly used both for his own entertainment. And she resented that more than anything.

"Now, now. Your claws are showing." His teeth flashed in an almost-honest grin.

"Why shouldn't they be? You've certainly used your superior position to rake me over the coals. You've put me down personally as well as professionally. You're taking unfair advantage and you know it. And by 'superior position' I certainly don't mean as a male; I mean as my employer."

Dropping his arrogant stance, he moved even closer. She felt hemmed in, but refused to retreat, facing him steadily as his look and his words challenged her. "Superior? Men *are* superior in many ways, as I'm certain you fully realize. Yet women hold the key to men's desires. That hardly puts man in a superior position, does it?"

The conversation was again moving in a direction she wasn't certain she wanted to pursue, considering her state of undress and his studied ability to stir her senses. He'd completely ignored as much of what she'd said as he chose to, seizing on the part he wanted to use to intimidate her. Still, she felt a need to express her thoughts. "I'd call that a position of equality. Neither is anything without the other, wouldn't you say?"

A glint appeared in his eye, a glint that could have

indicated anything from humor to a touch of anger. "At least you recognize the equality of the sexes in bed. That in itself is a plus for the liberation movement. I suppose you do subscribe to those ideas? I mean, you feel your position at Triad is one of considerable importance—a woman in a man's world, I suppose."

Unable to completely follow his meaning, Cara silently considered the face of the man before her. "My position with Triad was gained by hard work, not sex. I think I've proven that to you. I want only what I'm entitled to."

A touch of humor seemed to soften his mouth. "I'm glad to hear that, though what you're entitled to may differ, in my opinion, from what you're talking about."

She studied the implication of his words, her head tipped to one side, her dark eyes thoughtful. "What exactly do you mean?"

In that moment she knew the answer. But before she could move he caught her, drawing her closer before he bent to touch her softly parted mouth with his. "This. Just this."

In her astonishment she couldn't move. Gently, he gathered her to him, molding her pliable body to his own. She knew the robe barely veiled her soft curves, at the same time revealing his rock-hard form to her sensitive body. To her credit she hesitated, but his persistent mouth alternately teased with teeth and tongue until her lips opened beneath his to allow the plundering caress of his tongue against her own. A flicker of desire ran through her and she pushed it down, knowing that if he felt her response he would immediately take advantage of it.

Her arms moved to his shoulders to support her weakening legs as his tantalizing mouth continued its foray along the sensitive areas of her mouth and throat.

His breath was warm against her skin, his lips soft, demanding in their expertise. She lost all logic in her whirling response to this overwhelming kind of magic.

Only a corner of her mind was conscious of the loosening of her robe. When his hand moved to slide inside the loose folds, her breath caught. A fire began to burn through her when his warm hand slid across her ribs to the curve of her breast, and she arched blindly against him as he teased the sensitive tip to attention. A groan of satisfaction left him as her robe fell fully open and the length of her was revealed to him.

"Oh, Cara, you're beautiful. Even more than I'd imagined." But she was oblivious to his whispered words as her own hands ranged over his heated body.

With practiced ease he caught her mouth, the rough hair of his chest, revealed by his open shirt, teasing her sensitive breasts. His lips tantalized, answered her own desires as his hands slid provocatively along her smooth flesh, drawing her against him to feel the full extent of his own arousal. His hips were taut against her, moving with an urgency she recognized as her own.

Her fingers slid through the thickness of his hair. She lost all consciousness of what she was doing in the mindless response of her body. Again his tongue plundered the softness of her mouth as his leg insinuated itself between her willing thighs to move in a rhythm her body ached to answer.

This was crazy; it was idiocy. The words flicked through her mind, chased by other, stronger reactions, until they no longer had any meaning. All her mind knew, all her body knew, was the strength of her desire for this man in her arms.

"This isn't going to be enough, Cara, you know that." The husky voice, softened by his own desire, brought a kind of reality washing over the turmoil in her mind, overriding the hot fire for which her body demanded satisfaction.

As though drugged, her mind sluggishly began to function on a more sensible level. "I can't, Sloan. This isn't right."

He stopped her words with a kiss that demanded the satisfaction they both needed. Again arching her body against him, she felt his warm breath against her face. "You know it's right. What can be wrong about two adults wanting each other the way we do? You can feel what you're doing to me; you know I want you. You can't deny that you want me, too."

The words brought her sanity. What could she be thinking? She *wasn't* thinking. That was the problem. She, who prided herself on her logic, had thrown logic away and abandoned herself to blind reaction.

In her reluctance to let him go, her hands stroked the thick hair at the nape of his neck. She closed her eyes to keep the threatening tears at bay. "I can't deny that. But I still can't be what you expect. That's not my way." The words were inadequate, but at this point they were all she could say.

For a long moment he held her, before his hands slid down her body, as if to remember what had been denied him. "Maybe the wait will be worth it. It had better be." Then he let her go, her body swaying in reaction. With trembling hands she gathered her robe about her in defense.

Again he had changed direction when she least expected it. She had feared his anger, expected him to pursue their lovemaking, but instead he had let her go. Her emotions raged in a turmoil of contradictory reactions. On the one hand she wanted him to go as far away as possible; on the other she clamored for him to finish what they had started.

While she stood in indecision, Sloan stepped past her toward the door. "We're not finished. Just remember that."

And then he was gone. It was only then that she allowed her reaction to the last few minutes to take hold. With tears streaming down her face, her whole body trembling with unsatisfied need, she sat on the couch, shivering as if bereft.

For long minutes she sat staring into space before rising to pace the floor. Sloan. Sloan Montgomery. What kind of man was he? The question kept repeating itself in her mind as she went over each word again and again, each feeling, each reaction. The hidden meanings in his words, the way he baited her, tested her, twisted her words to suit himself. He was a mystery unsolved. A man who saw, wanted and took. A man who had known all along what he wanted from her but had abstained from revealing anything of it for all these weeks. A man who knew now the response he could draw from her, knew it would not be long before she would be unable to deny him what her own body demanded.

Chapter Four

Cara arrived at the Complex early, heavy-eyed from the hours spent rewriting the progress report and the disturbing dreams awaiting her when she was finally able to sleep. She sorted through the correspondence, quickly assigning several things to Lea for handling. Precisely at ten Sloan strode into the office, tossing an indifferent wave in her direction before disappearing behind closed doors for the rest of the day.

Cara was surprised by his abruptness, by his renewed rejection. His seclusion made all her anxiety over what to wear that morning seem foolish and childish. She'd chosen a pale rose linen two-piece suit to serve as armor between herself and Sloan, but he hadn't even seemed to notice her.

Choking down her confusion, she determined once more to maintain her own aloofness. If he could be so cold-hearted, then she could, too. And she pushed away the knowledge that, even if holding her had meant nothing to Sloan, it had made clear to her that she was no longer able to think of him only as her employer.

The sleek gray Jag was in its space near her own slot when she arrived a week later and her senses stirred when she saw it. Not even the passing of time and her acceptance of Sloan's casually indifferent attitude toward her could still the heightened awareness she felt whenever she encountered him or anything that reminded her of him. In his rebuff of her she sensed a kind of waiting on his part, a waiting for something he expected her to do, though she didn't know what it was. The past week's uneasiness between them was getting on her nerves. The waiting had honed her senses to a screaming pitch and his avoidance of her tuned it higher with each day that passed.

Lea was not yet at the reception desk as Cara entered the quiet suite. Slipping quietly into her own office, Cara dropped her purse into a lower drawer and prepared to organize her day.

Taking her appointment book, notepad and pen, she tapped on Sloan's closed door. When she entered, she frowned to herself on seeing the stack of new tapes that was waiting for her. Her amazement at the continued volume of work he accomplished startled her into speech. "When did you come in? Daybreak?"

Glancing up at her statement, he lifted a corner of his mouth in a sort of half-smile. "Early, obviously." His eyes flicked over her slim figure in its soft-mauve straight-cut dress. The simple style was attractive in a classic way, pointing up her dark hair, the color bringing warmth to her pale ivory skin. His quick appraisal set up a tingling in her that was becoming a habit whenever he was near. She quickly fought it down, clenching her hands to still their trembling.

Turning back to a legal pad filled with his bold writing, he completed a line before ripping off the page and sliding it across the table toward her. "That's an agenda for a meeting Monday morning. Make certain all department heads get it today, so they'll have time to prepare for it. You'll need to be there to do the official minutes, though I'll take my own notes."

Without hesitation he went on in clipped tones. "Set a noon meeting, lunch, for tomorrow with Finance. Also a dinner meeting with Legal. Notify catering for board-room service." He glanced over his notes. "And I need to see Advertising about a new campaign approach. I'm not satisfied with what we have now. Better get Marketing in here, too. I need to know what they think about how to reach the market we want."

Cara scribbled furiously, as Sloan ground out more instructions. When he stopped, as if going over a mental checklist, Cara took a moment to look over his desk. The surface was covered with papers, but there was an organization to it all. He was fully in control, as usual.

The now familiar husky voice broke into her thoughts. "I think that's it. Any questions?" Running a hand through his thick, already ruffled dark hair, Sloan leaned back for a moment to stretch, his hands locked behind his neck. The movement molded the soft fabric of his white silk shirt to his body so she could see the shadow of the dark hair across his chest. Her breasts tingled in remembrance of the feeling of that hair against them and she gritted her teeth to quell the reaction churning within her. She could ill afford for him to know—and use—the knowledge that his every movement affected her.

"No. I'll let you know the appointment times I set

with Advertising and Marketing and add these others to my book.'' Picking up the tapes, she ventured to question him in a slightly teasing tone. ''Are you sure you were here only early, and not all night?''

He had settled back to work and looked almost startled at her comment. But he didn't pretend to misunderstand her. ''Have to keep the wolf from the door.'' Again there was no smile to accompany the comment. Shrugging indifferently, Cara turned to her own office, carefully closing the door behind her.

After dropping the tapes on her desk, Cara stepped out into the reception area. Lea had just arrived and was putting away her jacket when Cara approached. Dressed in buttercup yellow, the normally bouncy girl looked even brighter than usual.

''My, my! You're an early bird, Cara.''

Cara had to grin at Lea's turn of phrase. It was so typical of her. ''Yes, but Sloan is even earlier.''

''He generally is. I sometimes wonder if he ever goes home, except he always looks so great in fresh clothes every day.'' Lea grinned impishly. ''Or does he have a whole wardrobe hidden away in there?''

Cara had to match Lea's infectious gaiety. She really enjoyed working with her. ''I'm beginning to think that, too. What I'm wondering, though, is whether the cafeteria serves breakfast. You'd think I'd know, as long as I've been here.''

Lea regarded Cara carefully. ''Yes, simple things. English muffins, toast, eggs almost any way. What are you planning?''

''Well, seeing that the boss eats breakfast, for one thing. I have the feeling he neglects the things that make us mortal people run, in favor of work. Besides, it might just aggravate him enough to crack that tough shell of his.''

Again the elfin look returned to Lea's face as she grinned delightedly. "I'd love to see that. What shall I order?"

"Well, how about an English muffin, two eggs over easy and coffee. That should do and not make too big a mess if he throws it at me."

The younger girl giggled delightedly. "If anyone can get away with it, you can. I'll bring it in when it arrives—about twenty minutes, I'd say."

With that settled Cara returned to her own office to find Sloan standing impatiently beside her desk. "If you need to 'powder your nose,' do it when I'm not here. Where's the Jacobson file?"

Cara fought down a grin at Sloan's attitude, anticipating his reaction to the arrival of breakfast. Moving quietly, she found the missing file and silently slid it with exaggerated caution across her desk toward him before turning to her own work. A narrowing of his eyes was Sloan's only reaction as he abruptly returned to his own office.

Cara was busy with her correspondence when Lea quietly popped her head around the outside door. Her button nose wrinkled in anticipation of Sloan's reaction to being served an unrequested breakfast. Cara accepted the tray with an assurance she hardly felt.

"Thanks. Just listen for the crash, then come pick up the pieces."

Like conspirators they flashed quick smiles, and Lea left Cara to face Sloan alone. Drawing a deep breath to steady her nerves, Cara quickly pushed open Sloan's door. As she hadn't knocked she caught him leaning back, eyes closed, his hands behind his head, apparently deep in thought. At her entrance his brown eyes blinked open, instantly alert, and a crease appeared between his brows. His eyes narrowed as he sighted the tray she set on the corner of his table.

Refusing to be intimidated, Cara removed the covering from the hot plate, turned the mug over and filled it with steaming coffee from the small pot. Carefully avoiding Sloan's gaze, she laid out the silverware, moved the mug within reach and left without comment.

After standing outside the closed door for a moment, expecting an explosion of some sort, she finally relaxed and moved to her desk when she heard nothing. More than an hour passed. Cara worked while keeping an eye on Sloan's door. She had finished most of the correspondence when it suddenly opened. Her heart skipped several beats in anticipation, but waiting for any comment from him was like waiting for the second shoe to drop. It didn't come.

When Cara finally looked up, Sloan was shrugging into his suit coat, obviously on his way out. "I'm going across town to Cameron's office. I'll be back about twelve-thirty, in plenty of time for my next appointment." And with that he was out the door before she could make any comment.

Surprised, Cara reentered his office to find the remains of his breakfast shoved to one side on the wide table, the crushed napkin in the center of the empty plate. She gathered the dishes and was just closing the inner door when Lea slid around the outer one.

"Well? I saw him leave. No battle scars?"

"No. He licked the platter clean, you might say." She indicated the cluttered tray.

"And what did *he* say?" Lea cocked her pert head to one side as she relieved Cara of the tray.

Cara shrugged. "Nothing. Not one word. It was as if it had never happened."

The younger girl nodded. "I understand he does that.

When he has words with anyone, which he seldom does because no one argues, you'd never know later that it happened. It's as if he just wipes that off the slate. Tom and I talked about it. He says that's good; it means he doesn't hold a grudge. But it seems so unnatural to me; no one can be like that."

Cara agreed, remembering her own experiences with him. "It is difficult to believe. Even when you forgive and forget, you tend to remember the incident and it colors your relationship later, if only to make you think twice about dealing with that person in the future."

"I know. I keep expecting an explosion of some sort. Sloan is always so controlled, never visibly upset or angry, or even happy, come to think of it. I can't understand it." Lea laughed. "Tom says it's because I'm such an open book about my feelings. What I am, I am, and it sticks out all over."

Smiling at Lea's open face, Cara brought up another subject that had occurred to her concerning Sloan. "Surely he relaxes in some manner, sports or something. He can't live in this pressure cooker without a release of some sort." Cara leaned casually against the desk as she spoke.

Lea's look was thoughtful as she balanced the tray with one hand. "Not that I know of. I think he plays handball, but not with anyone in particular. Just picks up a game a couple of times a week. He belongs to a private club, a temporary membership, but from what I hear from the good ole rumor mill, he plays alone on the golf course. As for women—well, you're as up on that as I am." With a raised eyebrow to indicate her feeling on the subject, Lea continued. "I hear that Susan Stafford has tried her considerable charms on him, but with no success, much to her dismay and the delight of everyone else."

Cara laughed. "For being here such a short time you've certainly caught on quickly; Susan is a well-known shark where men are concerned."

Lea matched her laugh. "That's no secret. Seriously, though, how Sloan's escaped marriage this long I'll never know. As far as I'm concerned he's a dream served up in a gorgeous package." Dimples glinted in her round cheeks as she flashed a grin at Cara. "How about you? You're of marriageable age, and certainly attractive. How have you escaped so far? What about you and Sloan?" One lifted eyebrow indicated Lea's enjoyment of the thought.

"Thanks for the compliment." Cara smiled at Lea's infectious good humor. "As for my being of marriageable age, that's certainly true. But I'm not actively in the market. I have a lot of things to do before settling for one person. I enjoy friendships, not relationships. At least for right now. And Sloan"—she thought seriously for a moment—"so far he and I mix like oil and water. In the same glass but never together." And that's not likely to change, she added mentally.

She had feelings for Sloan that she wasn't ready to examine too closely yet. Though they rarely spoke outside of necessary business talk, she was aware that her feelings for him could easily change to the point that she would no longer be comfortable working for him. Then there would be trouble. Finally, she spoke. "Who knows? He may change his mind and decide I'm not the person he wants here, after all. You never can tell."

Lea shrugged expressively. "Okay. Have it your way. But I think Sloan is something really special. What could be more natural than two very special people getting together?"

"You're a born romantic, a regular matchmaker."

Lea cocked her head to one side with a shrug. "Why

not? Tom and I are happy. When he graduates from the university we'll be married and he'll go into a good job in his father's firm. Even though I'm not too certain that the job is the best one for him, I'm happy. I guess I just want everyone else to be, too.'' Her dimples disappeared. ''And I don't think Sloan is a happy man.''

Cara had to agree. There was nothing concrete to back it up, but she felt sure that Lea's statement was true. ''Everyone deserves happiness.''

''Yes. But maybe you can help on that score.'' Lea grinned again conspiratorially. ''Whatever you say, I think you could be good for Sloan.'' With a slight wave Lea turned to the door. ''Before you argue, I'll leave you to your work. See you after lunch.''

Sloan returned at the stated time, only to immediately attend another meeting and not return until well after three o'clock. From that time on he remained in his office behind closed doors.

At five-thirty Cara finished the last of her work. Hesitant to disturb Sloan, she finally tapped on his door and entered to find him still bent over the papers scattered before him. Though she knew he'd been working steadily for at least ten full hours, it wasn't evident from his unflagging zeal. Without looking up, he took the new letters she slid toward him and glanced over each one as he signed it with his bold black scrawl.

''It's been a long day. Time you went home, Cara.''

''You, too, don't you think?'' She ventured the opinion, gazing at his dark head and noting the latent power of his sinewy arms resting on the desk.

At her comment he glanced up, then let his eyes fall carelessly down her slim form. ''I have some things to finish up here, unless you're offering . . . ?'' He pushed the last of the letters toward her as he carefully watched for her reaction.

Fighting down the tingling awareness his suggestion fired within her, she called up all her icy reserve. "Is there anything I can help you with here?"

Leaning back, he once again let his glance fall over her. "No, not here." At her scornful look an almost-smile lifted one corner of his generous mouth. "Don't take too long, Cara. I'm not a patient man." When there was no response, he returned to business. "There are enough times when it's necessary for you to stay late. Go along tonight."

She gathered up the signed correspondence and was almost at the door before she turned to find him still watching her. "You'll get something to eat?"

A strange look crossed his face as he continued his scrutiny of her. Uncomfortable under his discerning gaze, she turned to leave, but his voice caught her in mid-stride. "Yes, I'll get something to eat." His look was again measuring and there was no answer to her hesitant smile before she turned and left.

After the heat of the late summer day the apartment was a refuge of coolness. Kicking off her shoes as she entered the small bedroom, Cara decided that a quick shower would renew her spirits and refresh her tired body. Quickly choosing well-worn slim-fitting jeans and a pale blue knit blouse, she threw them across the vanity to wait until she finished her leisurely shower. Turning the water to steaming hot, she reveled in the tingling water against her skin, then blushed. She was becoming much too aware of her senses, of herself, her body. And she knew that Sloan was the cause of her new self-awareness.

Refreshed, she stepped out of the shower and toweled off briskly, carefully keeping her thoughts away from the tall, forceful man who haunted her waking and sleeping hours. Shunning a bra, she slid into her clothes, then mechanically twisted her dark hair into a knot atop her head and secured it with a few pins. Several strands fell loose, making her face appear very young and vulnerable. Ignoring the errant strands, Cara considered the question of dinner, though she really wasn't hungry yet.

Cara loved her home. She'd chosen the colors and redecorated the three small rooms herself. The cheery red tile on the kitchen floor and counter tops stood out against the sparkling white of the stove and refrigerator. The dark natural wood of the cabinets mellowed the contrast of red and white and the checked cottage curtains at the wide double window lent a warm feeling to the small area. The dark woodwork continued throughout the other rooms, working well against the beiges and muted earth tones she had chosen for her walls and carpeting. Mellow maple furniture accorded with the ceramic lamps of terra cotta, casting a soft glow over the chocolate corduroy of a comfortable couch and chairs.

Cara had several plants in hanging baskets in a triple-windowed alcove to successfully create a miniature solarium, which she especially enjoyed.

The warmth and comfort of her decorating scheme continued into the bedroom, which was done in pale beige and rose. The dark oak furniture contrasted with the beige carpet and pale walls. A deep rose bedspread and covered chair warmed a room that might otherwise have seemed too cool in color.

Abandoning the thought of food, she picked up her mail and collapsed in a chair to sort through the various magazines and circulars.

She started at the sound of the doorbell, then rose to pad barefoot to the door.

"Sloan!" She couldn't believe she was actually seeing the tall man framed in the doorway. After the past week, when he had virtually ignored her, she had not envisioned his coming to the apartment again.

"You seem surprised." Lounging against the door frame, he smiled in his halfway manner.

"Well, this is unexpected."

"Possibly. Aren't you going to invite me in?" He straightened then, his lingering gaze taking in her somewhat juvenile appearance. His eyes fell slowly from her tousled head to the pink toes peeking from beneath the ragged hems of her old jeans, then moved back to her slightly open lips. She knew he hadn't missed the taut fullness of her breasts against the thin material of her blouse and the knowledge of his appraisal made them feel even fuller.

Flushing at his frank appraisal, she gestured vaguely, inviting him to come in. He seemed to fill the small room and Cara stood uncertainly; Sloan seemed intent on making her ill at ease.

"Am I allowed to ask why I have the privilege of your company?"

Almost belligerently, he answered, "Do I need a reason?"

Startled, she glanced at him quickly. "No, I don't suppose so. Though I never expected you to make a friendly call."

His reply gave her pause, as she considered its possible implications. "But I can be very friendly, given the right circumstances." Before she could reply, he continued, "I don't have a reason for coming; it was purely impulse."

Judging by the tone of his voice, it seemed to be an impulse he was already regretting. "Oh? Somehow I don't equate you with the word impulsive."

"No? Well, I hate to completely shatter your studied opinion of me, but since you're always so concerned whether I eat properly, I thought I'd give you the opportunity to make certain I do."

She frowned slightly. "Oh?"

A strange glint came into Sloan's eyes as he wound one of the loose strands of her hair around a forefinger. "You're repeating yourself."

That same warmth he had awakened in her before began curling in her stomach as Sloan toyed with her hair. "I do a lot of strange things. . . ." She stopped her too revealing words.

"Around me? And you thought there was going to be a nice, safe platonic relationship between us. You know there can't be."

"Sloan . . ."

"But for now, have a hamburger with me. I never work well on an empty stomach."

"Sloan . . ."

"You're repeating again. Get a jacket and some shoes. You don't need to change."

Relieved to be away from his disturbing presence, she slipped on a worn denim jacket and tennis shoes. When she got back to the living room she saw that Sloan had removed his tie and unbuttoned his shirt to achieve a more casual appearance.

In a short time they were relaxing over coffee in a small restaurant, awaiting the promised hamburgers. Cara's curiosity prompted her question. "What brought this on?"

"What?"

"This impromptu invitation."

He was as obscure as ever. "Does it make a difference?"

"Well, no. I'm glad you came by."

"Then why worry about reasons?"

"Okay. No more questions."

Though the questions nagged at her, she relaxed enough to enjoy this opportunity to see Sloan in a different light. The occasional silences between their comments concerning business began to feel less strained, and by the time they finished their meal they were more at ease with one another.

"This has been nice, Sloan. I like seeing you like this."

He hesitated in the midst of taking a sip of coffee. "Do I seem so different?"

She studied his relaxed features, her fingers toying idly with her nearly empty cup. "Yes, you are different. But then, I never know what to expect from you."

His only answer was a slight smile before he rose to pay the bill.

All too soon they were pulling up before her apartment building. The quiet of the night was broken only by the faint ticking of the cooling engine. She didn't want the evening to end. Somehow, it was important to her to keep him with her a while longer.

"Will you come in for coffee?"

His look was studied and she swallowed drily, waiting for his reply. "All right."

When he entered the apartment, Sloan stretched, moving his shoulders restlessly as if he were utterly weary. His gaze danced quickly around the room, seeming to take in the décor, the furniture, the colors, for the first time. "I like your apartment. It's warm and the colors are good. It fits you."

She was warmed by his compliment. "Thank you."

She went to put the coffee on to perk. When she

returned she found Sloan standing before a small framed watercolor that hung over her desk. It was a favorite of hers and his interest in it pleased her. At her entrance he moved to the couch, sitting down to relax against the cushions. Cara chose a separate chair and his eyes glinted at her choice. "Where did you get the watercolor?"

"In a little out-of-the-way shop that takes paintings on consignment for local artists. I don't really know why it appeals to me, but I was drawn to it. The greens are so lovely and the scene itself is so peaceful." She straightened to consider the picture, her head cocked sideways, her shining hair slipping a little more from its pins. "A misty morning, so fresh somehow." She stopped, embarrassed. "I don't know. Maybe it reminds me of a Missouri morning in the spring when the lowland is foggy, the sun shining through the treetops." She shrugged slightly. "It's just special to me."

"I've never known that." He glanced again at the picture, then back at her. "Peace. Is that what you look for—peace?"

Still looking at the picture, Cara carefully considered his words, wondering what motivated them. His face revealed nothing. "Yes. Peace is important to me. Inner peace more than just freedom from noise and confusion."

"And do you have it? This inner peace?" He stretched again, bringing one ankle to rest across his knee and lacing his fingers behind his head. She watched his light shirt stretch across his powerful shoulders. The desire to reach out and stroke her fingers across the cloth, to feel the warmth of him, the stretch and play of the muscles she could sense moving beneath his smooth skin, snaked through her.

Mentally, she shook herself. She couldn't let this happen. She must stay uninvolved. If he knew her feelings, he would run roughshod over her, take away her independence. He could totally dominate her if she let him. At least, he would do so until he had finished with her.

She forced her thoughts back to his question. "Most of the time. When I lose that, I lose a vital part of myself."

The coffee finished perking, and she went to get cups and fresh coffeecake. When she returned, the atmosphere seemed to have changed somehow and she felt at more of a disadvantage than ever.

Glancing at him as she set out the dishes, she was startled by the look in his dark eyes. It seemed measuring, as if he was judging her somehow. She poured the coffee, adding cream to her own cup, then settled back to sip the hot brew. Sloan tried a piece of the cake and in a short time had finished a second.

After refilling his cup, Sloan leaned back again. He seemed to be thinking of something but not ready to say anything just yet. Picking up some embroidery she had been working on, Cara switched on an all-music station on the radio before settling comfortably into her chair. The relaxed feeling between them felt good after the usual careful treatment of one another.

"What is that you're working on?"

"Oh, just a design I did for a pillow cover. A couple of mine are worn and I couldn't find anything I particularly liked in the stores. Besides, it's much nicer making it myself."

He continued to watch her for several seconds. "Why bother?"

She let the work fall into her lap, the shining threads

of the embroidery contrasting brightly against her jeans. "Because I want to. Because it makes it a part of me."

"That's important?"

"Yes, it is. All things are important in their own way, at least to me. Don't you think so? Don't you feel that each business you resurrect is a part of you? Aren't you proud of it for that, as well as because it becomes successful financially?"

He seemed to consider her words seriously for a moment. "Possibly, though this isn't the same; this isn't business."

"But I can see something in it. I'm producing something. I'll be able to look back on it and remember that I made it myself when I see it there on the couch."

His look seemed to delve into her thoughts as he digested her words. "Do you look back?"

She frowned at the question, wondering just how to answer it. "Sometimes. I look back on pleasant things, remembering events and people that meant a lot to me. Birthdays, anniversaries, weddings, Christmas at home, family dinners, the laughter and sometimes the tears. They're all important, worth remembering and looking back on."

"Even the tears?"

"Yes. Tears for happiness and tears for sorrow." She smiled in memory, her face soft in the lamplight as she held her embroidery and remembered special times with her family, times that were now past reclaiming. "My grandmother used to say that tears were nature's bath. They washed away the hurt and pain, helped heal broken hearts. Somehow it made it easier to cry and feel better without being ashamed." She smiled to herself a moment, leaning her head back against the chair. "Of course, I'm Greek. We're an emotional people, never afraid of showing affection or sorrow. My parents were very loving people; they freely shared the happiness and pain of everyone around them.''

He seemed to digest her words. ''Your parents. Are you still close to them?''

She picked absently at the embroidery threads with her slim fingers. ''No, they were killed a few years ago. An auto accident.''

He studied his cup, turning it around slowly in his large hands. ''It must have been a bad time for you.''

She was surprised, but warmed by the compassion in his words. ''Yes, it was. But I was grown by then, and I realized that though I loved them and would miss them very much, it was a blessing that they died together. I've thought about it often. Each of them would have been desolate without the other. They shared a very special love.'' She smiled softly, self-consciously. ''Of course, it seemed more so to me because I saw it from the inside and knew it was genuine.''

He was quiet for several long moments, absently continuing to turn the cup round and round in his long fingers. She watched him, wondering what was going through his mind. His next question surprised her even more than his earlier words had done.

''Do you want a family like that?''

Though she had not expected the question from Sloan, it was a subject she had thought about many times. ''Yes. When I have a family, I would like it to be as warm and loving as the one I grew up in. Anything less would be cheating myself and my family.''

''Then why haven't you married, if that's what you want from life?''

Her fingers smoothed the embroidery threads across her knee, sorting through the colors, stroking them one by one as she considered her answer. ''I want more than just marriage. It should be a beginning. And I haven't found anyone I want to begin a life with yet.''

"How can you be sure?" The smoothness of his words, the intimacy of the setting, made the question more provocative than she felt he had meant it to be.

"What do you mean?"

The perceptive dark eyes met her own. "Have you ever lived with a man?"

Even having become almost accustomed to receiving the unexpected from him hadn't prepared her for that question. She knew he expected an answer as straightforward as the question he had asked. Drawing a calming breath, Cara leaned toward him, catching his look as her full, well-shaped breasts swung against the close-fitting blouse. Her awareness of his reaction made her heart beat erratically. "Is that what this is all about?"

His gaze didn't flicker. "I want an answer, not a put-off.''

Remembering the many insinuations he had made, she fought down her growing anger at his audacity. "I don't think you deserve an answer. That subject has nothing to do with our working relationship. And despite what your previous arrangements may have been, that's all we have. I want you to understand that fully.''

Sloan almost smiled at her seriousness. "I thought we'd gotten past that. But I already have my answer. It seems I made a second error in my judgment of you. You've never lived with a man, for all your cool façade.''

His words challenged her. "Possibly, but you can't be certain. How do you know I live alone now? Perhaps he's out tonight. Perhaps we have a very casual relationship—to each his own. Hmmm?''

A tolerant look crossed his face at her efforts to retain her composure. "No, I don't think you could carry that off. You're too responsive to me for a woman who already has a current lover."

She answered in kind. "Perhaps I'm a very good actress."

Again the lifted corner of his mouth indicated a kind of amusement. "Women generally are. But you forget, I've seen you under some very adverse circumstances and you don't strike me as the type." The hesitation was meaningful. "Besides, I can tell by your apartment; no man lives here."

"And what have you determined, other than that I'm something unique in your experience? A woman who has to love a man before she sleeps with him. A woman to whom old-fashioned ideals are still important. One to whom marriage and the attached vows still matter."

"I think you're an all-or-nothing woman. And if you loved a man, or believed you did, you wouldn't hesitate over some outdated Victorian ideals. If you loved him, you'd sleep with him. Maybe you'd have some next-day guilt if he didn't do or say what you thought he should, if he didn't exactly return that love in kind. But you wouldn't be unique in that. Most women want to hear the words 'I love you' after they've been made love to. Something in your mental processes, I suppose. And they're not hard to say. Words are just words, after all."

Struggling with an anger she could hardly contain, Cara hesitated before attempting to respond to what she considered an insult. "What a perfectly egotistical thing to say! I think you really believe that garbage!" She was almost beyond words in the face of such thinking from someone she had considered a man of high intelligence. "Talk about ignorance! I've never heard such drivel from anyone, and I certainly expected better from you!"

Her anger affected him very little. "You have to admit it's true. Women like to hear certain words and men will

supply them if it fills the need. And you're no different.''
There was a kind of sneer on his face. ''If you'll own up
to it.''

Though she didn't care for the direction of this
conversation, nor the purpose behind it, Cara strove to
make her meaning clear. ''You may be right—for some
women. But not for all. Not for me. I have certain ideals
I've set for myself. If I truly loved a man, then I might
have to reevaluate those ideals, but that's really none of
your business, is it?''

''Maybe not. But I'll bet you haven't loved a man yet,
either. We tend to rationalize when we want something.
And you can't find a stronger drive, a stronger desire,
than sex.''

''But I'm talking of love, not just sex.''

Sloan almost snorted in derision at her words. ''And I
suppose that 'just' sex has nothing to do with this love
you speak of?''

Cara leaned forward in the intensity of her determination to defend her position. ''Of course it has something
to do with it. I can't dissociate the two. And I don't see
how anyone can. I know it's not uncommon. People play
musical beds all the time, but sex without love is . . .''

''. . . Is *not* animalistic, and don't tell me I'm rationalizing because I'm a man and women are more involved
emotionally. That's a tale some mother told her daughter
to keep her chaste. It's two people who care for each
other for the moment and can walk away, without regret,
guilt or recriminations, when it's over.''

She met his steady gaze. For a man who had suppos-
edly enjoyed so many relationships with women, he was
totally unaware of feminine emotional needs and she was
amazed. How could he be so cold, so unfeeling? The
differences between herself and Sloan had never seemed
so irreconcilable as at that moment. ''So you're just

satisfying a need, a physical need, and you say that's not animalistic? The feeling, the caring, is what makes us human.''

He was unswayed. "But aren't you rationalizing now? Excusing yourself for not taking chances? Weren't you the one preaching to me about taking a chance on being hurt? What was that? Just so much talk? The only difference between us is that you slant the justifications for a sexual experience to your advantage—because you love the man, and I slant them to mine—because I want the woman physically. I think mine is the more honest approach.''

"You're wrong, Sloan. I live my life as I feel I have to, in the way that will work best for me in the long run."

"So I have my answer."

"Yes, though I'm not certain of the question." And she wasn't. Had he been asking if she would consider a relationship with him? As dissimilar as they were, that hardly seemed possible, though he might consider that their differences would only serve to make the relationship that much more interesting.

Setting his coffee cup aside, Sloan stood, his height dwarfing her. She was confused by his questions, his attitudes. As usual, he had played havoc with her emotions, while he remained totally self-assured.

While she gathered her scattered thoughts, she lost track of Sloan. Suddenly, he swept the forgotten embroidery off her lap. His large hands encircled her upper arms, drawing her to him, molding her length to his hard frame.

Instinctively, she braced her hands against his chest to keep some small distance between him. She felt the steady beat of his heart beneath her palms and the warmth of his breath teased the smooth skin of her temple as she turned to look up at him. Her gaze fell automatically to his wide mouth. She wanted to feel it, yet she was afraid to want it. His somber eyes watched the play of mixed emotions across her face.

"Admit it, you want me."

She swallowed, knowing that his words were the truth. His low voice played on her senses, creating a reaction that began deep in her stomach, reaching upward with a fiery path where her sensitive breasts brushed his solid chest.

"Are you afraid of me?" He whispered the question, as his lips brushed across her mouth, taking her breath.

"A little."

"I won't hurt you."

It was almost a promise as his hands moved across her shoulders and down her back to press her lower body to him, to make her know the hard length of his thighs, the desire building in him. She felt the warmth of him burn through the material of his shirt, knew the taut strength of his need. She longed to hold him closer, to feel him against her, to know him. But she forced down the emotion growing within her. She knew the kind of man he was. And she would not fit the mold, could not be the type of woman he was accustomed to, the hold-and-let-go kind of woman he wanted. No matter what he intended, he *would* hurt her, though perhaps not in the way he meant.

Her answer was a whisper against his mouth as he tantalized her lips. "I know you don't want to."

"Then, what? I can tell that you want me as much as I want you. I've felt your response to me before and it's there again. Your body can't lie."

"I'm not sure. I think you're too much for me. I'm not the type of woman you're used to dealing with and you're not my kind of man. . . . I'm afraid of that."

As she spoke, his persuasive lips caressed her own, then her eyes, moving to the soft underthroat she exposed to him. He teased, persuaded, pleaded. "Afraid because I'm a man who admits he wants you, with all the rules laid out ahead of time? You're an attractive woman, Cara. I'm not the first man to want you, though I may be the first you've desired in return."

She knew the truth of his words. She wanted him, needed him. "But they weren't like you, Sloan. You're a different sort of man from those I've known and I don't know how to handle you."

"Handle me? Were those 'men' put off so easily, so easily led about by the nose? Did they cater to your every whim?" The whispered promises were gone now. "Were they so easily 'handled' that you don't know how to deal with a full-blooded man?" His voice fell again to caress her senses and her body responded in new ways. "Is that why you put on such a front, such a touch-me-not attitude?"

He continued playing on her senses as he spoke, both with his voice and with his hands, which slid familiarly over her body. "Those weren't men, they were boys. Boys playing boys' games. Grow up, Cara. Grow up with me. Let me show you what there can be between us." His lips toyed with hers before breathing his words into her waiting ear. "You want me; I can feel it in you, in the way you lean into me, the way you move against me."

She couldn't face him. He was too discerning, too sure of himself. Unable to turn out of his arms, she dropped her head against his chest and closed her eyes, unconsciously moving to lean against his strength. Giving in would not be her answer.

But Sloan would not let her be. He lifted her chin,

forcing her to face him. She felt his warm breath against her mouth just before his firm demanding lips took her own in a renewed assault on her senses that could not be denied. She didn't want to fight her responses. Sliding her hands up his chest and around his neck, she drew him closer, tangling her long fingers in the thickness of his dark hair. Opening her mouth to his questing tongue, she closed her mind to all sensible thought. Her senses whirled as, with an expertise she could only envy, his kiss took her places she had never been.

She did not protest as he moved with her to the couch behind them. Knowing, yet not knowing, she obeyed him; her only thoughts were of holding him. In her need she arched closer to feel the desire mount in the long body pressing her back into the cushions. His experienced hands explored her warm receptive body as his mouth smothered the sounds of desire low in her throat. She gasped as he deftly unsnapped her jeans to find the smooth hollow of her stomach, to raise her into new desire. She forced herself against him, her body begging for release from the gripping need growing within her.

In her desire to feel his body unfettered, her hands pulled his shirt loose and reveled in the smoothness of his long tapering back. She experienced with joy his reactions as she stroked the taut muscles along her spine before her hands moved to his flat stomach, following the path of dark hair to dip hesitantly below his belt. He shuddered and she moved again, her fingers kneading now at his firmly muscled shoulders.

At the warmth of his hands exploring beneath her knit blouse, she arched unashamedly into him and he cupped her throbbing breasts to suckle the hardened rosy points one by one in the warmth of his mouth. It was not enough. It could never be enough. His lips drew her very soul out of her as they continued their pathway from her breasts to her swollen lips, then back across the swell of her breasts to tease her responses to fever pitch.

"Cara, I want you." He breathed her name, until she stopped the whispers with a kiss.

Suddenly, he was still, holding her beneath him in a crushing embrace. Though her senses were reeling, she waited in his arms, not moving.

"Sloan?" Her voice was a whisper. She felt the tremors moving through his body and held him, knowing his need.

"Don't move." For long moments he lay, just holding her. Gently, she cradled him in her arms while the trembling ebbed, wanting to love him, knowing she couldn't. And the hollow meaninglessness of her words of a few minutes earlier came back to haunt her.

After several minutes he raised his head to search her flushed face. His eyes were dark with unfulfilled desire. "You get to me, woman, you really do." The thought seemed to disturb him. "I'm not accustomed to dealing with someone like you, either." When there was no answer he continued, a jumping muscle in his jaw the only betrayal of the strength of the emotions he was keeping under a tight rein. "We're both going to pay for this evening. I don't know why I'm letting you go. You don't want it, nor do I."

He rolled away from her to lie with his arm across his forehead. He still held her on the narrow couch, and she felt she belonged there next to him. She wanted to belong to him forever.

During those several moments Cara regained some of her own shattered composure until she was finally able to turn to him. She wanted to reach out, to touch him, and she almost obeyed the desire until she realized that he didn't want that now. She was stretched to the breaking point herself and knew he felt the same.

At last she rolled off the couch and escaped on still shaking legs to the bathroom. She splashed her face with cool water and decided that the person reflected in the mirror was a stranger. Her hair was all tumbled down, her face flushed, with something new in the eyes, a new knowledge, a new emotion she didn't want to examine just yet.

Sloan was shrugging into his suit jacket when she returned to the living room. His face had regained the familiar cold mask. Uncertain of herself, she stopped across the room from him. They were strangers now.

He spoke grimly, his eyes searching her still flushed face, lingering on her bruised mouth. "Now you *are* afraid of me."

Suddenly, her heart felt lighter. He was uncertain, too; he just hid it better. "No. Not of you exactly. Maybe of myself, of what I've learned about myself."

A flicker of something came and went in his eyes before he spoke. "And what's that?"

"I have to think about it more. I have to relearn myself." At his look she continued. "That sounds strange, I know. But I felt that I knew myself pretty well, but now I have a whole new dimension to explore, one that I'd never suspected before."

The questioning look was replaced with a kind of heaviness about his eyes. "Didn't you want to find out that you're a woman, with a woman's responses and needs?"

She flushed at the directness of his words, still unaccustomed to such open discussion of the feelings and relationship between a man and a woman involved with one another. "That's not it exactly. I knew that; at least, I thought I did. That's what I meant by having to think about it all. I'm a thinker, not a reactor. And tonight I reacted without thinking. That's a whole new experience for me."

"I see. An unwelcome revelation."

"I don't believe you do see. All the ideals I've set for myself were wiped away by what I was feeling. I thought I was stronger than that. I have to . . . to reassess my feelings, see where I go from here."

"You can think something to death, Cara. If I hadn't stopped, if I had taken you, as we both wanted, you would have thought yourself into a guilt trip later that would have overshadowed everything we would have had. You want too much."

"Do I? Don't I have the right to expect something when I care for someone enough to love him, care enough to give him myself? Don't I have the right to expect something just as special in return?"

He stood apart from her, in mind as well as in body. His hands were crammed into his pants pockets; his suit jacket was pulled back to reveal his hastily rebuttoned shirt, making her want to touch him again. He studied her serious face, her rumpled clothing, then came the words she didn't want to hear.

"I can't give you that. I want you; you want me. It's as simple as that."

Nothing could be plainer. But she wanted him to understand her feelings, even if he couldn't accept them. As he turned to leave, she found herself moving to hold him back, even if only for a few minutes longer.

"Sloan?"

His look was remote as he turned to face her. With her cheeks scrubbed clean of makeup she looked like an intent child, holding him back from leaving her.

"You don't know what you're playing at, Cara. You'd

better be sure before you make any decisions. I'm not a boy. I'm a man, with a man's needs. And when I feel you in my arms, feel your responses, then the time for playing is past. What you decide will be irrevocable.''

With that he dropped a quick kiss against her soft and waiting lips, then left her standing with rounded shoulders, suddenly desolate without him.

Chapter Five

$\int$loan didn't come to the apartment again. Their relationship remained a business one, totally impersonal. Clearly, he was expecting her to make the first move and intended to wait her out.

Cara persuaded herself that this strictly business attitude was best. She and Sloan were too different in background, in goals, in motivation. And she did a good job of convincing herself except when their hands brushed briefly over some papers and she felt a reaction that seared her carefully insulated emotions.

It was the small things that disturbed her. The freshness of his cologne could stir up unsettling memories. Sitting across from him during a brief lunch to finish up a business discussion made her lose herself in the play of expressions across his face.

When his attractive dark looks drew the attention of other women, especially if he indicated a corresponding interest, she felt a sort of betrayal. But Sloan indicated nothing. Confronted with his seeming indifference toward her, she doubted the strength of his desire for her. But she could not doubt the love she knew was growing within her for this difficult and complex man.

Weeks passed without change. Work progressed, responsibilities shifted as Sloan began to delegate more and more of the work at Triad. But the situation between Sloan and herself remained static.

Cara and Lea had become close companions. Though different in personality, Cara and the bubbly bright receptionist had built a special friendship, and during particularly rough days Cara grew to appreciate Lea's qualities of loyalty and humor more and more.

Like Cara, Lea had no parents. She had grown up in a broken home that had never been mended before her mother and father died at an early age. Cara had never before experienced such a closeness to someone with whom she could openly share memories of her parents and home as well as her dreams for the future.

It was over one of their frequent lunches that Cara detected a touch of unhappiness in Lea's usually smiling face. When asked, Lea hesitated, then began to outline a problem she and Tom could see no way to resolve without hurt feelings.

"You see, Cara, Tom's family are so important to him. I want us to be close and I don't doubt that they want the same. But they're smothering. They mean well; they want to do so much for us. Almost too much." Lea's expressive eyes brightened with tears. "The position in his father's company is perfect for Tom, but not if we have to 'report in' every night for dinner. I want to run our own home, live our own lives. And Tom does, too. But how do we tell them? And his mother. I love her, but she's helping too much with the wedding, the furniture, the gifts. I feel overwhelmed. I want to enjoy the wedding, not dread it.''

Cara saw that the problem was too large for Lea to see beyond it, and she let Lea regain her composure before speaking. "Lea, what if Tom just sat down with his parents, his father first, and put his cards on the table? They've always had a close relationship, from what you've told me. Couldn't he be completely honest and yet not hurt their feelings? Couldn't he make them understand that you two are adults, ready to live your own lives now, ready to be treated as a separate family unit, as well as a part of the total family? Is Tom willing to try that?"

The younger girl toyed with her salad. "It's such a touchy situation, Cara. I'd rather let things go on as they are rather than chance a break in the family. This is so important to me." Lea's lower lip trembled childishly as she tried to express her feelings.

"I know, Lea. But it's because it's so important that you have to try. It's difficult for parents to let go; they love almost too much sometimes. They want to give so much, see that your life is easier than their own. They fail to see that you need those same experiences to grow, just as they did. Can you see what I'm saying?"

She studied the unhappy girl for a moment before continuing. "It would almost be better to chance a break than to have the problem grow between you and Tom, don't you think?"

Lea's face brightened a little. "Yes, I do. I guess I was thinking so much about the problem, I couldn't think about an answer. It won't be easy, and we may have to do this a step at a time, sort of wean them away, but we'll do it."

Cara's smile met Lea's as they finished their meal.

She only wished there was a solution to her own problems, but none seemed to be forthcoming. She was glad, though, for Lea's openness, her sharing nature, the buoyant spirits that she envied. She valued their friendship and wished she could share such things with Sloan.

Sloan. The name, the face, were always there before her. But he remained out of reach. She loved him; she could admit that to herself now, but she also realized that her love would never lead to anything lasting.

Occasionally, she caught Sloan watching her and thought she detected a flicker of something in his face before the mask fell into place. But she was forced to chalk it up to her own false hopes when nothing further happened. It was depressing, this whole thing between them. He was playing a waiting game, a game he was a master at, a game she was sure to lose.

Cara sometimes saw Sloan with Susan, who had apparently succeeded at last. Never in the building itself, but sometimes in the parking lot. The sight of him leaning over her as she lounged against her car, the possessive way in which Susan smoothed an imaginary wrinkle in Sloan's jacket lapel, stabbed through Cara like a knife. At those times she realized more acutely than ever that Sloan was a law unto himself. She also saw that Susan fit in better with Sloan's way of life than she could ever do. She knew Sloan could ease his frustrations with Susan, while Cara had to fight it out alone in the darkness of the long nights.

And there were other things that kept Cara's wounds bleeding. Sloan had never been known to be a one-woman man. The society columns dutifully documented the evenings he spent in the company of various notables' lovely and eligible daughters. The smiling profile turned up appealingly to the handsome Sloan Montgomery was sometimes not so young. Widows near their mid-thirties, young divorcees, and even some that Cara would have sworn were forty or more, could brag about being escorted by the popular corporate head. Cara wondered, in weak moments, what else they could boast of in connection with Sloan.

Hints of marriage possibilities abounded, and each time she read them Cara threw aside the newspapers with a mixture of contempt and pain. She had had her chance. And if sometimes she allowed herself to dream of being on Sloan's arm at some special social function, then at least she knew that a dream was all it could be. He'd made his position, his proposition, very clear, and she had passed up the opportunity. And she was paying for it dearly now.

Out of frustration, she began accepting dates with men she knew were safe, men she knew would make no demands on her. She even enjoyed the evenings in a passive sort of way. But the excitement was missing. The heightened expectation, the response, was not there when they briefly held her, their lips brushing her own. Involuntarily, she always turned quickly aside and she knew that their reactions to her cool response ranged from resignation to anger. She didn't expect to hear from most of them again, and really didn't care.

Larry called and they renewed their friendly relationship, going out sporadically. But if she had been uninterested in a permanent relationship with him before, she was even more so now.

The gray Jag was in its place as usual when Cara arrived at the Complex one Friday morning. Weary after another in a succession of nearly sleepless nights, she knew that Sloan had probably been at his desk for a couple of hours already. How he kept up the pace of both his business and social engagements she didn't know.

Living on little sleep, endless cups of coffee, on nerves and adrenaline alone, he was becoming more and more machinelike. Yet he continued to be totally on top of everything, giving the impression that nothing was ever too much to handle. His cool appearance of total control and aloofness remained in place at all times.

Cara hurried toward the building, intent on getting an early start on her own work. Entering the elevator, she glanced at her mirrored reflection in the wall panels, noting the smooth line of her pale green two-piece suit. The collarless neckline lay gently against her skin falling in a V to the first button, hinting at the soft swell of what lay below. Absently, she straightened the belt that encircled her narrow waist and adjusted the straight skirt, which was split in front to show off her well-shaped legs. Her matching green pumps hugged her narrow feet, giving a flawless line to her calf and ankle. As she adjusted the three-quarter-length sleeves, Cara mentally ticked off the projects that needed to be accomplished before the end of the day as she strode toward her office.

Sloan's door was shut, as usual. The routine remained, Cara thought, as she picked up her calendar. He had no open-door policy where she was concerned. That closed portal was a personification of the emotional barriers between them.

Tapping briskly on his door, she entered when there was no answer. The room was empty. The drapes were drawn, leaving the office almost totally dark. The lamp lit only the desk top, leaving all else in shadow. Sloan must have stepped out for a few minutes, she thought, as she peered quickly around the room. She pulled back the drapes, flooding the room with bright summer light. Then, without giving further consideration to where Sloan might have gone, she turned to flip open his appointment book.

Leaning over both books, she ran a finger down the listed appointments, making adjustments in her own so it matched his. The day was fully booked, as always.

After a moment her senses tingled; she felt as if someone was watching her. Uncomfortable, she lifted her head to encounter Sloan's gaze focused upon her, his long frame draped over the leather couch along one wall. The phrase "cat-and-mouse" flashed through her mind. Her resentment flared, giving strength to her momentarily paralyzed tongue.

"Sloan! Why didn't you say something!"

Carefully unfolding himself, he came to stand before the table. Cara's hungry eyes noted the darker edge of his brown eyes, the natural wave in his hair as it swept back from his temples. She clenched a fist to keep herself from brushing back a wayward strand. His dark eyes slowly perused her appearance, moving along the smooth fit of the skirt over her rounded hips, lingering on the quickened rise and fall of the fullness of her breasts, more than half revealed as she bent over the desk.

There was a challenging edge to the movement as she deliberately straightened to discourage his fascinated gaze. Though her knees grew suddenly weak under his probing eyes, Cara determined to stand her ground, meeting the dark eyes that rose to meet her own.

His voice carefully controlled, his gaze unwavering, Sloan finally spoke. "It's my office."

For a long moment they waited silently until Cara shifted her gaze away. It was as if he were saying, "We meet on my terms.'' That the time of waiting had come to an end, and her inability to confront him hinted at her own futile efforts to withstand the slow attack he had mounted against her defenses. She wondered what had broken the stalemate. What had made him change the hands-off policy that he had lived by for quite some time now?

''True. But I have certain rights here, too. And I don't need to be spied on.'' She knew that her restless nights, combined with his unnerving presence, had made her temper short, her words too sharp for the occasion. But she must make her position clear. She deserved a certain respect from him and she wanted him to know that. What she didn't want him to know, to be able to use against her, was that her love for him made it increasingly difficult for her to maintain her outward coolness toward him.

His shrewd eyes narrowed again slightly. ''Why should you feel spied on if you were only doing your job?''

Though angry at his taunting, Cara carefully controlled her words. ''I would feel the same way in my own office, or my home, if someone deliberately kept his presence secret from me.'' His countenance remained unchanged. ''You wouldn't like it if the tables were turned. I'm sure you'd be very angry if you should find yourself in that position.''

In a sort of defiance Cara lifted her chin, awaiting his response. She knew that there had been something else behind his words, but she would not back down. She must hold on to some of her pride.

''You're quite bold today.'' The words were ominous in their caressing tone and Cara felt a small finger of apprehension slide down her spine. This was the same cold Sloan she had always known. Nothing had changed during that evening after all.

Breaking the hold of his intent eyes, Cara slid his appointment book back into place. But Sloan was too quick for her. Stepping around the edge of the desk, he effectively cut off her only avenue of escape. Cara, who had begun to move at the same time, found herself within inches of his hard, tall frame before she could stop her momentum. Forcing herself to look up into his face without flinching, it seemed she almost ceased to breathe at the taut anger she saw there. Unconsciously, her gaze fell to his firm mouth, remembering, longing to feel it against her own mouth again, yet wanting to run away from him at the same time. The realization of her reluctant, but ever growing love for this man came to her stronger than ever.

For long moments they stood, each refusing to give in first. The tension grew to an unbearable level in Cara. Suddenly, her appointment book dropped from her nerveless fingers. The thud of it, as it struck the table leg, broke the silence stretching between them. Glancing first at her feet and the book lying open on the floor, then uncertainly back up to meet Sloan's still unflickering gaze, Cara stepped back, breaking the hold he exerted over her.

But before she could effect a retreat he advanced, his long form moving steadily forward until there was nowhere she could go, no escape.

"When are we going to finish it, Cara?"

Her heart pounded within her; her nerves pulsated with its beat. When she spoke, her voice was a choked whisper. "Finish what?"

In a seemingly careless motion the back of Sloan's hand brushed her sensitive breast as he moved to smooth the neckline of her jacket against her tingling flesh, a movement that was both sensual and aggressive.

The response his touch evoked brought a gasp choked from her.

"You know the answer to that. You just felt it."

A flush burned across her pale cheeks as the familiar tightening began in her stomach, the uncoiling tendrils of desire burning through her.

As if in a trance she watched his mouth come down, her lips tingling in anticipation before she knew the firmness of his own against them. Without conscious thought she leaned readily into his embrace. She felt the hardness of his body against her, as she automatically molded herself to him. Her ears roared with the pounding of her pulse as she abandoned all pretense of reluctance. She accepted, even instigated, the caresses that woke the slumbering response she had been denied for so long.

The kiss that began softly, caressingly, deepened almost to savagery as his emotions rose. Standing on tiptoe to fit her body to his, she accepted and gave, her mouth hungry for the feel of his lips, of his tongue as he teased and plundered her softness. Her hands felt the play of his muscles against her sensitive fingertips as she splayed them across his back. She arched against him, her aroused breasts almost hurting as his hands moved around her to take them in his hands, to tempt them until the ache inside her became a pain. Gasping, she allowed her mind to float free in total sensual response to his expert lovemaking, knowing this would never be enough for either of them. Without acknowledgment she felt the buttons of her jacket loosen to give Sloan free access to the ivory fullness his mouth sought.

Suddenly, he realized where they were and the searching motions of his mouth against her stopped. They stood still, letting their emotions subside, their heart-beats slow.

"This isn't going to work, Cara. You know that. There has to be a change . . . soon." Idly, his fingers moved over her to adjust her clothing, lingering against her heated flesh, flicking gently at one taut nipple until she groaned, then sliding smoothly away.

She closed her eyes to hold back tears of frustration. She was unable to speak. Her mind was still whirling, her emotions still too chaotic to think coherently. Shaking her head in answer, she stood away from him to clear her mind. Without meeting his gaze, she drew a deep breath, then stepped around him and left the office. He let her go.

When she reached her desk, Cara sank gratefully into her chair, resting her head in shaking hands. This was more than she could cope with. They were still at a stalemate. She needed a commitment in a relationship, while all he wanted was a no-strings affair for however long it took him to tire of her. And feeling as she did at this moment, she could almost believe that even a short-term relationship would be worth the gamble.

Cara's moments of recovery were brought to an end when Lea pushed open the outer door. Her ready smile quickly faded at the sight of Cara's stark white face.

"Are you all right? Can I get you something?" Concern creased the younger girl's forehead as she approached.

Drawing a calming breath, Cara hastily reassured her. "I'm fine. A touch of a headache, but it's better now."

"If you're sure . . . I have some aspirin if you need any."

"Thanks, but I'll be fine."

A smile dimpled Lea's smooth cheeks. "Just wondered if you wanted to change Sloan's menu." At Cara's uncomprehending look she continued. "Breakfast. I know he was in early this morning; there are three memos on my desk already, and they aren't from last night. Do you want the same or something different?"

After their first success, Cara had made a habit of ordering Sloan's breakfast if he was in the office. So far, the venture had gone without comment from Sloan, but he ate the food.

"Well, might as well be twice a fool." Shaking her head wearily at Lea's uncomprehending look, Cara continued, "Order the usual, but add a large glass of grapefruit juice, unsweetened." She sighed, depressed, but regained her equilibrium quickly. "It will fit his mood."

Lea glanced warily at Sloan's closed door. "Oh, oh. Heads to roll?"

"They could, I think. I'm glad it's Friday and he has a full slate of meetings."

"Hmmm. This could prove interesting. Well, I'll order breakfast and leave you to face the tiger."

As Lea left, Cara turned to her own full schedule, forcing him out of her mind for the time being. Sloan had meetings scheduled all day. Marketing was due in first, in order to finish before noon, leaving time for Sloan to coordinate any new ideas before Advertising came in after lunch.

By the time Cara finished some filing, Lea had returned with Sloan's breakfast tray. With a fingers-crossed salute, Lea left Cara to gather her courage. Admonishing herself for being so wary of the man, she tapped on his door and entered.

As usual, he was bent over an array of papers. His

glance took in the tray, but there was no welcome in his eyes. Nor was there a rebuke, however. Relieved, she set the tray down and left, without any words passing between them.

Grouped to one side of Sloan's office, the Marketing staff sat together, as if needing mutual support. As the meeting progressed, Cara had her first real experience of the corporate side of her employer. Sloan Montgomery at his desk, throwing out thoughts and decisions, demanding immediate results, was not to be compared to Sloan Montgomery presiding over a meeting. If he was this way among his own people, how must he have been during negotiations to take over the business? She could almost feel pity for the retired former president.

In response to Sloan's request, the head of Marketing and two staff members had come armed with statistics to substantiate their viewpoint and verify their current direction. Sloan wanted to see results, she knew and, watching them attempt a presentation, Cara became more and more apprehensive as she sensed, rather than saw, Sloan's attitude.

Indecision and confusion were evident in their behavior. As a result, their thoughts were disjointed and they had nothing tangible to show either as a marketing plan or creditable efforts toward achieving one.

As they fumbled, Sloan's displeasure became painfully obvious. His impatient fingers drummed lightly on his chair arm, though his carefully controlled mask was firmly in place. His quick, sharp questions made the men grow even more uncertain as their presentation drew to a close and Cara felt the tension in the room tighten like a steel band around the group.

By the time Sloan turned the discussion toward the future, the Marketing representatives were obviously totally disconcerted. Almost in exasperation, Sloan stood and leaned over his desk to face the department head. His voice low, the cutting words showing his irritation in no uncertain terms, Sloan made his attitude clear.

"Collins, this is getting us nowhere. We'll meet again Wednesday morning, early. At that time I will expect to see a proposal on the direction you believe Triad should take, your reasons, and the eventual results we can expect. I want something concrete to work with, not just vague ideas." The theatrical pause hung heavily in the room. "Do I make myself clear?"

Dismay registered on Jason Collins' face. He knew his job, but apparently wasn't in the habit of doing it, if his latest reports were any indication.

As the Marketing group left, a markedly depressed atmosphere remained in the quiet office. Sloan collapsed back in his chair in obvious frustration, shoving himself away from the desk in abrupt anger. Turning in his chair to gaze moodily out the window, he appeared to be in deep thought for a few minutes, a line of concentration creasing his broad forehead.

Uncertain whether to leave or remain, Cara glanced over her notes. When she glanced up, she saw his profile outlined by the window light, softened by the draperies. For a moment she allowed herself the luxury of memorizing the strongly chiseled forehead, nose and chin, remembering the feel of that generous mouth against her own. For a second she luxuriated in the memory of the feelings he aroused in her. They were feelings that she hadn't known she was capable of, that made her come alive, made her the woman she could be—a physical woman, a woman in love with a thoroughly masculine and virile man.

Forcing down those remembered responses, she turned her mind back to the business at hand.

Finally, without turning, Sloan spoke. "What do you think, Cara? Can he do the job?" His voice was flat, tired. More than tired, even weary.

She was startled at the tone of his voice and at the question itself. After a moment, she answered, "I think he *can*. The question is, will he?"

At her words he leaned back, stretching in the now familiar way, his fingers laced behind his head. Again, her nerves jumped in reaction to his attractiveness and his pull on her senses.

"He has the background and, I think, the ability to do it. But maybe since he's been here he's gotten away from doing the job." She thought again for a few minutes. "I've heard Cliff say several times that things were stagnating here, possibly because Mr. Quinn was ready to retire but couldn't, until he had a buyer. He lost control of things. Carelessness became the rule, but you're well aware of that. Collins is just one of those who became slack. Not a good situation for you."

His mouth tightened in reaction to her words. "You've analyzed the situation quite well. Quinn did let things slide." He hesitated in thought. "Most companies begin to go bad because of either economic conditions they can't adjust to or plain poor management. Both apply here, but the second more than the first. There's potential here, but remotivating the personnel, getting them out of bad habits, is proving to be more difficult than I had expected. I think the right people are here. It's just a matter now of making them aware of what's expected and motivating them to redirect their thinking on their own."

He seemed to be talking to himself, clarifying half-formed thoughts. "This can be a viable, competitive company again. We can't let it die for lack of leadership or positive action; that would be a crime. Our economy needs companies that can provide both a product and employment at a functional level. In short, profitably. Not just for me personally, but for everyone. Too many once important and stable industries are barely surviving, even dying, and I refuse to let Triad join them. At least, not without a fight."

He seemed to reevaluate his statements before continuing and she waited intently. It seemed important to him to say aloud the things he felt about Triad, about his business interests in general, and she wanted to hear it all. "But the people have to be involved. I can't babysit for them. I refuse to. Some will measure up, some won't. And those who don't . . ." He let the words die, the end of the sentence unnecessary.

It was the most she had ever heard him say about his reasons for personally taking control of Triad. It involved the need to win. The challenge of motivating the people appealed to him as much as the potential financial gain. And this realization gave her a new picture of the man inside Sloan Montgomery, a picture she liked.

"Yes, I know. But if the reports I've read are any indication, I believe things *are* turning around. The people are sounding optimistic, realistically so. The departments seem to be formulating definite plans. At least, most of them do."

Suddenly, he swung around in the chair to face her, the movement so quick she blinked in surprise. His large hands dropped to the chair arms, his legs spread apart in a deceptively relaxed attitude. "And what are your plans, your direction?"

She could tell from his tone that he was asking about

her personal, as well as professional, plans. There was a challenge in the words, along with a note of sarcasm. It was time for a decision, a turning point in her life. And she spoke with a low-toned attempt at confidence in spite of her hammering heart. She intentionally used an impersonal tone for her first words, deliberately avoiding responding to the implication of his question.

"Just like everyone else here at Triad, my immediate plans depend on you. I want to help you turn this company into a successful part of your operation, not just a convenient tax write-off for the next two years, to maintain our jobs. Whatever that calls for, I'm willing to do."

He studied her closely, and she felt he could read her thoughts. Calling up her courage, she said, her voice hoarse with nervousness, "Other than that, well . . . that depends on you too, doesn't it?"

His expression remained unchanged. "Does it?"

The simple words sounded heavy with meaning. Or was she seeing meanings where there were none? Was she fooling herself? Could she afford an emotional investment in a man like him? Could she take a chance on a man who had admitted that he wouldn't allow a lasting relationship to develop? Though she had gone over it all in her mind a thousand times, when it came to the final saying of it, she hesitated.

Finally she spoke, her voice barely audible. "I think you know the answer to that."

Still, he sat, unmoving, unwavering in expression or attitude. "How far? How far will you depend on me?"

Her heart nearly stopped. Now was the moment of decision. She was on the verge of making a commitment that she knew he would not match. Would she listen to her heart in the final decision, or to her practical nature?

Would she be able to handle the repercussions of either decision?

When Cara did answer, her voice was tight with suppressed emotions. Her hands gripped the note pad in her lap to still their trembling, its edges cutting into her fingers.

"But that's the point. You don't want anyone to depend on you. Not really. So I suppose that's also up to you."

The silence between them was weighty. Tension tingled in the room.

"You know what you're saying?"

Vainly, she searched his face, his eyes, for some indication of his feelings, trying to read his thoughts as she knew he could read hers. But she could tell nothing from the controlled features she was longing to touch. This man could call forth reactions, feelings, from within her that no other man could. But could she allow him to have a hold over her without a like commitment on his part? And though she had made the decision countless times in her mind, she was still undecided.

Motionless, he watched and waited for her answer.

"Yes. I know what I'm saying."

"You're willing for me to make the rules?"

She forced the words from stiff lips. "Don't you always?"

Again, the pause lengthened, each of them studying the other.

Cara was nearly spent with tension and the emotions battling within her when Sloan broke the silence. "I hope you know what those rules are. You could get hurt."

Cara swallowed hard, trying to hold on to her composure. "I know." And she watched him closely, thinking,

Better me than you. But she spoke the words only in her mind. Sloan would reject as sympathy or pity the emotion she knew as love, enough love to want to take away the hurt he had suffered in his life no matter what that cost her. Enough love to want to spare him more hurt. But would that be enough?

Something flickered behind Sloan's penetrating gaze. But it was gone before she could determine whether it was acceptance or merely a smug acknowledgment of her surrender. Whatever his thoughts, they were not revealed in his next words. If she had expected tenderness or understanding of what her decision meant to her, it wasn't in his words. If he had any idea of how she had totally negated everything she had set as her way of life, he didn't show it. She felt curiously empty when he said, "Have you thought of the possible consequences?"

She allowed her gaze to shift to the window, to the world outside the room. Out there people were going about their own lives, but here, inside, so much was being said in so few words. So many changes were being determined in a life that, until she met Sloan, she had thought complete, content. Now, without him, there would be only emptiness and pain.

"Yes."

"And you can deal with them, should it become necessary?"

"Yes."

It seemed her voice came from somewhere outside herself. She was numb. The total realization of what she had committed herself to had not set in yet, she knew, and she wanted to keep that moment at bay for as long as possible.

There was nothing more to say; it had all been said. Silently, Sloan turned his back to her in dismissal. Like a sort of automaton she rose and slowly left the room, leaving him sitting alone.

Weak and trembling, she sank into her chair, dropping forward and leaning her throbbing head across her arms. She shut out everything except the pounding of her heart, which was full of the knowledge that neither of them had spoken of love.

By the end of the day she was totally drained emotionally, her nerves taut as bowstrings. Anxious to be alone with her thoughts, she hurried through the last of her work. Uncertain as to what Sloan expected of her, Cara chose to follow his lead and act as if this was just another day. She left the Complex without speaking to him again.

Cara drove home thoughtfully. Seeking solitude, time to think, she found herself walking the quiet shady paths of the park across from her apartment.

She followed the worn, winding ways through the trees around the small lake. Stopping for a few minutes, she watched children, accompanied by their mothers, feed the few ducks paddling around on the still water. Reflections of the early summer clouds rode the mirrored surface, which was laced with pink and white blooms from trees shedding the last of their late spring foliage. The atmosphere soothed her tangled thoughts.

Before she realized it, two hours had passed. Though she had solved nothing, she somehow felt more at ease with herself and was able to go home feeling that she could cope with whatever came in her relationship with Sloan.

As she entered the apartment, she sighed and rubbed her aching temples to relieve the tension headache that had settled there. In the darkness Sloan's face rose in her memory. The strong planes were softened, as she had sometimes seen them; then they sharpened in concentration and determination, as had more often been the case. She thought of the sadness she had felt upon discovering the barrenness of his childhood. She was aware of the responsibilities that had been thrust too early upon him; the pressures of corporate business had had a devastating effect upon a young man who should have been just learning to know himself. He had survived those pressures a driven man, but an incomplete one. It was all part of what made him important to her.

She thought, too, of the experience he had shown in his personal dealings with her, an experience that was the result of his encounters with the sophisticated women who were part of his world. She could hardly fault him for that. He was a man to take pleasure where it was offered. And she could hardly say she resented his expertise in lovemaking. Rather, she exulted in it. The memory of it made her long, even now, for the feel of him against her. Her body wanted the proof that she could arouse his desire for her to the same fever pitch that built within her with just his touch. But she recognized that it was an exercise in futility. She was so uncertain of him.

Darkness had fully come when she finally rose to snap on a chairside lamp, no closer to achieving inner calm than ever. She had made a commitment, a commitment that she knew Sloan would hold her to, would call upon when he chose. A commitment that, on one hand, she wanted to honor but, on the other, held back from, because the decision overthrew everything she had been taught since childhood, the limitations she had set for herself. The question was, could she live with that decision? Or would it eventually kill her love for Sloan?

And when he tired of her, could she follow through with her promise that there would be no recriminations?

With those dark thoughts, her body utterly weary, she switched off the light and went directly to bed, where she fell into an exhausted sleep.

Chapter Six

𝒜 persistent sound kept intruding into her dreams, a ringing she could not locate. By the time she had forced her spent mind to function and had reached for the telephone, she heard only the empty buzz of a dial tone. Wearily she replaced the instrument, noticed that it was still night and glanced at the watch she still wore. Only nine o'clock. Exhausted, she eased back for a while, willing sleep to return. She listened to the early summer night, alive with the sounds of people out in the neighborhood, but sleep avoided her.

Finally she rose to stand at the window and watch as the street lights began to blink on along the thoroughfare. It was a sight she normally enjoyed, finding a certain magic in it, but tonight Cara turned wearily away from it. None of it meant a thing. She felt drugged, her energy sapped, her mind incapable of functioning.

Despairing of a return to the escape that sleep provided, she brushed back her tangled hair and slipped on a pale pink brushed nylon robe. The robe clung to her slim frame as she moved in her naturally graceful way, loosely tying the sash. Hoping that food might help her sleep, she padded barefoot to the kitchen. The abrupt ringing of her bell interrupted the quiet of the apartment.

Sloan stood in the doorway, the light from the hall creating shadows and hollows in his face. His casual dress indicated that he had gone home to change before coming. Her attraction to him overcame her surprise and wariness, as she appreciated the fine physique outlined by his hip-hugging casual slacks, their dark gray contrasting with the lighter gray of his close-fitting silk shirt. It was open halfway down his chest, and the deep V revealed the small medallion resting in the mat of hair against his tanned skin. Unconsciously, she licked dry lips, the tip of her pink tongue catching and holding his appraising gaze.

"You shouldn't come to the door like that. Looking like you've just come from bed. It's too enticing."

With fascination, she watched him close the door and slip the lock. Turning to her, he questioned, "Are you all right? I called earlier and there was no answer."

Drawing a deep breath to calm her racing heart, she switched on a lamp, bathing the room in a soft glow. "I was walking. In the park across the street."

She moved to the small alcove, staring out into the night again, crossing her arms to hug her trembling body. "I sat in the shade and watched the ducks on the pond. It was peaceful."

She sensed him move directly behind her. He didn't touch her, but she could feel him as surely as if he was branded upon her.

"Again that word—peace. To look at you, one would think that was the last thing you needed."

She felt the power he could exert over her by his

presence alone. She refused to face him, feeling safer in avoiding the potency of his direct gaze. "I'm not like you, able to totally control my feelings, though I've tried. You're able to set things in categories, take them out to examine, use them when you choose. I guess I can't do that."

"Maybe I've simply had more experience." His voice was closer, touching her, caressing her with its huskiness.

She stretched her neck backward, her hand massaging it to ease some of the tension there. "I'm sure that's true." In reaction to him, her voice was sharper than she had intended. "I'll grant you that you do," she said coolly, finally recognizing the double meaning that had been obscured by the calm word game he was playing.

She could smell the familiar scent of him, feel the warmth of his body. She longed to turn into his arms, to let go, feel him, love him. But she couldn't.

"Then why fight it? Why deny the pleasure we could give each other?"

A sadness came over her. "It seems we've had this discussion before. It makes little difference, though. I'm like all the rest. A few words, a few kisses, and you'll have what you want. Everything is so easy for you."

"But I don't have what I want. Not yet." The low tones of his naturally husky voice plucked at her nerves, setting up a reaction she found almost impossible to hide with sharp words, though she tried.

The changes in her life were too new. She felt used already. What would she feel later, when he left her? And she had little doubt that he would. Her attraction for him would pale and there would always be someone else to take her place. That knowledge and the pain of it gave an edge to her words. "That's what you're here for, isn't it?" She could sense his withdrawal, though he hadn't moved. Cara forced herself to face him, searching the cold remoteness of his face for something she could hold onto.

"Regrets already?" His tone was mocking, cutting her deeper yet. "But you're a woman who knows her own mind. At least, that's what you maintain."

"Yes, I always have been."

"Then?"

He wasn't making things easier for her. He seemed to be deliberately forcing her to voice her doubts. But why should he bother? It was of no consequence to him, as long as he got what he wanted. Nothing ever changed.

She couldn't lie to him. "You upset my equilibrium. The ideals I've lived with mean nothing when you're here. That upsets me; you upset me." The last was spoken in a near-whisper as she realized that nothing she could say would make the least difference to him.

"Yet you agreed, agreed to a relationship that you knew would be more than you were prepared to give." He half-turned away as if to leave.

Obeying a blind impulse, she laid a shaking hand on his arm to hold him. At his look she let it drop, clenching the fingers into a fist to stop their trembling. She could see the tight lines of his averted face. But she determined to make him understand, even if it stripped her emotions raw.

"Not more than I wanted to give." Her mouth trembled as she fought back tears. "That was never in question."

"Then what?" His voice was flat, rough.

Drawing a deep breath, she plunged on. "I'm a strong person; I like to think I'm as strong as you. But, also like you, I have my own fears—when I choose to face them. Oh, not the same ones, but real fears, nonetheless. They have no outside source, but come from within."

She swallowed, trying to rid herself of the nervous dryness which claimed her throat, making her voice hoarse. "I'm not immune to hurt. I haven't always lived in the cotton-lined protection my parents would have preferred for me. I've been hurt. Not in the same way as you, but hurt all the same. And I don't want to feel like that again. So I'm afraid. Afraid I can't be what you need, what you want. Afraid you'll soon grow tired of me and go on to someone else. I know that eventually you will, and it will hurt, maybe more than I can bear. But even more than that, I'm afraid I can't be enough for you."

Her tears flowed freely now. She felt stripped naked before him, more vulnerable than she had ever been before. But if she had expected comfort from him, there was none.

"Wasn't that part of the agreement? That I make the rules? That you could cope with any eventual changes in our relationship?"

Blinking back her tears, Cara searched his face for any trace of understanding. She fought for control over the pain that stabbed her when she saw none. "Yes, but that doesn't change the fact that I want to avoid that kind of pain whenever I can." And yet she couldn't turn away from him; she knew that. Why, she thought, why doesn't he just leave now? I can't stand all this. The words alone are killing me.

"Self-preservation? You should have thought of that. You're a grown woman, aware of all the things that can happen in a relationship with a man." He studied her carefully for a moment. "You care too much, Cara."

There it was again, that same accusation. If only he knew how much she wished she didn't care so. A coldness wrapped around her heart, making her want to strike out against the unemotional shell he persisted in pulling around himself while she felt more and more vulnerable. "And you don't care at all! You don't know what it is to feel." She wished she could scream at him, attack him.

He was obviously unaffected by her words, and she reflected briefly on the type of man he was. He was untouched by any emotion other than physical desire or anger.

"So where does that leave us?"

He was unreal. She was tied in emotional knots, her nerves at the breaking point, and he was calmly analyzing the extent of her compliance with their verbal "contract."

"Exactly where we were. There hasn't been any change."

"You would live with me in spite of your personal reservations?"

That set her back; her thinking hadn't advanced to that point. "No, I won't live with you. I couldn't do that and work with you as closely as we do."

"It won't be necessary for you to work. And I suppose you could continue to live here if you prefer. It's of little consequence to me."

She flinched at his unfeeling words. "I can't do that. I have to have something to fill the hours; I have to work." Mentally, she added, I have to have something left when you leave.

The seeming normalcy of this conversation appalled her. They might be discussing a grocery list instead of something that would affect her whole life.

"You'll have a generous allowance. I've never yet seen a woman who couldn't fill her time if she had the financial resources to do so."

She felt as if she was up at auction and resented it. Quick anger flashed in her black eyes and stained her pale cheeks. "No! I won't have it! I'm not something you can buy! I'm not a puppet to be manipulated in that way!" She faced him directly, her anger blazing out toward him.

He seemed almost amused at her sudden temper. "No? Then what do you want? Surely something."

"A price? You think I have a price? Is that really all you think I am? A piece of merchandise? A piece . . . a piece of baggage. Isn't that the term? A glorified prostitute—aren't those your words?" Involuntarily, her hand flashed out to strike him flat across the face. The sound echoed in the tension-filled room.

With a kind of horrible fascination she watched her handprint on Sloan's cheek change from white to deep red before registering the rage that formed as her words struck home.

Unadulterated fear gave Cara's shaking legs strength as she turned to run toward the bedroom. She cursed her habit of sleeping nude, which prevented her from leaving the apartment to seek refuge elsewhere in the building. Grabbing the door to push it shut, she glanced frantically about the room for escape. But before she could think she was flung backward as the door slammed back against the wall with a resounding crash.

Clutching at the footboard of the bed, Cara tried to stop the momentum of her fall. Landing heavily on one hip, she scrambled away from the menacing figure standing over her. With one hand she tried to hold together the robe that fell open to reveal a flash of long leg as she struggled to regain her feet.

Sloan's hand snaked out, pinning her to the carpet as he knelt over her. Fear and exertion had her gasping for breath; the rapid rise and fall of her full breasts straining against the thin material of her partially open robe drew his angry gaze. Frantically, she turned and twisted in his grasp. His strong hands grasped her flesh, but still she struggled to avoid the look of hatred burning in his narrowed eyes. But even as she struggled, she knew it was useless. She was held physically, as well as emotionally, by the strong hands and desire-darkened eyes of the man above her.

Still holding her with one hand, Sloan forced her to face him, ignoring her attempts to twist out from under him. With his body he held her to the floor. The knowledge of his intention suddenly filled her, giving added strength to her efforts to escape. Heaving, she almost dislodged his grip, forcing a muttered oath from him.

"Damn you! If that's the way you want it, that's the way it will be." The words were forced from between Sloan's clenched teeth, the rage and bitterness that poured from him flowing over her shaking body.

His taut frame stretched full-length over her, weighing her body down, successfully halting her escape attempts. Her mind whirled with the heat of the rage he directed at her. His breath, heavy with the exertion of battle, fanned her face, his darkened eyes cold and glittering as they moved over her flushed face and tangled hair.

It was no use. She was desolate, defeated. Closing her eyes, Cara forced herself to relax. Tears of pain and frustration rolled from the corners of her eyes, falling into the silken hair at her temples. Her breath caught and held as she fought back sobs of despair welling up within her spent body.

Her soft mouth trembled, then jumped in response

when his hard mouth came down to claim it, crushing her lips against her teeth. Fiercely demanding, he held her mouth, taking what he willed.

Knowing she was no match for him physically, she fought back in the only way he understood. She opened her mouth to accept his anger and hostility with a fierceness born of love and desperation. She felt his hesitation before he joined her in a demanding expression of need that erased all her fear and eased his own aggression.

A heat grew within her, starting in the pit of her stomach and licking through her veins as his expertise began to fire her passions. She warmed and responded as she fed his questing tongue. At her sudden and unrestrained response to the ravishment of her mouth, he hesitated, then softened his assault, taking her response and forcing it to grow in answer to his need.

He released her numb wrists, sliding his hands slowly to her shoulders to mold her to him. He moved against her as his breathing slowed and deepened in awareness of the charged tension between them. Cara buried her fingers in the thickness of his hair, gripping him to her in a desire to hold him emotionally, as well as physically.

With a smothered groan, he covered her aching body with his own, grinding into her an awareness of his full intention. It was not enough. Of their own volition her fingers slipped the buttons of his shirt, sliding it loose from his belt to reveal the smooth texture of his skin as she slipped his shoulders free. With her hands she worshiped his torso.

Sloan's mouth teased, explored, trailing down the sensitive column of her throat to the hidden valley between her breasts, shifting and licking them to attention, to an aching awareness of his expertise. In moments all fear, all reasoning, left, as she gave herself up to him.

The warmth of his hand moved against her as he slid loose the tie of her robe. She arched blindly against him as he explored the length of her responsive body. Feverishly she kneaded his shoulders as his knowing fingers awoke her full response, sliding against her in his growing knowledge of her.

Insinuating a leg between her thighs, he heightened the agonizing need for release peaking within her. Her mind screamed with the need crying out in her body as his mouth once more sought the swollen softness of her lips. Her nails sank convulsively into his flesh as his teeth gently caught her nipples, swelling the already taut orbs of her breasts to fill his knowing hands. The rhythm of his body against her own cried out for an answer.

She heard his almost inaudible whisper against her mouth. "I don't want to hurt you, Cara. I don't want to hurt you."

In answer she whispered feverishly, mindlessly, against the lips teasing her own, "I love you, Sloan. Please love me, just a little."

Time stood still as the kisses stopped. She felt his ragged breathing, his body trembling as he lay against her, and knew she was not alone in her emotional turmoil. Though he held her, she felt him begin to draw away again. And she felt cold and more alone than ever.

In a few minutes he shifted to rest his forearms on either side of her, his long fingers brushing her tangled hair softly back from her flushed face. He shifted to drape the lapel of her robe across her exposed and throbbing breasts, his fingers brushing the hardened nipples, deepening the aching need of him inside her. She gasped, then bit her lip as his gaze fell over her in accusation. He was visibly forcing himself to control his labored breathing, the only sign that his emotions were still as involved as her own.

His voice was hoarse, tight with tension. "Damn you, lady, you want too much. You don't know what you're playing with. You give and then pull back. And one day soon it will be too late to stop. As it is . . ."

The words trailed off as he heaved a deep breath and rolled to sit up beside her, his head resting on his thick forearms bridged across his knees. She watched him, watched the control he exerted over himself, over his emotions, and didn't remind him that she hadn't been the one to pull away.

The silence stretched before he spoke again; his words were not what she had expected, certainly not what she wanted to hear. "I'm leaving town for the weekend. I'll be away Monday."

The unspoken command to arrange things at the Complex was there. She nodded in compliance, striving to put aside the aching hollow left inside her by his refusal of her offer of love. In too short a time he rose and was gone, leaving her empty and alone. She ached with frustration and anger, devastated by her own emotional contradictions.

For long minutes she lay curled into a tight, miserable ball, loving Sloan, yet filled with the knowledge that she was an expendable item in his life. She knew he was just biding his time until she fully accepted his terms, knew he would not wait much longer.

The bedside clock showed nearly noon when Cara awoke. She was as drained as she had been when Sloan left. There was no answer to it all. She loved him, needed him, had poured out that love to him in every way but the one he wanted. And he had rejected them all. He didn't want her love, only her body, for however long he chose. And it hurt. It hurt more than she had ever imagined it could.

Refusing to think or examine her feelings further, Cara rose and showered, letting the hot water cascade over her.

Finishing a light meal of toast and coffee, which was all her stomach could stand, Cara decided to tackle the laundry. She hoped, as she walked down the back stairs, that she would be late enough to avoid meeting anyone. Luck was with her and she filled the machines and settled down to listen with closed eyes and mind to the gentle swish of the agitating water. She kept her mind carefully clear of any thoughts.

After stacking the freshly cleaned clothes in her basket, Cara retreated again to her apartment. As she was struggling through the door with her burden, the phone jangled. Dropping her basket, she hurried to answer, half hoping it was Sloan, knowing it would not be.

"Cara, it's Lea. Have you read this morning's papers?"

Cold fear clutched at her. "No, I haven't been out."

"Well, brace yourself. Sloan's father died. It's front-page news. Everyone thought he had died several years ago. Apparently, he's been in a hospital under psychiatric care for alcoholism and related illnesses." Lea's voice stopped for a moment. "I tried to call you last night at about nine, when I heard it on a special newscast, but I guess you weren't in."

Sinking onto the couch, Cara almost gave in to the lurching of her stomach. He had come, knowing his father was dead, and she had failed him. She had been so concerned with her own feelings that she had failed to see his need. The very thing she longed to do was to keep him from further hurt, and from the first she had fallen short. He had needed her and she had turned him away.

Tears filled her eyes and fell onto her pale cheeks as she thought of all the terrible things she had said to him, the awful things that must have brought back memories of his bitter homelife, his father and his mother's desertion of him.

Lea's voice drew her back to awareness. "Cara? Are you all right? Have you heard from Sloan?"

Slowly, she gathered her thoughts. "No, I haven't. What else does the paper say."

"Well, it says he was 58 years old. Was active in business and financial circles until some fifteen years ago. He was at Riverdale when he died of a massive stroke. There's a picture of him from years ago and of Sloan. It says the funeral is Monday."

Monday. There was no doubt—Sloan had known. "Does it say where the funeral will be held, or who is in charge?" She waited for Lea's answer, her mind working frantically.

"Let's see. Yes, Bacon-Abbott here in the city is in charge of arrangements, but it's to be a private service."

"Thanks, Lea. I'm glad you called. Talk to you later."

She rang off at Lea's quick goodbye. Within minutes she had checked with the hospital and Sloan's home to find that he was at neither place. There was only one place he could be.

With her decision made, she ran to her bedroom to rummage through the closet. She dressed quickly in a simple front-buttoned dress of dusty pink. Its simple lines hugged her figure, the shade giving color to her naturally pale skin.

In a short time Cara guided her car into its space at the Complex. Quickly checking the lot, she finally spied the gray Jag pulled into an alcove between the buildings, well hidden from view. After hurrying through the private entrance, she impatiently punched the elevator button, willing it to hurry before she lost her nerve. As the doors slid open, she stepped inside, nervously working the clasp of her purse, the clicking sound loud in the confines of the elevator as it rose.

When the doors slid open once more, Cara glanced down the corridor. The silence was frightening. She was almost certainly alone in the building with Sloan and the thought made her doubly aware of the tap of her heels across the tiles before they were silenced by the carpet.

When she pushed open the outer office door she could see no light coming from beneath Sloan's closed door. For a moment she felt that she had been foolish to rush out looking for him. He might even be trying to reach her at the apartment. But she had come this far; she couldn't leave without making certain.

Her steps made no sound on the carpet as she crossed to his door. Quietly, she pushed it open. The room was in semidarkness, the drapes pulled only partially back. Stepping inside, she waited until the door had closed again.

At the click of the latch the broad-shouldered figure sitting before the window moved. As Sloan turned fully toward her, she could see the cold glitter of his eyes, and she almost quailed, her courage suddenly shrinking.

"What are you doing here?" The flat sound was back in his voice.

Without speaking she moved toward him, dropping

her bag onto the table as she passed. Carefully, almost warily, he watched her, his taut figure aggressive even as he sat. Holding his gaze, she came to stand before him, forcing him to look up into her face. She moved between his spread legs, leaning to brush a kiss across his still mouth before dropping to her knees and sliding her arms around him.

A muscle worked in his jaw, but the brittle coldness in his face remained the same. Knowing that she had gone too far to back out now, and fully aware of her own vulnerability, Cara laid her head against his chest. She felt the solid beating of his heart beneath her cheek, the warmth of his body against her.

For long moments he was still, then slowly, very slowly, his arms came around her, folding her into him, holding her so closely she could hardly breathe.

She didn't count the time, content that she was here and he was responding. Finally his hands slid to her shoulders, setting her back away from him. His hands still held her as he leaned forward to be more on her level.

"Why?" A little of the coldness was gone, but the mask was still in place.

"Because you need me. Because I need to be with you."

Her hands rested on his corded forearms as he continued to hold her. When he spoke again, his voice was colder than ever. "I don't *need* anyone. Especially you. And I don't *want* anyone who isn't mature enough to handle a relationship with a man without hiding behind the legal armor of a mere piece of paper—a marriage license. I don't want a woman who measures her worth in terms of what she can get out of a man when the loving is over, a women who can't decide whether the man alone is really worth the risk."

He was like a surgeon who worked with words, cutting away at her with each syllable, pouring anger and frustration and bitterness into her open wounds as he went on. "What's a piece of paper, anyway? It's just as easily replaced by another. Divorce is easier to say and simpler to get than a marriage license." She felt the anger in him; the tautness of his body, the tight-lipped expression on his face as he clipped out his words told the story.

"But I won't be caught by either one." The silence was short, only a small respite before what was to come. "Do you know what a tease is, Cara? Well, lady, you are one. A superb one. And I don't much care for the tactic."

Numbly, she sat before him, letting the words stab into her like a knife. "You offer all the goodies with one hand, but strike out with the other when someone attempts to pick up the candy. You know what that does to a man. You're not so innocent as that. But you're using it. Using it to strengthen your case, hoping I'll remain a 'gentleman,' make an 'honest' woman of you before I get you into bed. Well, two can play that game. I can make you hurt as much as I do after one of your blow-hot, blow-cold ploys." The narrowed eyes and tense mouth, the clenched muscle in his jaw, told her that his anger was genuine.

She felt as if she were in shock. She had come here to help him. She wanted to love him, comfort him, and he was striking out like a cornered, injured animal. She prayed that her control would last until she was alone again. She couldn't let him see that he was slowly killing her.

Swallowing the cotton in her mouth, Cara managed a nearly normal tone of voice. "Don't you think that I *did* feel the same as you? The same ache, the same emptiness. Women aren't so different.''

Sloan's hands still gripped her arms, but she wasn't aware of that pain, only of the tearing she felt inside at his attack. But loving him, she somehow stood her ground. As she tried to think what to do, she began to realize that he was even more like a cornered animal than she had realized at first. He was attacking her in his own pain, his own hurt, his own aloneness. If so, then it was a sign he could at least feel something. It meant that the loss of his father did mean something in his life.

Suddenly, he changed the subject. ''How did you know I was here?''

''I just knew.''

''Am I that transparent?'' he said, leaning back in the chair.

''No, you're very complex. But I knew you would be here, keeping hidden.''

''Hidden?'' The idea seemed absurd to him. ''Why should I hide?''

''Because you always do. You keep yourself hidden, afraid to be alive. So you try to be a machine, unfeeling and mechanical.'' Then her voice softened. ''But I know better. You're very much alive, very much a man.''

His mouth tightened for a moment before he spoke, his remoteness fully returned. ''I perform like a man. Remember? Performance is what counts.'' The bitterness etched across his face wrenched her heart. ''At least to most people.''

''But it's not all. There's more.''

''You didn't think so last night. You would have given up your pious morality willingly and been satisfied. But I chose not to have to listen to your 'maidenly recriminations.' The word love doesn't enter into what I want from you and I want you to fully understand that. I'll be responsible only to a point. Beyond that, it's up to you. I won't carry your self-indulgent guilt for you. I can give you satisfaction, but as for the rest . . ." He let the words trail off, anything more unnecessary.

Her whole body flushed at the implication of his words, the curt dismissal of what had happened between them. But she refused to let him frighten her away. Not yet. "Anyone can 'perform' like that. The difference is in the caring, the loving involved. We've discussed this before, and nothing has changed for me in that sense."

"How would you know?" His words were deliberately belittling.

"Because no one has ever affected me the way you do. Because I love you. Because I do care." The words seemed so inadequate somehow and she wished she could better express her feelings.

"You confuse desire with love. Desire is a healthy, physical response. Love is debilitating, crippling."

"How can you say that? Love is a tender thing, something to be nurtured, encouraged, cherished."

His voice fairly dripped with scorn. "Romantic drivel. Your body in my arms wasn't responding from love. That was desire, a physical response I can arouse anytime I hold you, and you know it. You just don't want to admit it and take advantage of it. But don't confuse that with love. It just isn't there."

"Not for you, maybe. But for me, love is necessary. And it *is* there. I love you. I love you even now, when you hurt me, when you ignore me, when you frighten me."

"You make me sound like a brute." Again, the muscle was moving in his jaw, a sign of his agitation.

"No, just a man who's been hurt tremendously and is

striking out. A man determined not to feel, but who can't help it. A man who is lashing out at something and someone who affects him in a way he doesn't want.''

Her voice softened even more as she gambled against great odds that he could care for her. ''I see a man who needs to love and to be loved, but one afraid to be hurt anymore.'' She leaned forward, placing her arms along his muscled thighs, feeling them jump in involuntary reaction. ''You're the man I love, the man I want to love me, hold me, to let me hold him. Please, Sloan, let me love you. Even if you can't love me in return, just let me love you.''

There it was. All her feelings, her hopes, her heart, were laid out before him, open to be ridiculed, trampled in the dust or—perhaps—taken up and cherished. She could see something, possibly indecision, flicker momentarily in his intense gaze. His look held hers for long moments before dropping to her parted lips.

Roughly, almost as though against his will, Sloan jerked her to him, his demanding mouth capturing her own. Unrestrainedly, she answered, slipping her arms around his neck to hold him to her. Sliding her across his lap, his hands blazed a path where they touched. Pushing back the open lapels of her dress they sought the soft mounds of her breasts, which were straining toward him, as his mouth deepened its quest for her own.

In answer to his need she held him, her fingers tangled in the thickness of his hair, sliding down the smooth column of his neck and inside the collar of his shirt to feel once more the smoothly moving muscles of his shoulders. When he would have drawn away, she held him, whispering against his mouth, ''Let go, Sloan. Let go and love me, just a little.''

Burying his head against her neck, Sloan held her quietly as if struggling with a decision. Finally the low voice, raw with spent emotion and another tone she did not know, answered. "I don't know if I can. I don't know if I can love anyone."

She slowly let out the breath she had subconsciously held. He'd made a big step, admitting even that much. "Then let me teach you."

Turning, she caught the momentary crease of a frown between his brows as he looked away. Catching his face, she brought it back to meet her own. "What is it? You've gone this far. Be honest with me, at least be that. I'll accept no less from you."

Absently, his hand caressed her shoulder, straying to fall around her neck, his thumb softly rubbing the hollow of her throat. "You've changed. I don't know if I want to be responsible for that."

She smiled gently, brushing a kiss quickly across his mouth. "I haven't changed. I'm sure of my feelings now, that's all, and not afraid to be responsible for them myself." And it seemed to be enough for him.

Together, they left the office. As they rode the elevator down, Sloan avoided looking at her, while she feasted her eyes on the tall, broad-shouldered man who she felt closer to at this moment than ever before. He was a man of confidence when dealing with facts and figures, a ruthless man in business, but a man who could not bring himself to accept any kind of real personal commitment to another person. A man afraid to let love make him vulnerable.

After escorting Cara to her car, Sloan leaned back against the door to pull her to him. She surrendered willingly to the teasing of his lips, finally taking the initiative to hold him close without reserve, to let him know she needed him.

Eventually she drew a deep breath and leaned back. "How about me fixing dinner? Would you come?"

The tension between them eased. A small smile played around his lips. "Are you a good cook?"

Playfully, she crinkled her nose at him. "Beast. Yes, I am. You should see what I can do with a steak."

He nuzzled her hair. "Hmmm. You should see what I could do with you."

Her breath caught in her throat. "Let's go home."

"Coward." And dropping a quick kiss across her mouth, he handed her into her car before turning toward his own. They had faced the subject of her love for him, and he still had to deal with the death of the father he could not forgive.

They spent a comfortable evening, though Sloan tended to pace, prowling about the apartment restlessly, thumbing through books, listening to record albums at random. Cara prepared the steaks, seasoning them carefully before grilling them. Salad and hot bread completed the meal. Before long they were dining to the accompaniment of soft music and candlelight.

Over coffee they watched a variety show on television, and Cara marveled at the normalcy they achieved. Cara honored Sloan's reluctance to talk, waiting quietly for his determination of what would come next. She sensed that Sloan needed some time. Something nagged at him, something he could not put into words, and as much as she wanted to share whatever it was with him, she knew it was best not to force the issue. At the end of the program she switched off the television and chose another album to play.

Sloan finished his coffee and leaned over to set his empty cup on the table. His elbows rested on his knees as he ran a hand through his loose hair. "The reporters must have given up by now. I'd better go."

She watched his weary features. "Was it bad?"

He rubbed a hand down his face. "Enough. A lot of questions, naturally. Questions that need no answers, as far as the public is concerned." He sighed deeply. "They're like vultures, always probing for something rotten and unsavory."

"It's their job, I suppose, but not a very nice one. It seems like they become callused to the hurt of other people. Anything is acceptable as long as they get their story."

Standing, Sloan again ran a hand through his hair, failing to smooth it at all. Seeing his intention, she stood with him. A renewed tension invaded the room. "You don't have to leave yet."

As he halted, she swallowed with difficulty, knowing the totality of the commitment she had just made. Sloan stood before her, considering her pale face. She licked her dry lips in her nervousness, afraid of his next move.

Slowly, he touched her cheek with a fingertip, running it along her jawline. Her flesh tingled. Closing her eyes, she turned her face into his hand, her lips kissing his palm with a sensuousness that drew a sudden gasp from him. As if a floodgate had opened, he drew her roughly to him, his mouth bruising as he took her own, demanding satisfaction. She clung feverishly to him, a whimper finding its way from her throat as he roughly crushed her against his solid frame.

Without a word he swung her up into his arms, the dark glitter of his eyes answering her silent question. Moving into the darkened bedroom, he held her a moment before allowing her body to slide against his own to the floor. He cupped her face in his hands, his thumbs tracing the fragile bones of her cheeks as he drew her mouth to him to taste again the sweetness of her lips.

She felt the firmness of his hungry mouth, tasted the bitterness of coffee, smelled the aroma of his cologne as he demanded and received an answer to his needs.

While he held her near him, he loosened the buttons of her dress, allowing it to fall softly from her hips to the floor. In moments the clip of her bra was loosened and she heard his half-choked groan as her breasts swung free against him.

Her own fingers were busy freeing him from the confines of his shirt, her hands needing to feel the warmth of him beneath her palms. His belt dug into her middle as he tantalizingly brushed her aching breasts against the mat of hair across his chest and she clung to him for the strength to stand.

Her fingers fumbled with his belt and he helped her loosen the barriers between them. Her body burned with recognition of his need as he slid her half-slip and panties away from her hips.

Lifting her out of the soft mound of clothing, Sloan carried her to the waiting bed. She felt the give of the mattress beneath her and reached for him, unwilling to let him go for an instant. She arched toward him as his body slid along her own willing form to lie next to her. His hand roamed at will, sending waves of desire rippling through her. All reasoning was gone. Only emotion, feeling, reaction, remained to feed the need, the giving, the taking her body craved. In a need for reassurance her hands moved first tentatively, then in newfound abandon, over the heavy muscles of his back and shoulders, clutching him to her as his fingers teased the places now exposed at last to his tenderness.

In the pale light falling through the draperies and across the bed, she watched without embarrassment the reactions of his strong body. With no sense of self-consciousness he met her curious gaze. Sensuously, he slid the length of his ready body against the softly curved warmth of her, the roughness of his thigh insinuating itself between her tightly closed legs. His breath whispered against her face.

"Cara, let me feel you. Let me know you."

And together they explored, reacted, learned one another. With her hands and lips she learned the hard rippling muscles of his chest that led to the hard flatness of his stomach. As she searched, she felt him arch against her, trembling. And the stifled her own cries of reaction as he sought and found the places that made her body ache for release.

While her hands learned his body, his searching mouth trailed across the swell of her breasts. When he took their erect points, rolling each in the softness of his lips, she cried out with the mindless searing of her senses.

"Sloan, love me. Teach me what you need."

His warm breath fanned her face as he whispered a hoarse reply. "You're what I want. I want to feel your warm softness around me. I want to hear you when I take you. Talk to me, touch me."

Again and again, he brought her to the brink of completeness, only to draw away to further heighten her awareness, her demands. And she met his every whispered desire, fully and completely, unquestionably. He was everything she had hoped for, everything she had dreamed of. He was Sloan. Filling her whole life, her whole being. It would always be Sloan. And in her delirium of aching need, she whispered his name again and again as she rose to the heights of unutterable joy.

Her fingers clutched him feverishly as she begged for the release only he could bring. And he shivered against her with the strength of that same desire.

"Oh, Cara. It's got to be now." He smothered her

involuntary cry as he led her past the one brief pain into womanhood.

Tasting her tears, he whispered huskily against her swollen lips, "It's all right, baby." After a moment in which he calmed her tense body, he began to move in the rhythm that the ages could not change. And a new tension began to build within her to erase all else in its strength until its explosive release brought a shuddering groan from the depths of Sloan's taut body.

With tenderness and understanding he brought her down from the dizzying heights they had achieved together. She felt his breathing calm under the sensitive palms of her hands as she held him against her, unwilling to release him. She felt the dampness of his sweat-slick skin, the roughness of his face, the crisp mat of hair across his chest still teasing her tender breasts. The weight of his body crushed her into the once crisp sheets, while the night surrounded them in its all-enveloping darkness and quiet.

Sloan. The repetition of his name in her mind brought a new awareness of him and of what they'd experienced together. Absently, she fingered the crispness of his tousled hair, marveling at the texture of it, knowing she was absurd in her musings. He'd called her a romantic and maybe she was. At least some of her dreams had been realized. Loving Sloan was everything she had dreamed it could be, everything she could ever want or need.

She dozed, thoroughly satiated, completely fulfilled in the knowledge that Sloan was with her, at least for the present. When she awoke, it was with the knowledge that she was alone.

She lay for a moment, listening, hoping for some indication that Sloan was still there. Then she heard the shower and relaxed. He hadn't left yet and for that she could be happy. Contented, she stretched languidly, her muscles gently complaining.

"You look like a sleepy cat." His voice from the bathroom doorway startled her. Jerking around, she saw him buttoning his shirt and drank in the sight of him, remembering the feel of him against her.

"I feel like a cat. A cat full of milk that's slept in the sun and is waiting to be petted." Her eyes ran over him in open invitation.

For a moment he watched her, idly buttoning the cuff of his shirt as he moved toward the bed. She curled toward him as he sat on the edge of the bed to lean over her. She could smell the freshness of soap, see the beads of water still dancing in his hair.

With the ball of his thumb he traced the bruised outline of her mouth. "You purr when you're stroked. Do you know that? And you bite and scratch." A corner of his mouth lifted at the flush of red that crossed her cheeks. "And you still blush like a schoolgirl."

He hesitated for a moment, his gaze falling over her. "Who would have known what lay beneath that cool exterior? You're quite a lady, Cara. Very much a woman." His long fingers caressed her face as he spoke. His face was serious, his eyes searching, moving over her with a strange look she did not understand.

She felt a touch of panic. The realization of her actions almost overwhelmed the satisfaction she had received from his lovemaking. Could he already be regretting his actions? Could it be over so soon? Her doubt must have shown in her eyes.

Sloan's husky voice soothed her fears. "You're everything I thought you would be, Cara, and more. I've never before been a woman's first lover, but with you . . ." He seemed to have trouble expressing his feelings, and she sensed that he had his own doubts now, in spite of all his earlier words.

"Sloan, *I* made the commitment. *I* made the decision. And I'm not sorry, so please don't make me sorry."

There was no flicker of emotion across his face as he searched her mobile features. "Nothing has changed. Nothing can change." And as he spoke she recognized the bleakness of his words and saw that bleakness mirrored across his face.

He rose then to finish dressing, his gaze never leaving her face as she struggled with her sudden desolation. He tossed her robe to her and turned to leave the room. Without looking at her he said, "Come with me to the door."

As though in slow motion she shrugged into the robe, standing to tie it securely around her. He was standing in the middle of the living room when she entered, his hands thrust into the pockets of his trousers. At her entrance he allowed his gaze to drop over her, noting the tangle of her hair, her bruised mouth, her fatigue-smudged eyes.

She glanced around the suddenly too quiet room. It was like her life without Sloan—full when he was there, empty and without purpose when he left. But there must be something of him for her. Something she could hold onto.

Remembering the heights to which they had risen together, the completeness of their union, hope sprang alive and vibrant in her. But considering the barriers between them, Cara realistically saw the problems and pain ahead for her. She was resigned to it now, but the pain would not lessen merely because of her resolve to endure. Added to it were the possible repercussions

Sloan had made certain she was aware of, had made certain she realized she would be coping with alone.

Watching the reflections of her thoughts move across her face, Sloan saw the vulnerability of her, the childlike insecurity imprinted there. And turning to him she saw the mask back in its place, the tightness of his jaw as he turned to the door, leaving only the empty click of the lock sounding in the silent room.

Chapter Seven

*M*onday arrived sunny and beautiful, but Cara saw none of it. She felt drained of life as she arrived at the Complex. She steeled herself in case someone noticed a difference in her, saw Sloan's mark upon her somehow. But the mark was inside, in her own mind.

Shortly after Cara's arrival Lea made an appearance, two cups of coffee in hand. Concern was clearly written across her face. "Have you talked to him?" Lea waved a hand toward Sloan's vacant office.

"Not since Sunday. The funeral is this morning. If I know him, he'll try to come in later today, but I mean to forestall that." She sipped the welcome coffee. "The reporters have been a nuisance."

"I can imagine. The news was startling; no one suspected that his father was still living, much less in a nursing home like Riverdale. It must have been terrible for him."

Remembering Sloan's reactions, Cara nodded absently. Lea's next words brought her back to the present. "What about you, Cara?"

Startled, Cara stammered. "Wh-what about me?"

Lea cocked her bright head to one side, studying Cara's pale face. "I mean, what about you and Sloan? There's more here than you're telling. I would hate to see you hurt."

Tears stung Cara's eyes and she quickly turned her head, blinking them back. "I know. Thanks. But I'm a big girl now, have been for a long time."

Lea's voice was soft with concern. She wasn't fooled by Cara's evasive ploy. "You love him, that's evident. But be careful, Cara. I know you don't want to talk about it right now, but if you ever do, I'm here. All right?"

Cara hoped that her smile was convincing. "Thanks. Everyone needs a friend, but I'm all right."

Lea tactfully changed the subject. "Are you going to the funeral?"

"I think I will go to the cemetery. It's a private service, but I think someone should be there."

Lea smiled indulgently. "Just 'someone'? I thought so. I would, if it were Tom's father. I can handle anything here. No one in the Complex will expect him to be in anyway, so things will be quiet."

Suddenly efficient, Cara sought to put things on a more impersonal basis. "Thanks. I'll just finish up a few things before I go."

After Lea left her office, Cara became so involved in her own work that she was startled a short time later when the door swung violently open to admit a stormy Susan Stafford.

Instantly, there was a charged atmosphere in the room. Cara forced her voice to sound normal while carefully controlling her features. "Why, hello, Susan. Is there something I can do for you?"

The classic blonde profile was hardened in anger. The pale blue eyes, sharp with intense dislike, were directed at Cara, who was far from unaware of Susan's only marginally successful campaign to snare Sloan. Cara also recognized that Sloan's neglect of Susan during this particular period of his life gave fire to the woman's evident anger.

Susan's words were bitten off. "Don't use that condescending tone with me. Is Sloan here?"

Taken aback by the ferocity of the other woman's verbal attack, Cara did not immediately respond. A look of cunning replaced the anger in Susan's face, changing her whole attitude. "Yes, Sloan. Don't look so surprised. Where do you think he goes when he's finished here? You don't think he spends all his waking hours behind these four walls, do you?" Susan continued to pin Cara with her piercing, spiteful gaze. "Didn't you ever wonder what he did after the parties were over? I'm sure you've seen our picture in the papers."

Struggling to maintain a calm appearance, Cara was stung by the woman's cutting words. Susan continued her attack, pacing agitatedly back and forth across the floor in front of Cara's desk, a venomous look playing over her face.

"Thought you had him in the palm of your hand, didn't you, working with him up here in this isolated office? Did you think those newspaper photos were just so much publicity?"

Cara registered the sly look, the slightly narrowed blue eyes, as Susan leaned toward her across the desk, lowering her voice meaningfully. "How long do you think you can keep a man dangling, especially one like Sloan? He isn't cut out to be celibate. He's a man used to having a woman available to him whenever he chooses. He doesn't play games, especially waiting games."

Susan straightened, a smug look crossing her features. "I may not completely understand your plan, but I know you have one. And I do recognize a lost cause, and that's all you have. You're not unaffected by him, no one in her right mind could be, not even you, with your ice-lady reputation. But believe this, and take it for what it's worth, ideals don't warm the bed and Sloan likes a warm bed."

The dismay that registered on Cara's pale face seemed to give impetus to Susan's tirade. "No, it doesn't take a mindreader to know how it stands between you and Sloan. Either you haven't given him what he wants or you're not enough for him. Maybe there is ice in those veins of yours, or maybe your experience isn't varied enough. Whatever the reason, Sloan isn't satisfied, and I mean to change that situation."

Susan moved angrily across the floor to face Cara directly. "Oh, yes, I've played second to you long enough. 'The beautiful Cara, the bright Cara, how intelligent she is.' I've heard your name often enough to choke. How they grovel at your feet, and you don't even see them."

At Cara's widened gaze Susan continued: "You never even noticed, did you—you in your ivory tower? So above everyone. So untouchable, so regal. Taking everything for granted while the rest of us took your leavings. You even had Mr. Quinn as your footstool. And now you want Sloan, no matter what you said to me. You never miss a trick, do you? Well, that's over. I'm going to see your tower fall. And nothing will give me more pleasure."

Cara had nothing to say. She was stunned, both by the openness of the attack and by Susan's words and heated emotions. She'd never realized that Susan hated her so much.

But foremost in her mind was Sloan. Just how much did he have to do with this? How could Susan have known anything about their relationship unless he had told her? Susan would never have the nerve to attack her this way unless she had been given the right to do so by Sloan. Cara was unable to fit the puzzle together, but even thinking that the two of them could have discussed her made her stomach churn.

Cara held a tight rein on her emotions, even as the doubts of Sloan began to seep into her mind alongside the hurt Susan's words had brought. Susan glanced casually around the office, her countenance calm once more. "I'm giving you fair warning, Cara. Your stay here"—and she gestured to the room—"is only temporary." And with that she strode confidently from the room, leaving Cara stunned.

The door was hardly closed before Lea pushed it back open. "Need I ask what that was all about?" She dimpled a slight grin in Cara's direction. "After she swooped back through the outer office I thought I'd better check that you were still in one piece."

Cara smiled grimly; Susan's words had hurt more than she wanted to admit. "Nothing important. I wouldn't worry about her," she said, wishing she could believe her own words.

By ten o'clock Cara had rearranged Sloan's scheduled appointments and left instructions for the rest of the day. Having dressed appropriately in a thin-knit form-fitting navy dress and matching pumps, she drove straight to the cemetery and searched for the Montgomery burial plot, carefully avoiding any thought of Sloan's reaction to her uninvited appearance.

The warm early-summer weather had brought the flowering trees and shrubbery to full bloom. Yellows, pinks and whites created a pale mist over the newly green leaves. Several graves were honored with bouquets of red tulips and the last of the early jonquils, bobbing in the light breeze. The white gravel that marked the winding drive and the predominantly white stone grave markers lent an air of serenity where sorrow was normally the overriding emotion.

Cara slowed her car to a crawl as she searched the names cut into the markers. She caught sight of a caretaker idly snipping grass around some of the headstones and asked him for directions. With one green-stained hand he pointed to the far side of the cemetery.

Following his directions, she wound along the narrow road until she reached a striped awning stretched over an open scar in the earth. Pulling to one side, Cara kept the plot in view as she waited in her car. Before long the stillness was broken by the muffled sound of motors.

Glancing behind her, Cara saw the black hearse and watched as one lone mortuary limousine drew up beside the bare, tent-covered plot. The loneliness of the whole scene gripped her and tears sprang to her eyes, threatening to spill onto her pale cheeks. The memory of the hundreds of flowers and the many friends and relatives who had crowded around with comfort, love and concern at her own parents' death was in deep contrast to this barren scene and made her heart ache for Sloan.

As she watched, a plain bronze casket was lifted from the hearse and placed on the waiting rack. The lone spray of flowers sent from Triad stood in place like a guarding soldier at attention on its wire tripod. The young minister stood to one side, waiting, until Sloan finally emerged from the limousine to stand beside the attendant at the edge of the open grave.

Unable to stop the tears that were now flowing freely, Cara swallowed back a sob as she quietly left her own car. Her footfalls muffled by the short grass, she stepped quietly to Sloan's side as the dark-suited minister began to read. His words of comfort and acceptance brought an extra ache to Cara's already burdened heart.

Glancing up into Sloan's set face, Cara took his arm before turning her attention to the service. He maintained his self-contained stance and they stood, without moving, until the words stopped and, with a slight hesitation, the casket was lowered into place. The sound of earth thudding into the grave finally drove them to turn away.

The minister, sensing their wish to be alone, left without the usual words of comfort. The limousine driver waited awhile, but finally followed the departing hearse when Cara and Sloan walked together toward her waiting car. Still without speaking, Cara slid into the driver's seat as Sloan leaned wearily back in the passenger seat, his eyes closed, his face deeply lined with weariness.

"Want to go home?"

His voice was flat, emotionless, when he finally answered. "Home? Where is that?" It was a tired, empty question, indicative of his fatigue.

Instead of answering, she turned the ignition and drove toward the exit. In a short time they were entering the apartment parking area. When they got upstairs, the still-silent man seemed to have his mind on faraway matters. Taking control of the situation, Cara held out her hand. "Give me your jacket and relax. I'll fix coffee."

After she had hung up his suit coat, she found him stretched out on the couch, his long, long legs hanging over the end. While crossing to the kitchen, Cara slipped off her high-heeled pumps and padded about in stocking feet to prepare coffee and sandwiches. The fragrance of fresh coffee filled the room as she brought the loaded tray to the coffee table.

Turning from her task, she found Sloan's gaze on her. She settled into a chair opposite him, indicating the food. "It seems we're always eating."

He swung upright to lean over the table, still watching her strangely. "Yes, usually at each other."

Smiling slightly, she ignored the implication of that remark and poured the coffee. After adding cream to her own cup, she leaned back, keeping her attention on the hot brew and letting Sloan retain his detachment as he ate.

Later, his hunger satisfied, Sloan leaned back against the cushions as Cara carried the few dishes through to the kitchen. Returning, she sank into the corner of the couch opposite him, to wait for him to lead the conversation. She knew that something more than the loss of his father was on his mind.

In a few moments he turned to her. "Cara?"

"Yes?" Her voice was soft, questioning.

At that moment a change came over his face. "That's what I want to hear—yes."

He pulled her to him, his mouth moving searchingly against hers. She felt the tension in his body as she willingly settled against him, her hand tangling in the crisp hair curled at the back of his head. This was where she belonged, where she wanted to be always.

Sloan shifted to a more comfortable position, almost reclining on the couch as he turned her willing body to his. Sliding a hand across her back and around her ribs, he pulled down the long zipper at the back of her dress, easily setting her shoulders free. His warm lips played across her face, feathering down to the hollow of her throat. The warmth of his fingers against the fullness of her breast quickened her breath, reawakening senses thirsty for experience.

Following his lead, Cara slid her hand down his neck into the collar of his shirt, where his loosened necktie left a way. Sliding her hand across his chest in a kind of possessiveness, she felt the strong heartbeat beneath his heavily muscled flesh and absorbed the feel of him. His shirt buttons slid free almost of their own will as she sought the knowledge of his body. Sloan explored her mouth, then he held her above him and his lips met the rosy points of her breasts to play for long moments before leaving them so he could draw her back against him.

With his warm mouth against her temple he held her in his arms and moved until they were lying full-length on the couch. She wanted him again. Needed to hold him against her, feel once more the fire between them, know the mastery of his touch, experience that desire in her which he answered so skillfully, so satisfyingly.

She arched against him, willing him to know how much she needed him. It was then that Susan's words penetrated her mind.

The doubt was potent. Involuntarily she wondered if the words were true. Had Sloan gone from her arms to Susan's? In spite of herself, her uninhibited response to Sloan's lovemaking became woodenly mechanical.

He sensed her withdrawal. Moving away slightly, he studied her flushed face and half-closed eyes for a moment. Though brief, the break was long enough for Cara to regret allowing Susan's vindictiveness to affect her feelings for the man she held and long enough to break the mood of the moment.

Instead of condemning her actions Sloan seemed to accept her withdrawal, though he couldn't have known the reason for it. Brushing her lips lightly with a kiss and releasing a long sigh, he turned to lie beside her, his arm still across her body.

"Why did you come this morning?"

His question didn't surprise her. In fact, she had expected it sooner. "Because I felt you needed some-one."

"Just someone?"

"I hoped you needed me. At least, I needed to be with you."

"That was reason enough?"

"For me it was."

As they spoke she turned to watch his carefully immobile face. Though his expression didn't alter there seemed to be a somewhat thoughtful look about Sloan's eyes. She waited, watching him, wanting to reach out to him. She wanted to feel the smoothness of his brow, the roughness where his beard was beginning to show already. The light played across the rise and fall of his bared chest, the contours smoothly muscled, but she held back the desire to feel the dark mat of hair shadowing the broadness of his chest and dropping in a V to his belt line. The desire for him burned within her, but the moment was permanently broken. She'd failed again. She had let Susan come between them and had fallen short once more in her resolve to be whatever Sloan needed.

Finally, he arose and unselfconsciously tucked his shirt back into his slacks. Though she wanted him, needed him and felt acutely his withdrawal, she knew that there could be no other decision right now. He had sensed her doubt and it had caused a barrier between them.

For a while it had been good, almost too good, but she had hesitated, and now he was closed to her again. He had let down the walls in his loneliness after the funeral, but now that edge had worn off. He was back behind the walls and building them higher than before. And she had only herself to blame for her lack of fulfillment, her frustration.

She still had not moved when Sloan slowly leaned to brush a kiss across her swollen mouth and trace a finger over the swell of her exposed breasts. Then he straightened and left the apartment without a word. In spite of herself, she wondered if he would go to Susan and, hurting, knew he might.

From that point their relationship took on a new dimension. Or, rather, returned to the old footing of strictly employer and employee. They had both come to a near-commitment, only to discover that neither of them was yet ready, no matter how much she wished it otherwise. She had made a promise, sealed it with her body, her total love, but Sloan could not meet that promise with one of his own. Nor was she certain she could keep that promise without one given in return. They were at a stalemate, neither one willing to push toward a final answer to their unstable situation.

The weeks that followed fell into a pattern. Once the new marketing plans were formulated, new advertising plans were soon ready for approval. Production gains continued at an increasingly optimistic rate, and new-product plans progressed well. The days were long and demanding and for that Cara was grateful. The long hours left her less time in which to contemplate the deterioration of the fragile thread of feeling she thought had been developing between herself and Sloan.

As new elements of the job were introduced, Cara was able to work alongside Sloan with efficiency, often anticipating his requests. She took on added responsibilities, which included some projects involving other companies in the conglomerate structure, passing on more of her work to Lea and gaining the girl a title change and a raise along with it.

Her friendship with Lea had deepened, but she was still unable to share her feelings and doubts concerning Sloan. She was too insecure, too uncertain, about the status of Sloan's feelings toward her.

Several days after the funeral Lea had broached the subject over lunch in a small fast-food restaurant. "I know this really isn't the place, Cara, but, well, I'm concerned about you."

Cara stopped stirring her coffee to glance at Lea's unusually sober face. "Why? There's nothing . . ."

"I know, I know you're okay. At least on the surface. But, well, what happened between you and Sloan? I thought things were working out between you two. Now all of a sudden it's back to the deep freeze."

"That's an apt description. But there's nothing to be done about it. Sloan has to work things out in his own way. He can't be rushed into changing. I'm a threat to his chosen way of life, it seems. In any event, he's very thoroughly freezing me out. And there's nothing I can do about it."

Lea recognized the finality of Cara's words and, with a look of sympathy for her friend's pain, let the subject drop.

Cara continued to push herself as unmercifully as Sloan, though she doubted that it was for the same reason. She constantly strove to curb her awareness of him as they worked together, keeping in check her reactions to the careless brushing of hands as they exchanged papers or one of the endless cups of coffee.

Sloan certainly appeared to be unaware of her. She might as well have been an inanimate object, part of the machine that was Triad. And to cover the hurt that knowledge brought, she slowly began to build a sort of defense against him.

She knew that Susan Stafford was more than ever a part of Sloan's social life. She often saw them together in the cafeteria, the two of them sitting alone and talking familiarly over a meal. It seemed that Susan had second sight, for whenever Cara appeared on the scene, she made certain that Cara was fully aware of the relationship between her and Sloan. Cara felt like a fifth wheel, totally unnecessary. It was like insult added to injury to see Sloan's careful avoidance of her at such times and Susan's smug recognition of his actions.

After her third attempt to carefully keep her countenance and cover the anguish the scene brought, Cara began avoiding the cafeteria again.

Sloan was as enigmatic, as painfully impossible, as ever. He almost flaunted his relationship with Susan, while he treated Cara to a total absence of personal conversation or contact. The night spent in his arms that had meant so much to her had been nothing more than a one-night stand for Sloan. An event that had caused such upheaval in her own life had left his feelings uninvolved, rendered his words meaningless. And she died a little each time she remembered her own words, her own uninhibited actions, which had made so little impression upon him. To counteract her heartbreak, she lost herself in work.

A new marketing plan was formulated, accepted and implemented. Advertising layouts were submitted, reflecting a different and more innovative approach. It seemed that the various departments were now working up to standard, having realized that the expectations of their new employer were not to be lowered but lived up to.

Summer was in full force now. The long evenings, filled with the sounds of laughing children and picnics in the small park across from her apartment, began to wear on Cara's nerves. She envied their air of abandon, as if life had few complications. And she felt more sharply than ever the break between herself and Sloan.

The situation between them did not improve as the weeks went by. Finally, almost in desperation, Cara accepted a dinner date with Larry. His call had been a pleasant surprise, coming so long after their last meeting, and she was glad to hear his voice, thankful for his easy conversation, and found herself actually looking forward to seeing him again. It seemed to matter little how much time passed between their meetings; they were always able to pick up their relationship as if it had been only yesterday that they had spoken. Cara valued their unique friendship highly.

As she got ready, she thought about Larry. She was always comfortable with him, secure in his unromantic affection for her. She wondered why she never felt the excitement rush through her when he was near, when he touched her, that she felt with Sloan. Comfortable. That was certainly the word for Larry. Just as exciting was the word for Sloan.

Not only were Larry and Sloan different in their looks and in their attraction to her, they were totally diverse in personality. Larry was a brown-haired, blue-eyed All-American type, the kind of man you could depend upon. Sloan was as unpredictable as he was exciting. Larry comforted her frustrations; Sloan fired her passions.

Sloan. He was her hope, her nemesis. Her love, her despair. She hated him for his ruthless abandonment of her, loved him because she understood so much of his motivation and wanted to ease his pain. She loved him in spite of herself. No one else had ever affected her in such a way. No other man threatened her independence, left her both devastated and uplifted, nor made her feel as needed as Sloan could. She was an emotional masochist with Sloan. She continually hoped for something he would never provide. She continually asked to have her love crushed mercilessly without a sign of regret on his part.

In spite of that, just thinking of him, remembering the times he'd held her, the feel of his body against her own, could bring a surge of emotional reaction that left her shaken. She'd felt very young and vulnerable when he made love to her, very beautiful and womanly in the aftermath of their passion. The memory of feelings aroused to fever pitch in Sloan's strong arms was enough to set her pacing the floor once more in an agony of wanting.

It was at those times that her own naïveté embarrassed her. Her inexperience was painfully apparent when measured against the expertise that Sloan had attained with women who willingly accepted his rules for living.

Her giving fell so short when measured against the women who met Sloan's demands, who took what they could for as long as they could, perhaps hoping to be a permanent part of Sloan's life, but accepting the impossibility of that when the time came.

Cara could understand their hopes; they had been her own. But now she fully realized the futility of hoping. She must begin to rebuild her life using her new knowledge, and her dinner date with Larry would be the first step.

Choosing a dress she especially liked, one that Larry had never seen, Cara dressed carefully. She spent a moment critically viewing herself in the full-length mirror, turning to see the back, finally satisfied that the close fit was not too close. Her tall, slim figure was set off elegantly by the straight skirt of the simply cut black knit. The skirt was slit up the side seams to show quite a length of shapely leg and thigh, set off by dusky sheer stockings with a lacy pattern woven in.

The high-necked bodice fit closely over her full breasts to show their youthful thrust. It fastened with a single loop at the collar front, leaving a provocative opening that tempted with a promised, but unfulfilled, view of rounded cleavage. The tight sleeves fell to the wrist, emphasizing Cara's long, slim-fingered hands and the oval perfection of her nails.

Pulling her hair straight back, Cara fastened the chignon securely. The severe style gave her a slightly exotic look. Translucent powder, silvery eye shadow, and mascara to emphasize her naturally long lashes lent a hint of mystery to her black eyes. Faint blusher beneath her high cheekbones completed her makeup. Tiny diamond studs winked in her ears, matching her mother's diamond cluster ring, a family heirloom that graced her right hand.

Satisfied that she had achieved the look of a confident woman ready to enjoy an evening with a charming man, Cara picked up her bag and snapped out the bedroom light. And if a tiny, niggling wish that Larry could be replaced with Sloan entered her mind, she quickly pushed it aside.

If Cara had any doubts that her efforts had been successful, one look at Larry's face reassured her. He was obviously reappraising their previous relationship as he escorted her toward his waiting car.

Sliding in next to her, Larry hesitated before reaching for the ignition. He brushed her cheek with a knuckle as he carefully considered her profile before turning her to face him. "I'm glad I booked a reservation at the country club. Nowhere else could measure up." He searched her face, his direct blue eyes perceptive as they renewed his remembrance of her. "There's something different about you. What is it—or shouldn't I ask?"

Frowning slightly at his astute observation, Cara studied Larry's intent face in return, carefully phrasing her answer. "There's nothing different. It's just been a while since we were together, and I thought a special evening with a special friend warranted something fancy."

His thumb gently caressed her chin as he considered her further. "All right, I'll accept that for now. You always were an independent creature. I can see that that part of you hasn't changed."

Cara knew a twinge of relief. Larry knew her so well, better than anyone, she supposed. He was good for her; he honored her reluctance to go beyond friendship. She wasn't ready for anything serious with anyone at this point. Her feelings for Sloan were still too raw. And in that moment, as she sat beside another man speeding across town, she realized that she could no longer continue to work at Triad.

When they arrived at the club, Cara knew that she had been correct in deciding that the evening would be cool enough for her long-sleeved dress. The air conditioning in the popular Twin Pines Club was working overtime and she would have been uncomfortable in something lighter.

Twin Pines was a membership-only club with an exclusive restaurant and separate lounge. The décor was an elegant mixture of antiques and the clean lines of somewhat more modern pieces. A few private rooms for small groups and the lounge led off the foyer, as did the restaurant offering a choice of privacy or the opportunity to see and be seen.

A soft-spoken hostess led them across the quickly filling restaurant to a well-situated table. Larry glanced around with satisfaction at her approving comment after they were seated. Membership in the club was one of the benefits Larry enjoyed through his company now that he had risen to the upper-executive level.

After he had placed their order for a light wine to sip while awaiting the first course, the conversation touched easily on many and varied subjects, including several trips Larry had taken that he described as business and pleasure. By the time their entrées arrived, they had caught up on each other's activities and progressed to more current matters. Cara carefully avoided more than the occasional reference to her employer, hoping she wouldn't give herself away when Larry tried to question her more closely about the newsworthy corporate head. In addition to her own reluctance to speak of Sloan, the corporate part of him demanded that his staff honor his wish for privacy in his business and personal life. And Cara was more than willing to comply with that wish at the moment. She concentrated on the Club instead.

Cara studied the newly added panels of leaded stained glass, which lent a particularly warm feeling to the club's décor. Display lights showing dimly behind the antique panels gave relief from the indirect lighting, which itself was cleverly concealed. The interior of the dining area was done almost totally in natural wood, the large room divided only by carefully placed high-backed booths affording privacy to those who wished it. Individual tables situated in seemingly random pattern about the room, in dark corners or beneath skylights, filled the middle section of the large room. The food and service were excellent, and Cara relaxed for the first time in weeks.

Both of them had a distinct preference for seafood, and Larry had ordered two lobster dinners. When the plates arrived, the bright red shellfish bordered by bursting baked potatoes, overflowing with sour cream, chives and butter, tempted even Cara's flagging appetite. The tidbits of delicious lobster dipped in a specially prepared melted butter brought a smile of satisfaction to her face.

Cara glanced at Larry with a warm look as she remembered their first meeting. It had happened quite by accident during her last year of college. He had been dating a friend of Cara's at the time, and she had heard a great deal about him. When an exam was rescheduled, Cara had been commandeered as a messenger to explain her friend's failure to meet Larry at the appointed time. After delivering the message, Cara had accepted Larry's invitation to have coffee in a nearby restaurant.

By the time his date had arrived Larry had decided

that the delay had been a fortunate happenstance. But Cara was determined to stem his obvious interest, for her friend was definitely sorry she had made the arrangement. Though Cara refused to date Larry as long as her friend expressed an interest in him, they were attracted to one another on their occasional meetings.

When her classmate ended her relationship with Larry in favor of the attentions of a young instructor, Cara and Larry had become quite close for several months. Slowly they had realized nothing but a close friendship would ever be the result of their relationship, and that friendship had survived.

Immersed in their conversation and appreciation of the meal, it was some time before Cara looked about the room at their dinner companions. As they were relaxing over coffee, having nearly exhausted conversation for the time being, she became aware of a couple at a nearby table.

Cara nearly choked on the hot liquid as she recognized the intent gaze of Sloan Montgomery slicing into her from across the room. All color left her face as she concentrated on setting down her cup without spilling its contents. She also noted, in that instant, Sloan's gloating dinner companion. Susan's triumphant smile was evidence that she had noticed Cara's presence long before Cara became aware of them and was relishing Cara's discomfort.

Unaware of the developing situation, Larry continued to glance idly over the room until, noting Cara's lengthy silence, he followed her gaze toward Sloan's table. On seeing the stormy look on Sloan's face and Cara's pale profile, Larry immediately understood her reluctance to discuss her employer, as well as her disinterest in reconsidering a relationship between themselves. A kind of sadness rose within him, but he was also wise enough to realize the futility of any hope on his part, if the situation was even half as explosive as it appeared.

Laying a hand across her cold fingers, where they rested on the table, Larry leaned toward her. "Cara, don't let him know. Don't let him know you're hurt. Smile at them, even if it kills you. We'll finish in a moment and leave as if we'd planned it that way."

His calm words penetrated her paralyzed mind. His reasoning was sound and gave her a way to save face. With a great effort she forced her stiff lips to move into a slight curve before tearing her eyes away from Sloan's cold gaze.

When she saw Larry's concerned face, Cara's frozen thoughts began to thaw. "How did you know?"

His slight smile hid Larry's own disappointment. A case of "too late wise" for himself, he supposed, and he could accept that. "A single look at both of you. Have you told him?"

Her voice was tight with the effort she was making to control it. "Told him what?"

"How much you love him."

What a question. Told him? She'd thrown herself down like a rug and he'd casually wiped his feet on her. But what did that prove? Only how little regard she had for her own self-esteem.

Drawing a deep breath, Cara strove to calm the trembling inside her. "He knows. But he doesn't need anyone. He takes what he wants and then discards it when he's done. I could almost stand that. Almost, but not quite. He really isn't capable of loving anyone, and I'm human enough to need to be loved."

Aren't we all, Larry thought, as he watched her white face and signaled for their check. As soon as she was certain she could walk out with some semblance of dignity, Larry took her arm to escort her outside. In a few minutes they were out in the cool, fresh air and Cara breathed deeply, feeling as if it had been a long time since she had been able to breathe at all.

She was hardly aware as Larry guided her quickly to the car and helped her inside. Their ride through the busy streets was leisurely, uninterrupted by conversation. It seemed that Larry was giving her time to regain some of her lost equilibrium. Immersed in her shattered feelings, Cara was passively grateful for Larry's support.

By the time they arrived at her house, Cara had regained some of her composure. Mindful of Larry's comforting silence, Cara was doubly thankful for the long-term friendship that had enabled him to understand that what she needed right now was acceptance, not questions. She only wished that Sloan could understand her needs so well.

Sliding the car into a parking space in front of her building, Larry spoke for the first time. "Feeling better?" His voice was low with concern as he took her still-cold hand in his.

"Yes, but very foolish. Thank you. Thank you for being you. I don't deserve it." Tears pricked behind her lowered lids.

"Yes, you do. And you deserve more than you're getting from him. It was just bad luck I chose the club, but at least we had a good dinner." His words were accompanied by a gentle smile to lessen the misery he felt in her.

Cara managed a faint smile in return. "Yes, it was good. And I'm glad we went. At least it proved to me that I'm fooling myself if I think I can get over Sloan that easily." Her voice softened as if she was speaking to herself. "But I will get over him, even though it's going to take a while." She turned to face him then, leaning forward to place a gentle kiss at the corner of his mouth. "Thank you, Larry. I appreciate your being there and being so understanding."

The man beside her drew a long breath of resignation. "Yes, well, I don't know about that, but I hear a note of finality in those words."

Nervously, Cara smoothed her skirt against her leg. "It wouldn't be fair to take advantage of your good nature anymore. I think I used you tonight to try to forget. But it won't work. It's something I have to do on my own. I'm sorry I involved you." Tears glistened on her lashes, and Larry gently smoothed them away as they slid onto her pale cheeks.

"It's all right, Cara. Maybe I exorcised a few ghosts tonight, too." At her questioning look, he continued. "I think I used you tonight, too, in a way. I've been seeing a woman I think I could care for very much. But a certain dark-eyed beauty kept getting in the way. Now I can go on with my life, knowing we can care for each other, but never love each other. You're totally committed to Sloan Montgomery and, for whatever it will get you, I wish you the best. But remember this, I'm there if you need me. Call me. Will you do that?"

Cara laid her hand against Larry's jaw and gently kissed the opposite cheek. "I'm glad for you, Larry. She must be very special."

He studied her as if memorizing her face. "It could have been good for us, Cara, but we waited too long."

Knowing he was right, and knowing she would never call him, Cara turned with an audible sigh. Just as she reached to open the door, it was abruptly jerked out of her grasp. In the moment before her arm was taken in a punishing grip that pulled her from the car, Cara saw, in the glow of the streetlight, the tight, angry face of Sloan Montgomery.

Larry's quick protest was cut off by Sloan's terse command. "Tell your friend good-night, Cara."

In a moment all three of them stood outside the car in full view of any passersby. Larry's usually placid face was flushed with anger, his knuckles white as they gripped the edge of the car door. Knowing Sloan's capacity for deliberate antagonism, Cara sought to avert a direct confrontation between the two men by turning to Larry. "It's all right. I'll talk to you later."

For a moment she thought he might pursue the situation, but at last he nodded in her direction, keeping an eye on Sloan's still-angry face. Showing no alarm, only concern for Cara, Larry slowly reentered the car and pulled away from the curb. A last backward glance evidenced his reluctance to leave her in an obviously uncomfortable situation, but Cara waved him on to ease his doubt.

Watching the disappearing red taillights, Cara was very much aware of the taut figure beside her and the cruel grip he maintained on her arm. Deliberately, she turned to Sloan and pulled her arm free. She realized, however, that she could not have done so unless he had allowed it.

Her physical and emotional reactions to this man overwhelmed her. In spite of her resentment of Sloan's intrusion into her evening, the arrogant manner in which he had forced Larry into retreat, Cara knew she would never really want to be free of him. Even now, she felt the tight curling in her stomach that was the first stage of her physical hunger for this man she loved.

Sloan's rough voice, tight with tension, broke the lengthening silence between them. "Shall we go in, or do you want to do this on the street?"

The coldness of his demeanor and voice angered her into a swift retort. "It's your choice. You started this, and since you seem to feel you have to control everyone and everything, I'm sure it makes little difference to you where you make a scene. You've done well enought at it already.'' Anger fairly sparked from her narrowed black eyes.

In answer, Sloan again took her arm in a painful grip, half-dragging her into the building and up to her door. His obvious anger and her retaliatory indignation made her fingers tremble as she searched for her keys. They were snatched from her hand as she fumbled with the lock.

The door swung open and Sloan's hand at her back nearly shoved her into the room as he snapped on the light. Taking her bag, he dropped her keys back into it and threw it onto the couch in a gesture that illustrated his rage.

Unyielding, Cara stood in the middle of the room, watching as Sloan paced the floor. He was a commanding figure and even now her senses tingled in awareness of his total masculinity and pure physical power. That he was furious, too much so even to speak, and evidently trying to walk off some of it as he paced, grated on her already taut nerves as she struggled with her own fury.

Suddenly, Sloan's rough voice broke the silence. "Who is that man you were with? What is he to you?"

Ignoring his question, Cara countered with one of her own. "What did you do with Susan? I'm sure she didn't take—"

Sloan cut into her words, "Susan is no concern of yours." At Cara's look he relented. "I put her in a taxi. Our relationship is no news to her."

"Just as yours with her is nothing new to me. She made that very clear to me recently." Her mouth firmed as she faced him squarely.

His face tight with tension, his words sharply separated with deliberation, he demanded again, "Now that that's settled, who is that man?"

Adamantly, Cara faced Sloan's narrowed, threatening gaze, her voice nearly matching his imperious tone. "Why should I answer a question like that? I live my own life, just as you choose to live yours."

He advanced closer, forcing her to back away from him in an effort to keep sanity and space between them. "I want answers, not more questions. No cute little female tactics. Who is he? Your new lover?"

Inflexibly, she hissed back at him, her anger thoroughly incited now by his attitude. "You're not really entitled to any answers, are you? You want no commitments, therefore we're both free to do as we please. That's what you want, isn't it? No commitments?"

With a small twinge of guilt she continued stubbornly, facing his flushed, angry face. "Maybe he's willing to make the commitment you won't!"

In one angry movement he had her backed up against the wall, pressed to it by his intimidating body. "Commitments! I'm sick to death of hearing about commitments!"

Her eyes widened as she saw the dark blaze of his anger run almost out of control at the same time as she felt the wall at her back. He ran a deceptively gentle finger along the side of her jaw and down her throat to loosen the closing of her dress. As he invaded the shadow between her breasts she caught her breath at the desire that shot through her. "Does he make you feel good when he touches you? Does he make you feel like that?"

His voice caressed her as he spoke. He ran his hands down her body with a possessiveness that took away her breath. His thumbs hooked in the slits of her skirt to raise it and reveal the entire length of her thighs as he pressed closer to her. His mouth brushed across her open lips and she tasted the liquor he had consumed earlier at the Club. Caught between the wall and his demanding body, she could not think, only react. Her half-closed eyes disclosed the extent of his command over her senses. Almost without being aware of it, she felt him pull her body to his, his hard hands sliding up her exposed thighs to rock her hips to his own. She could not deny the yearning ache of her body as she reciprocated his arousal. She melted against him in a surrender that she could not deny, her arms encircling his neck as she strove to assuage the hunger in her body for him.

His words were breathed into her ear. "Does he make you feel like this? Can he set you on fire like this? Give it up, Cara. Stop fighting it. . . ."

His words brought her back to sanity. She thrust away from him, able to escape only because she caught him unaware. "No! No one makes me feel like you do, but I have to have more!"

The muscle jumping in his jaw indicated the force of his tension, as he strove to control the fury evident in his whole body. His voice was ominously threatening. "Damn you, Cara! You go too far!"

Almost beyond control herself, Cara matched his threatening tones as she glared back at the tense figure. "And you don't go far enough, Sloan."

It was a repeat performance of things done and said before. They were killing each other emotionally, cutting one another to ribbons. Cara knew it, felt it, saw that same knowledge in the dark eyes boring into her own before the absolute and inflexible look of the Sloan Montgomery she knew so well returned. That mask was replaced immediately by one that was invidious, almost malicious. And at that moment she felt the touch of real fear. Maybe this time she had truly gone too far in antagonizing him. It would be so easy for him to totally lose control at this point.

Evidently, some of her fear transmitted itself to him and Sloan suddenly stood back from her. He seemed to regain his usual attitude of disdain, while he continued to watch her carefully.

Relentlessly, he pursued a conversation she had thought finished. "You knew the conditions. You keep saying one thing, but doing another. Whatever your game is, I'm not joining in, Cara. I never play games like that."

Her fear gone, Cara again faced Sloan directly. "Yes, you do, Sloan. You play your own games, by your own rules, that's all. I was ready to do that, but only to a point. I had too much to lose. You lost nothing, but I've already lost." Her almost whispered statement was rewarded with a slight flicker of reaction before it was smothered. "That's not quite fair, is it?"

Angrily, he considered her white face as he taunted, "Quite a number of women felt they got a fair trade."

The sheer arrogance of the man fed her own anger. It didn't matter that she had lost so much, had gambled that he could love her and lost. Her downfall was of no importance to him. "Oh, we're back to that, are we? It's performance that counts, Sloan Montgomery's slogan. We mustn't forget that! That should make all the difference!"

His eyes glinted dangerously in the dim light, but she continued recklessly, no longer caring what happened. "I'm sure you're right. You're The Great Montgomery. One snap of your fingers and we all do your bidding. Especially women—that expendable commodity." She sank into a chair in exhaustion as she continued. "Women—your opinion of us is degrading. We're to be used and cast aside. Of no more value than a piece of crockery. We can always glue ourselves back together and go on to someone else. It makes no difference to you. We have no real feelings.''

Refusing to capitulate to the threat in Sloan's face, Cara continued, determined to finish what she had started, ''But your sexual prowess isn't at question here! Your emotional capacity is! Your ability to care for someone other than yourself. And as much as I care for you, I cannot find it within myself to sell myself so cheaply. Believe me, I wish I could. You may have made a conquest, but you'll never win this war.''

In spite of her resolve, tears of anger and pain began to flow down her cheeks as she tore her gaze away from him. She felt subjugated. Her pride, her emotions, her love for him were broken, lying in shards. Now he could do what he wished. She had little desire to continue this verbal sparring with him. She wished he would just go and let her put her life back together again.

But he persisted ruthlessly, his words emphatically spaced for emphasis. ''You never answered my question. Who was that man?''

She was tired of it all. Resting her pounding head against one hand, her elbows propped up on the chair arm, she answered dully, ''A friend. A friend I felt I could trust not to make demands on me. Someone I could relax with, feel comfortable with.''

''And you needed that?'' His voice came from somewhere near her chair, but she refused to face him again.

''Yes, I needed that.'' Her voice was weary with spent emotion and stress.

But he continued ruthlessly. ''From the look of that little scene in the car as I arrived, I would say you didn't get the 'comfortable friend' you say you wanted. It looked quite cozy from my vantage point.''

Empty in spirit, Cara turned to face Sloan, who now

stood across the room from her. "But looks can be deceiving. You've misjudged me before, if you'll remember. I'm not going to bother explaining anything to you except to say that Larry and I understand each other. We've had a very close, friendly relationship and nothing has changed that. He's going to marry a woman he's been seeing and tonight was a last fling for him."

Again Sloan agitatedly paced the floor. "You expect me to believe that? Damn you, Cara, I've held you, felt you respond. A woman like you can't live like a nun. You expect me to believe this platonic friend story? What innocent would believe that?"

Resignedly, Cara laid her head down against the curved arm of her chair, completely depressed by this whole scene. "Well, I do, but I can't very well play the innocent now, can I? You very effectively took care of that little obstacle. Oh, yes, I admit I complied willingly, maybe instigated it. And your 'performance' was top-notch—not that I have anything to compare it to. Yes, you certainly know how to get a response. Your reputation is secure there." If she had expected a reaction, she received none. "No, I expect nothing. I can only tell you the truth; you make of it what you will."

With a smothered oath Sloan turned angrily to stand before her tensed figure. "Don't pull that martyr act with me."

She came out of her lethargy then. She had had enough. As she rose to face him, a smaller but equally angry figure, it was as if someone had flicked a switch inside her. "Just who do you think you are—almighty Sloan Montgomery? You manipulate people to suit your own devices, planning their very thoughts to suit your own ends! Oh, yes, it's quite all right for you to do just as you please—with me, with Susan, with your companies. We're all just pawns on your private chessboard. I was right that first day. You're egotistical, arrogant, patronizing, selfish, inflexible and cold.

"Well, this is my message for you, Sloan. Get out of my life. I've lived this long without you and I can make it just a while longer. I loved you, but I can get over it. I'm not yours to control any longer. I won't be around to be manipulated. I resign my job and I resign you and your autocratic ways! Get out of here! Get out of my life!"

The two of them stood like opponents in an arena. The sudden quiet of the room was broken only by their harsh, angry breathing. Rueful tears flowed down Cara's white face and her breasts heaved with the last of her anger as she struggled to control her desire to run from the look on Sloan's face.

His quietly spoken words were like a dash of cold water on Cara's burning, emotional upheaval. "You have your wish. You have two weeks vacation unused, I believe, and with two weeks' notice, which I will waive, you will have a full month's pay coming. That should give you sufficient time to find a nice, unemotional niche in which to build your nice, uncomplicated little life."

A knife turned inside Cara. The pain took her breath away as she watched Sloan stride confidently to the door. With his hand on the knob he turned, his face perfectly controlled, his voice flat. "In face, I already have your replacement in mind. Susan will do very nicely. At least her opinion of me is several notches above yours, by any account. Too bad, Cara. We could have had something good between us, while it lasted."

Through her tears she watched as Sloan walked through the door and quickly closed it behind him. Sinking into the armchair, she knew an emotional pain that was almost physical in its intensity. It was then that

Cara heard the roar of the powerful Jaguar as Sloan pulled away from the curb and out of her life. In a moment almost of desperation she cried out "No! What have I done?" Then she thought ironically about the two men who had said almost the same words to her within the past few hours: "It could have been good."

Chapter Eight

$\mathcal{S}$unrise found Cara still awake. Throughout the sleepless night she had struggled with her love for Sloan. She had suffered over his cruel rejection of that love, had shed endless tears for herself and Sloan, agonized with her emotional pain. How they had hurt one another! She was almost unable to believe the ferocity of their last encounter, unable to comprehend the absoluteness of the ending of a relationship she had so hoped would turn into something lasting.

Toward dawn she had finally managed to get a grip on her emotions and to force her drugged mind to begin to function with some measure of normalcy. Now she ordered her weary body to move. Standing in the shower under needles of icy water, she began to think ahead to the next few days. Further than that she knew she could not go right now.

The next several days were spent job hunting. Her month's pay was sent by messenger Monday morning in a cold, impersonal gesture that was typically Sloan. Lea was her only friend, it seemed. During her lunch hour that first Monday she arrived at Cara's apartment, her face registering shock when she saw Cara's ravaged face.

"Oh, Cara. I knew something was dreadfully wrong." In a take-charge attitude Lea gathered Cara in her arms in a warm gesture that twisted Cara's painfully bruised heart. She sobbed as though she had shed no tears through the long hours of the night.

Leading Cara to the couch, Lea held her friend's cold hand as she considered how best to help. "Come on, tell me what's going on here. What has Sloan got to do with this?"

Forcing down more tears, Cara struggled for control. "Lea, I made a fool of myself. I knew what Sloan was, but I did it anyway."

"Oh, honey. I'm so sorry. I know you love him, and I so hoped he cared for you. I think he does, in his own way."

"Maybe. But it's not enough. He can't love anyone, and now he doesn't feel anything but hatred for me. Oh, Lea, the things we said . . ."

Lea knew better than to argue. Nothing she said would make any difference to Cara at this point. Instead, she limited her concern to an offer of help if needed. Cara truly appreciated the empathy she felt coming from her friend, but, as tempting as confiding fully might have been, Cara could not yet bring herself to repeat any of the painful things she and Sloan had said or discuss the complete emotional devastation she felt. She could hardly face it herself.

The days lengthened into weeks as she haunted the personnel offices of the larger companies in the area.

Time and again she heard that there were no positions available, even for someone with her considerable skills. Somehow, every time she thought an interview had gone well, something happened and a ''regrets'' letter arrived in the mail. Even low-paying clerks' positions were not offered to her, on the basis she was overqualified. And though she understood their reasoning that she would become bored with the routine, she would have welcomed the uninvolved work.

Nearly a month passed before she became convinced there was nothing for her and signed up with a temporary agency. From time to time she remembered Sloan's blackmail threat, but refused to relate her current problems to his statements. Cutbacks in personnel for economic reasons had to be the answer.

The temporary offices were always on the lookout for competent secretarial staffers. It was a solution Cara would not have chosen, given an alternative, but there was no choice. Her employer at the service was sympathetic to her situation, which helped when Cara's list was particularly exasperating, full of dull positions and long distances to travel.

The summer brought vacations and there were never enough people to fill the requirements. Cara grew accustomed to the work and was not too dissatisfied. Slowly, the haunted feeling began to leave.

Lorene Lawson managed the agency Cara had signed with. A nervous, highly strung woman in her late forties, she was more than happy to count Cara among her staff of temporaries. Though somewhat disorganized herself, Lorene was quick to recognize the sought-for qualities of organization and logic in applicants for her service. She knew she had a real find in Cara, who on her part was thankful not to be asked too many questions concerning her abrupt departure from Triad Industries.

Glancing at her first week's paycheck, Cara was thankful that money was not the prime motivation for her life. She could manage on what the temporary positions paid, but there wasn't anything left over.

Recognizing that she needed time for recuperation, Cara filled her days with as much work as Lawson Temporary Services could give her. She even worked most Saturdays during the heavy vacation season. She filled her evenings with cleaning her small apartment until that became a ridiculous ritual. Then she began running in the park to revive her flagging spirits and appetite. She soon found she thoroughly enjoyed the exercise and became serious about it.

Since her lowered income prevented her buying much in the way of a new wardrobe for the approaching fall, Cara once again took up sewing. Her mother had patiently taught her to tailor clothing so a homemade frock looked like a more expensive purchased one, and Cara soon regained the skill she had exhibited at an early age. She enjoyed the small challenge and the results brought her many compliments, which bolstered her badly battered confidence.

Lea called often during the evenings, but respected Cara's reluctance to speak of Sloan. Their conversations dealt mainly with Lea's approaching marriage. Cara listened patiently to the tale of woe that Lea recounted when the chosen wedding colors didn't suit the bridesmaids, the story of the ringbearer who came down with a severe case of chickenpox, and to a thousand other anecdotes. Lea recounted each incident with her usual good humor, making Cara laugh as she visualized the situations.

Cara was able to rejoice with Lea over her sense of triumph when she and Tom overcame his parents' wish to dominate their married life. Tom had finally spoken to his father about the position in the family firm and the relationship such a decision would entail. Surprisingly enough, to Tom's delight and Lea's happiness, Tom's father saw his point of view and, though he hadn't foreseen a problem, agreed with Tom's expression of doubt about their ability to work together. After a conversation that brought father and son even closer, a workable solution was reached and Tom decided to take the position, with the understanding that, should insoluble differences arise, he would be free to join another firm without a disruption of family relationships.

Following closely on that decision, Tom's mother called Lea and apologized for any problems she might have caused. Together they had openly discussed Lea's thoughts about the wedding and other potential differences. All in all, it had worked out well.

Cara listened and was happy for Lea and for Tom, whom she had met briefly. But she also found herself wondering if such a simple solution could be hers, or if happiness was forever beyond her reach.

She received a wedding invitation from Larry and dutifully chose a gift to be delivered, feeling that it would be inappropriate to attend. That was an experience she didn't need at this point. Her feelings, though healing, were still too raw.

As for Sloan, he apparently shared none of the shattered emotions Cara was trying to knit back together. The gossip columns often carried bits about Sloan's apparently active social life, which included a number of women besides Susan. He was still a news item financially, also, and was frequently interviewed for his opinion on the economic swings of the nation and business trends in general. Triad's new advertising campaign was evidently very successful and the company was back on its feet and doing well.

Sloan had not yet moved on to another challenge, which faintly surprised Cara. Susan *had* been prominent in a number of the society-page photos, which might account for Sloan's remaining in Springfield. Cara strove to ignore the sharp pain those pictures brought, the misting of tears for something that might have been but would never be a reality now.

Late summer brought long hot days of sweltering heat and humidity, with temperatures frequently at the 100° mark. Time lay heavy on her hands and her lethargy grew. Her thoughts turned more often to Sloan and she knew the wounds were still unhealed.

Fate seemed to take a hand in Cara's life when her schedule of jobs for the week listed one day at Triad. Hesitantly, she took her schedule into Lorene Lawson's office, unwilling to reveal her reasons, but determined not to take the position.

"Yes? What is it, Cara?" Peering over the glasses perched on her nose, Lorene spoke expectantly as Cara entered.

"I'd like to request a change in my schedule." She rushed on at the look of irritation on the harried woman's face. "I know it's unusual, but I have reasons, good ones I'd prefer not to discuss."

Glancing at the mass of paperwork on her desk, the older woman sighed, fidgeting nervously. "You realize how very busy we are and how very understaffed we are with people of your capabilities? In fact, at this point, you are the only girl on our rolls who can qualify for the position of executive secretary, though I realize your capabilities far exceed that. All those positions on your schedule fall within that range." Uncharacteristically curt to the point of rudeness, she continued. "I'm sorry, there is no way I can alter your schedule. And, at this time, I cannot discuss it with you further."

Though surprised by the woman's attitude, Cara realized that she must accept the situation if she expected to stay with the agency. She was apprehensive, but knew that the office to which she was assigned was far enough removed from Sloan's domain that there would be little likelihood of her seeing him. And she convinced herself that, with a little planning and a little luck, she could complete the assignment with no problems.

The next morning, however, it was with more than a little trepidation that she dressed carefully in a crisp linen two-piece suit she had sewn and tailored for herself. Cara surveyed the completed picture she presented in the full-length mirror in her bedroom. She saw the changes reflected back at her. She was somewhat thinner than she had been, though her curves were still in evidence. Her shadowed dark eyes had a warier look than she had realized. Her thinner face gave her high cheekbones more prominence, lending an exotic look to her small face.

The cool lime color of the suit complemented her coloring perfectly. Out of indifference more than design, she had let her hair grow past her shoulders and she wore it pulled away from her face for comfort during the hot months. The more severe style lent a somberness to her countenance that bothered her a little. She looked older, wiser, almost marked by her experience. Sloan's mark, her mind echoed, then she hurriedly pushed the thought away.

It was only as she pulled into the familiar parking lot that she experienced a moment of panic. Luck was with her as she went unerringly to the department to which she had been assigned. She strode quickly down the long halls, not seeing a single familiar face.

Even in the short length of time she had been away, a

number of changes had taken place. New faces and a feeling of productivity and anticipation pervaded Triad now. She noticed the change immediately and was unselfishly happy about it. She had been a part of the beginning of this new era for Triad and felt pride in that.

Her supervisor for the day was one of the new employees, hired to accommodate the expansion necessary to deal with the influx of new orders and line expansion. Settling down to work, Cara began to believe she would be able just to do her job and leave at the end of the day.

Working alone in an isolated office near the end of the long main corridor, Cara was totally absorbed in her task until a footstep behind her attracted her attention. Expecting her supervisor, she swiveled around in her chair, only to meet the angry blue eyes of Susan Stafford.

Controlled arrogance was evident in the woman's stance and in the set of her mouth. "Well, well. Just couldn't stay away, hmmm? Sloan will be surprised to hear you're here. When did Mark hire you?"

Cara's stubbornness stood her in good stead as she refused to allow herself to be intimidated by Susan. Leaning back in her chair, Cara gave the impression that Susan's sudden appearance had no effect upon her. "Mr. Ferris hasn't hired me. I'm here on a temporary basis until the new employee comes in tomorrow. These reports had to be finished before then."

A raised eyebrow evidenced Susan's skepticism. "Still, I'm surprised you would venture back here, whatever the reason. Have you no pride at all? I'd have thought that Sloan's dismissal would have been enough, even for you." Susan leaned a rounded hip against the desk in an insolent manner, which grated on Cara's already taut nerves. "Or don't you know when to quit?"

Cara stood to busy herself straightening the already

finished reports before answering. The move also served to rid her of the feeling of subservience that came from having to look up at the arrogant woman. "In the first place, I'm really not certain what you're talking about. Sloan didn't fire me; I resigned. In the second place, my presence here has nothing to do with either you or Sloan. So, if you'll excuse me, I'll get on with my work. I'm sure you have things to do elsewhere."

Successfully concealing her nervousness, Cara left Susan fuming in obvious anger that her unwarranted attack had failed.

Returning to the office later, Cara was grateful to find that Susan had departed. As she determinedly set herself before the typewriter, Cara forced herself to concentrate on the job at hand and not on the possible repercussions of Susan's unfortunate appearance.

Cara lunched at her desk on a sandwich she had brought from home. Thankful for a few minutes' peace, she was dismayed to hear the approach of someone confidently striding down the long hall toward her office. Wishing she had closed the door before spreading out her lunch, she rose quickly to push the door to, when she saw Sloan's tall figure hesitate a few steps away.

Their eyes caught for a moment, and she saw that same "something" flicker across his face before it assumed the controlled look she recognized and hated. Breaking their gaze, his dark eyes perused her slim figure from head to foot, as if analyzing the changes she knew he had immediately noticed. Holding his look when it returned to meet her eyes, Cara firmed her mouth and deliberately gave the door a shove, closing it in Sloan's face.

Frozen, she realized how he would interpret her move. She waited to see if he would pursue the issue, but when the steps retreated after a few minutes she knew that her point had been taken.

Somehow she finished the day. The longer she worked, the more certain she was that Sloan would not allow the insult to pass. Every step in the hall made her freeze in anticipation. She worked feverishly to finish the work so that she could leave, although she knew the dangerous time was five o'clock, when everyone headed for the parking lot. There would be people she knew, people who would ask questions she couldn't answer.

Shortly after five the reports and correspondence were completed. Mark Ferris congratulated her on her speed and efficiency and even suggested that she might want to consider Triad for permanent employment. Somehow she got past that moment. It was completely ironic that the only company to welcome her was the one place she could not possibly work.

Checking the hall to see who was in the immediate vicinity, Cara felt like a fugitive. She straightened her shoulders and stepped out with determination. When she reached the door, she headed toward her car, concentrating simply on reaching it and leaving for the sanctuary of her home.

Set on getting to her destination without discovery, Cara failed to see the tall figure lounging against the gray Jaguar parked just beyond the door. Out of the corner of her eye she caught the movement as he straightened, stumbling as she automatically sidestepped to change directions and avoid a confrontation. Sloan's tight face became even grimmer as she turned quickly away, her only goal to escape.

Her flight was effectively halted by his large hand encircling her upper arm, nearly cutting off her circulation in the process. Firming her mouth, she glared

209

silently at the figure looming over her in the hot red glow of the evening sun.

Sloan's harsh voice grated on her already tautly stretched nerves. "Running away accomplishes nothing, Cara. I'm here for a reason."

Gathering an armor of pride and anger about her, Cara faced him directly, hiding the rawness of the emotions he stirred in her. "Oh, I'm sure you have a reason. One that entirely suits your purposes."

The wide mouth set angrily. "You will listen to me . . ."

Struggling to release her numb arm from his grasp, Cara backed away from him as far as his grip would allow. "We have nothing to discuss. We've both made our positions abundantly clear and there's no point in belaboring the issue. It wasn't my choice to be here today, whatever Susan may have told you. And I won't be here again if I can help it. Now, let me go; I don't want to be here with you."

A quiet anger dominated the two antagonists as they faced each other in a battle of wills.

"Then why are you here?" His dark eyes flicked over the smoothness of her profile as she turned away to avoid his probing gaze.

"Just doing a job. One that I tried to avoid, believe me." She stumbled over the explanation, not wanting him to learn where she was working if he didn't already know. "I had no choice." His eyes narrowed as he absorbed the bitter words: "Being within your reach is the last thing I would choose."

His words were tightly controlled, spoken quietly with a deliberation both taunting and caressing in its cruelty. "What happened, Cara? What happened to all those fervently spoken words of love you whispered while in my arms? Was that love so superficial after all?"

Her pale face turned paper white as his sarcasm reached her. Pain twisted deep within her at his mockery of her unselfishly given love. Her head thrown back as if in an effort to absorb the brunt of his attack, her answer was a whispered rasping sound escaping from her tear-clogged throat: "You killed it, killed it . . ."

Suddenly, Sloan released her arm as if pushing her away in disgust and anger. The abrupt movement caused Cara to stagger against the rough brick building. She gasped in pain as the heel of her hand scraped against the roughness, bringing blood welling to the surface of the wound. Stunned by the violence they aroused in each other, she watched as the blood began to seep across her palm.

Sloan seemed on the brink of moving to examine the injury, but Cara took advantage of her freedom and his hesitation. Turning quickly, she ran awkwardly toward her car. Gaining it, she reversed out of the parking space as quickly as she dared, hoping that Sloan wouldn't attempt to stop her. As she entered the stream of traffic, she glanced in her rearview mirror to note with relief that Sloan was still standing where she had left him. He watched her small car as she guided it out onto the avenue and into the anonymity of the traffic.

As she drove, Cara searched out a tissue from her bag and wrapped her hand to keep the blood from staining her clothing. She kept careful control of her feelings until she could reach the security of her apartment. She parked her car and quickly climbed the back stairs of the building; in moments she had gained the quiet refuge of her home. She slammed and locked the door as if pursued by an actual being rather than merely the specter of an unfulfilled dream.

Reaction to the experience began to set in as she washed the scrape. The tissue had adhered to the wound and cleaning it started the bleeding again. She stood by the sink, running cold water over the torn flesh of her hand. She was mesmerized by the rosy water running down the drain, her hand shaking so badly she could hardly hold it under the stream. At last she was able to apply a light bandage.

The pain in her hand abated, but her emotional pain overrode the physical. The tears that had been held back began to well up as she sat there. She hugged herself tightly, a defensive posture assumed against the overwhelming agony which twisted like a live thing inside her. How could things have gotten to such an impasse? How could something so beautiful have become such a morass of despair?

She *loved* him, he *wanted* her, and yet they could come to no comfortable compromise. Compromise. When it came down to it, that was what it would have had to be and Cara couldn't do that. She had compromised her own ideals for Sloan, but she could not compromise her love for him. And all the pain she had somehow held at bay for weeks rushed over her in a drowning tide as she sobbed helplessly into her hands.

During the long dark hours of the night, Cara convinced herself that Sloan would not bother to take any retaliation for her actions. She wasn't important enough to him, she finally decided, and pushed that worry forcefully from her weary mind.

But the worry returned the next morning when Lorene specifically asked how her day at Triad had gone. That sort of question seemed unusual enough in itself, but the look on the woman's face at Cara's noncommittal reply was even more so. The strangeness of her attitude began to sneak into Cara's thoughts later.

Thinking about it again, Cara suddenly realized that the job she had been assigned to at Triad had not really required her skills, not even those of an executive secretary, as she had been led to believe. Any fairly competent typist could have done the job and she knew of three who were available.

With that in mind, Cara tapped on the clouded glass door of Lorene's private office. Carefully closing the door behind her, Cara noted uneasily the somewhat suspicious look in the older woman's eyes.

"Lorene, what was the purpose behind sending me to Triad yesterday? Surely you realize, as I do now, that the position could have been filled by any one of the service typists."

Clearing her throat in an agitated manner, Cara's supervisor shuffled papers nervously across her desk, avoiding Cara's intent gaze.

Sensing the answer for herself, Cara continued. "Shall I guess, then? You got a call from Sloan Montgomery." Lorene's surprised upward glance confirmed her suspicions. "He asked for me specifically, didn't he? And he told you to keep that a secret, right?" Scornfully Cara held the woman's gaze. "And what did he use to 'convince' you—charm or blackmail?" Already certain of the answer, Cara angrily paced the room.

Lorene's voice held a pleading quality as she watched the agitated girl before her. "Now, Cara, it wasn't like that at all. Mr. Montgomery said he wanted the opportunity to talk to you, and that you would refuse to see him."

At Cara's incredulous look a touch of sympathy crossed the older woman's face. "I didn't see any harm in it when he asked me not to say anything to you about his request. He said it was a sort of lovers' quarrel.

Besides, well, he could see to it that several of our most prominent clients no longer needed our services.'' A kind of wheedling quality came into her voice. ''You can see the position that put me in. I couldn't afford to . . .''

Anger replaced dismay as Cara realized that Sloan's tactics had actually bordered on threatening. ''Did he openly threaten your business contacts?''

Almost shamefacedly, her employer began, ''Not exactly, but the hint was strong, and, well, I couldn't take the chance . . .'' Helplessly, the woman allowed her statement to trail off at the look on Cara's face.

Cara knew the hopelessness of the situation. It was futile to attempt to combat the power Sloan could exert. Cara interrupted the woman's explanations. ''Well, it matters very little now. He won't have the opportunity to try that again. I'm leaving the service, Lorene.'' And with grim resignation Cara turned to leave. ''That way, you won't be forced into any more embarrassing situations because of me.''

When she reached her car, Cara sat behind the wheel to regain her composure. She forced her mind to function practically once more. Now that this avenue was closed to her, what next? She could not allow Sloan to control her life in this manner. He had no right. When personal intimidation had failed he had gotten to her through her job. She had ignored his threats that first day, but now she recognized his determination to ruin her. Ignoring anything Sloan said was a mistake.

With renewed determination, Cara reviewed the list of agencies and once more began her search for employment. By the end of the day she had reestablished contact with a number of agencies dealing in permanent positions and signed with three temporary offices. The Clark Temp-Service promised work by the end of the week. Though it was not the best-paying service, nor very attractive personnel-wise, it would fill the gap and help her flagging cash flow.

By the time she reached the apartment that evening she was utterly weary. Just as she unlocked her door, the ringing of the telephone spurred her movements. She hurriedly snatched up the receiver and collapsed onto the couch.

Lea's welcome voice greeted her tentative hello. "Cara? Are you all right?"

Wary now, even with Lea, Cara carefully questioned her greeting. "Certainly. Why shouldn't I be?"

Ignoring the sharpness in Cara's voice, Lea hurried on. "Because I heard something about what happened. How on earth did you ever let yourself get caught into working at Triad?"

Relaxing a little, Cara nudged the apartment door closed. She kicked off her shoes and flexed her tired feet, then answered Lea's question. "Believe me, it was certainly not my choice. In fact, I tried to get out of it as soon as I saw the name on my schedule."

Lea was persistent. "Well, tell all. What happened?"

Reluctantly, Cara recounted the story, even to having encountered Sloan outside the building. That part of the tale brought an instant reaction from Lea.

"Hmmm. Any theory as to why he was waiting for you? Seems a little incriminating to me. Like maybe he cares more for you than he wants to admit?"

Grimly, Cara discounted that theory. "Hardly. More like getting a little revenge, I suspect. I didn't fall into step with his plans, and that's a new and annoying experience for him. No, Sloan and I have nothing to say to each other. All I want is for him to leave me alone. He hates me."

But Lea was adamant. "Then why would he take the trouble to phone the service and request you to fill in at

Triad? Seems to me he was looking for a way to see you without seeming to make arrangements, especially with the story he told your employer. Did you ever consider talking to him? Listening to what he had to say?''

Cara was certain Lea was wrong. The whole idea of Sloan setting up a meeting of that type was ridiculous. ''No, I didn't. We've said all we can say to each other. All that's left now is more hurt and I can't take much more of that kind of abuse. I've found another service and I'll work there until I sort things out better. I may have to leave the city, whether I want to or not.''

''Oh, come on, Cara. Surely that won't be necessary.''

''I hope not. But if Sloan won't let me work here in peace, I may have to.''

In spite of herself, Cara was intrigued by the thought that Sloan's unusual actions might have some meaning after all. Lea's idea might have some value. ''I can't think why Sloan went to the trouble of forcing the service into assigning me to Triad. If he wanted to get rid of me he could have arranged it outright. Something doesn't fit.''

Lea hesitated a moment before she spoke, refuting her own theory with her next words. ''Well, what if it wasn't Sloan? Maybe it was Susan.''

Cara frowned slightly as she considered that. ''No, that hadn't occurred to me. But it has to have been Sloan; Lorene Lawson spoke to him herself. Besides, why would Susan make that kind of effort? She has what she wants—my job and Sloan.''

''Well, I don't think things are going as smoothly as she'd like. From what I've seen, Sloan certainly doesn't make any effort toward making any relationship they have permanent. Susan goes to great lengths to convince everyone that she has him right where she wants him—in bed and out. But you know Sloan better than I do. He's totally unreadable. Maybe she convinced someone on staff to pretend to be Sloan.''

Cara winced at the scenes Lea's words had conjured up in her mind. ''But why would she make any effort to put me into a compromising situation? I'm certain she was genuinely surprised to see me yesterday, too. She's not that good an actress.''

''Maybe I'm wrong. But that's the only thing I can come up with. That things aren't going as well as she would like between herself and Sloan. What if he's grown tired of her, or didn't want her in the first place? What if she feels you're the reason for Sloan not being quite so compliant as she thought he would be?''

Cara frowned again as she considered these new ideas. She rubbed a hand across her throbbing head. ''Well, whatever the reason, it's past. Susan has a free path to whatever she can get from him, and more power to her.''

''I don't think you really mean that. If I read things right, well, they're both so short-tempered that something isn't going as planned. It's my bet that it won't be long until there's a new executive assistant in that office. And none too soon for me, let me tell you.''

Cara could hardly ignore the note of triumph in Lea's voice, but it brought little comfort to her. Whatever Sloan decided to do had nothing whatsoever to do with herself.

Changing the subject, Cara asked Lea about her wedding plans, and the younger girl moved willingly into the new area of conversation. Lea renewed her request that Cara be a member of the wedding party, but understood Cara's refusal. Though she had few friends as close as Lea, Cara could not bring herself to be quite so public, where any Triad people might ask questions. Several minutes later they hung up, leaving the subject of Sloan Montgomery unresolved.

Within a few days Cara was maintaining a somewhat steady schedule with the Clark Service. And if the positions weren't as prestigious as with Lawson, she ignored the fact, satisfied that at least the days were too busy to allow any unwelcome thoughts of Sloan.

Fall approached and Cara was gripped by a restlessness that found no relief. She tried to busy herself planning changes in her wardrobe. She even toyed with the idea of a change in hairstyle, then decided against it. The longer length gave her more choice and she didn't want to limit herself. She admitted that it could be just plain lack of interest, too.

Cara knew that the leaves of the tall, stately maples around her apartment house and in the park would soon turn bright yellow and red. The Missouri Ozarks could well boast of their picturesque fall colors. The multicolored maples in their vividness appeared painted with an artist's brush against the greens and oranges of neighboring trees. Blue skies would soon be changed to slate gray, warning of the harsh midwestern winter yet to come. Autumn rains would rush down the leaves to be crushed underfoot and washed away in thoughtless rivers of muddy water in the grimy gutters along the street.

Fall was a melancholy time for Cara, at best, but this year she especially dreaded the rainy gray days to come, the long evenings to fill. And her restlessness grew more acute.

Soon the air turned crisp and the trees began their change. As Cara walked the deserted trails of the park, her serenity was often disturbed by thoughts of a tall, dark man who lived in the recesses of her memory. The long nights brought haunted dreams, tears soaking her pillow as she faced again the hopelessness of her love.

Unable to shake her depression, Cara delayed buying a gift for Lea's wedding. She dreaded entering the department stores to see other, happier girls going over their gift lists. Finally, on one relatively warm Saturday, Cara girded herself with false courage and drove to a downtown mall to look for an appropriate gift.

The store was crowded with people there for the annual Fall Sales. After much jostling and searching and rejecting of suggestions, Cara finally settled on a set of intricately carved napkin rings and a matching carved basket. After adding a set of colorful napkins, Cara was confident that the gift would suit Lea. Standing in line to have it wrapped, Cara was unaware that her chief antagonist was approaching until far too late.

Cara's whole body stiffened as Susan's low purr reached her. "Looking for a gift, Cara? Or are wedding plans in your future?"

Glancing up, Cara noted with chagrin Susan's chic appearance in a matching beige dress and coat, which contrasted with her own well-worn and faded denim suit. Gathering her confidence like a cloak about her, Cara faced the other woman. "I could ask you the same. Wedding plans in your future?"

Susan's regard of Cara was intent, watchful for any reaction to her words as she answered, slowly and with deliberation, "No, Sloan and I have discussed it, but I'm not ready to set a date yet. You know how Sloan is, though, don't you? So demanding. I may not be able to put him off for much longer."

Cara watched grimly as Susan allowed her fingers to slide over an ornately carved piece of serving silver. It took all of her willpower not to strike out at the woman. Summoning extra reserves of control, Cara managed to appear unconcerned by Susan's not so subtle digs. She resolved never to allow this sort of thing to happen again. It seemed almost a foregone conclusion that she would have to leave town to get a permanent job. She needed a fresh start in life, and a new location and a new job would give her that.

Before Susan could again take up her attack it was Cara's turn to have her gift wrapped. Handing it to the clerk, she waited impatiently as Susan lingered to examine another silver piece before continuing her conversation.

"Of course, you know that Sloan and I are very close. I hope you weren't laboring under the misconception that you made a lasting impression on him. I would think that your last encounter at the Complex would have been sufficient to quell that hope."

Both the words and Susan's arrogance penetrated Cara's carefully constructed emotional armor, as they were designed to. The thought that Sloan and Susan had discussed her made sudden anger almost overshadow the hurt such a thought brought to her heart. Sloan was a wound that had never healed properly, a wound that could break open to bleed afresh with just the slightest pressure. And she was tired of bleeding, tired of hurting.

Noting that her package was nearly wrapped, Cara drew a deep breath for control before turning to meet Susan's watchful gaze. Speaking very precisely, very clearly and with all the coldness she could command, she carefully held back the anger striving to break loose. "Susan, I won't even dignify that with a response. It should be perfectly obvious, even to you, that we have nothing in common. That I prefer not even to see you if it can be avoided. And, as far as Sloan is concerned, I'm sure you deserve each other. In any event, neither of you is of any concern to me." She hesitated significantly to make her point very clear. "And now that we have that out of the way, I'll say goodby and hope we never meet again."

With all the dignity she could muster, Cara reclaimed her package and left the surprised Susan blinking before an astonished counter girl. Cara could almost smile as she entered the elevator, turning as she punched the down button to see both women still standing just where she had left them.

Though she resolved daily to improve her attitude, Cara found her work more and more depressing. With the Lawson Agency she had always been assured of top-rank positions with good companies. But with the Clark Service her assignments continued to be in small two-office situations where all that was required was that she answer the phone and type a couple of letters. It seemed to her that an answering service would have served as well, though the leers of the employers gave her a hint as to the reasons why they hadn't sought that simple solution.

On a couple of occasions Cara had been caught unaware and had barely escaped an embarrassing encounter. She counted it a blessing that she did not have to report to those same offices again and managed to calm her apprehensions before another such situation arose.

Daily she searched the Help Wanted columns and sent out letters of application, but without success. The employment agencies seemed to make no better progress. Her financial situation became more precarious as she was forced to dip into her savings more frequently. She continually considered the possibility of moving away, but put off making a decision until after Lea's wedding.

To alleviate the situation, she began to skip lunches

and after the first few days she even told herself that she wasn't missing them. She stopped sewing, too, both from boredom and the cost of fabric. Her interest waned in almost every area and she found herself going to bed earlier and earlier as a form of escape. Her haunted dreams made even that escape untenable and her shadowed eyes began to tell the tale of her growing anxiety.

She passed almost a month with the Clark Service. It was a month she hadn't enjoyed, but she accepted it as necessary until something better came along. On the Monday after the incident with Susan, Cara went to the agency to check her assignments. Glancing at her card, she saw that it was filled with the least attractive of the positions she had previously been assigned. With a questioning frown she rechecked and found that her suspicions were correct. With a flash of anger she stormed into the supervisor's office unannounced, a new determination giving her the courage to question the assignments.

Catching Norman Fair by surprise, she was only vaguely aware that he quickly hung up the telephone without a sign-off at the look on her normally expressionless face.

She tensed as his insolent gaze swept over her from head to toe, making her skin crawl in reaction. His voice oily, Fair leaned comfortably back in his armed swivel chair, totally unmoved by her answering look of disdain. "And to what do I owe this visit, Cara? A question about your schedule?"

Clenching her fists in frustration, Cara paced the floor to control her anger. Suddenly, all the repressed feelings of the past surfaced, making her almost incoherent when she finally spoke. "You know there is! You know I'm capable of more than these jobs require!" She angrily threw the job list down on the desk in front of the man.

"You know the types of offices these are! You persist in sending me to them when I know there are better positions going to some of the other temps who have half the skills I have. It's not fair and I want to know when you're going to change things!"

Fair leaned forward in the chair, his pale blue eyes pinning Cara to the spot. "In the first place, Cara, you're out of line questioning any position I send you to. In the second place, I am the full judge of your talents . . . and I judge that you are not using the full extent of them." Having let that soak in, he continued. "I do have better positions, you're right, and they're given to the girls who, shall we say, cooperate. And they are fully compensated for their, ah, talents. Am I making myself clear, or shall I spell it out further?"

Cara was rocked with the force of his implications. As the full knowledge of what he was saying penetrated, a flush rose over her face and Fair's complacent look became one of triumph.

As he leaned back in the chair again, a screech of complaint emanated from the overloaded springs, scraping Cara's raw nerves. "I think you have the full picture now, Cara. I'll give you a couple of days to think it over, if you need to, though I shouldn't think you would. This is nothing new for you."

At that Cara found her tongue. "What are you saying, 'nothing new for me'? Just what do you mean?"

A sly look crossed her opponent's face. "Why, the word's out on you, honey. And I must say, Sloan Montgomery's cast-off does carry some weight. Makes your price higher . . ."

The room whirled as Cara took in what he had said and suddenly understood everything that had been happening to her. All the questions about the types of positions she had been assigned, the reason behind being sent to Triad by the other agency were suddenly clear. The knowledge that she had been so unfeelingly used made her physically ill.

It was not only learning how she had been manipulated into her current position, how her name had been smeared, but the total disregard Sloan displayed for her feelings, for her love for him, that sickened her. How he must have laughed. How he must be enjoying her dilemma. That must have been what he wanted to tell her when he confronted her at the Complex. He'd wanted to let her know just what he could do if she didn't cooperate. Oh yes, it was all very clear now. She had been so ignorant, so naïve, so unaware of the extent of his power, his need to illustrate how wrong she was, to imagine she could fight against his plans for her.

With her legs trembling uncontrollably, Cara sank silently into a chair across the wide desk from her employer. His chair squeaked in protest again as he leaned back, satisfied that he had made his point successfully.

For several moments Cara sat with her head down, her long slim fingers kneading her temple as a nagging headache began to grow. Aching tension and an enveloping despair descended upon her as she realized just how insidious Sloan's plan had been and how well it had worked.

Gathering her composure, Cara faced the smug Fair across his cluttered desk. Her gaze fell over his unkempt person in disgust. One of the things she had always disliked about the man was the litter of papers, used coffee cups and overflowing ash trays that always spilled across his desk. Now the revulsion she had swallowed in order to work bubbled up, nearly choking her as she took in the self-satisfied countenance of the man facing her.

"Mr. Fair, let me make myself very clear. I am not,

nor was I ever, Sloan Montgomery's 'woman.' In fact, it was because I would not become one of his women that I left Triad. Whether you believe me or not is immaterial to me.''

As Norman Fair leaned abruptly forward to interrupt her, Cara rose, holding up a hand to halt his speech. ''No. You have nothing to say that I want to hear. I should have foreseen this development. I should at least have suspected something amiss when I was sent on some of these 'jobs.' I just never thought Sloan would stoop to this.'' She did stop then to study Fair's slowly reddening face. ''Just how did you get your instructions? The last place was threatened with the loss of several good clients. What was your price?''

Fair realized that Cara was past intimidation and relaxed in his chair again, the angry red leaving his round face as he brought himself under careful control. ''Well, well. I may have misjudged you, Cara. I figured you one of two ways. Either looking for some good money after being thrown over by Montgomery, or desperate for work because the word was out on you. Both, maybe. You must have something else going if you can afford to drop this opportunity.'' One fat hand stroked his rounded cheek as he considered her coldly. ''You catch on quick. There could be something in this for you if you play along, Cara.''

Contempt for the man and what he represented was evident in Cara's attitude as she turned to leave the room. Never in her wildest imaginings would she have believed this could happen to her. It seemed ridiculous, but Fair had used some of the same words Sloan had used, phrases about misjudging her, missing an opportunity. That only made the hurt slice deeper as she began to realize exactly what Sloan had done to her.

Fair continued as Cara reached the door. ''Don't buck

the system, Cara. Montgomery has put out the word that if you don't work for him, you don't work for anybody. Not even temporarily. You must have really gotten to him." His eyes slid over her again. "I can see that you could."

Purpose stiffened Cara's resolve as she turned to face him. "And just how did he get to you?"

A greasy smile crossed the man's face. "A few well-placed calls, a few subtle suggestions, are usually enough for a man with Montgomery's power. And he's gained a lot of that in the months he's been here. Even a verified call from someone in his organization is enough. It doesn't have to come from the big man himself . . . and usually doesn't, unless you're important enough." The hesitation was intentional. "And his women acquaintances are rarely important enough. A few hints will do the job."

For a few moments Cara thought, hoped, that she was dreaming the whole thing. How could she ever have gotten into this kind of situation? The absurdity of it was overwhelming.

Realizing that she was still standing in Fair's office, she turned abruptly and left the room, carefully closing the door behind her, then walked from the building with stiff-backed determination and went directly to her car. When she reached it, she sat quietly for several moments, breathing deeply to regain her composure. For the second time in as many months she was faced with having to find another job. And she knew that this time would be even more difficult than the last two.

The magnitude of what was happening to her was too much to comprehend. A few ill-chosen words at an inopportune time had brought all this about. Sloan's determination to get his way, her own determination to have what she needed from him in order to love him, had fed the original wrong and brought about her utter humiliation today. How could she have been so deluded? How could she ever have thought she meant something to him? All her love counted for nothing. She was just one of the many in Sloan's life. And not even a very important one, if he could treat her in this manner.

Suddenly she realized that she was still sitting in her car, so she turned the key and headed for the refuge of her home, fighting the depression that hung over her as the repercussions of her latest set-to nagged at her weary mind. She needed a clear head, logical thinking, if she was to work her way out of this situation. Tears again stung her eyes. It was so unfair. Her mind, her nature, fought against it. Even now, she could hardly believe the vindictiveness of the man. Relentless as Sloan was, this determination to control or destroy her life, though he was no longer personally interested in her, was totally beyond her comprehension. She had thought him fair, at least. But he was a destroyer. She had not known him at all.

Pulling herself together again, Cara searched the papers for positions. Finally she was able to obtain a three-month position as a typist for a private researcher, forcing herself to overlook the small lie she had told by omission. In retyping her résumé she left out the years spent at Triad. When questioned concerning the gap between the present and her business school graduation, she made vague reference to her parents being involved in an auto accident and let the interviewer assume that she had undertaken responsibilities in that regard. She salved her conscience by telling herself that she never really told the lie and that desperate times needed desperate measures. And she was fast becoming desperate.

227

Three months was not a long time, but the pay was good and the work would be soothing to her frayed nerves. Besides, it would keep her out of business circles where she might have any contact with Sloan. It gave her breathing space to decide what she would have to do next.

She began to believe that things would take a turn for the better. And even if her dreams were still sometimes haunted by Sloan's face, her resentment of his treatment of her began to overshadow the love she still held for him, which she saw as a good sign.

Chapter Nine

$\mathscr{L}$ea's wedding day arrived. The perfect fall day dawned sunny and crisp, as beautiful a wedding day as anyone could hope for. Rising and showering, Cara's thoughts were on Lea and all the times they had shared over the past months. The hopes Lea had expressed about Tom's gaining his degree, his graduation, his acceptance of the position in his father's organization, the cohesive family unit that had been forged from a near-crisis flooded back to her mind. Lea deserved happiness if anyone did, and Cara would not have changed anything in that. She did catch herself wishing, with a touch of envy, that she could have some of that same happiness in her own life. But she could see none in the near future.

Cara decided on a high-necked long-sleeved knit dress in muted shades of brown and green. The gored skirt was designed to fall just below the knee, swirling gracefully around her long legs as she moved. The fitted bodice skimmed her slim shape, accentuating the contours of her high, firm breasts before the skirt flared out over her rounded hips. Though she had lost more weight during the past several weeks, her feminine curves were still unmistakable.

The church was something from a bygone era. She smiled fondly on seeing it. The exterior was gray stone featuring double wooden doors with long iron hinges extending across the front. It was a building that spoke of solidarity, of unity, of a time when life had centered around the family and the church. Cara could see why Lea had chosen it.

The short flight of steps up to the entrance could have been a hundred feet high for all Cara's awareness of such things as she climbed them. She strove to keep her mind carefully blank as she followed the other guests inside and signed the guest book.

The late afternoon sun slanting through stained-glass windows bathed the interior in jeweled shades of blue, green and wine as Cara stood in the doorway of the chapel. Soft organ music wrenched her heart. The flickering of candles as each wick was carefully lighted wavered momentarily in Cara's misted eyes.

Unbidden, her own dreams of such a wedding surfaced, a wedding that would join her to the man she loved. She had dreamed of love, of tenderness, of a home and children, a fulfilled future with a man she could depend on. A man who would cherish her, whom she could cherish in return with her whole being, who would answer her love with the same intensity and devotion she brought to the marriage. But that was a dream she would never realize now.

None of that really mattered, Cara thought, forcing her thoughts away from what might have been and back to the present. Both sides of the church were filled with the friends and families of the bride and groom. Cara noted several familiar faces among those seated on the bride's side of the church. Eluding the usher, she slid, gratefully unobserved, into one of the last pews.

As the soloist sang a traditional wedding song of love and promise, Cara's hands clenched together until her knuckles were white, her nails digging into her palms. It was not until several moments after the last note had faded that she noticed the pain and forced her trembling hands to open.

Drawing a deep breath, she steeled herself not to react as the first notes of the wedding march began. The stirring of the crowd indicated the approach of the first of the bridesmaids in their floor-length gowns of varying shades of rust, apricot and yellow. Their sashes of deeper tones of brown and orange velvet made a lovely parade of the colors of fall. As the audience stood, Tom and his groomsmen approached from a side entrance to take their places, watching expectantly as the attendants in turn reached their stations. The look of pride and anticipation, of longing and love, on Tom's face as Lea stood framed in the entrance nearly tore Cara's heart from her body. Swallowing drily and unconsciously standing straighter, Cara fought to bring her building emotions under control.

The tiny blonde flower girl stepped slowly down the aisle, intent on her task of carefully dropping bronze mum petals along the way. At the rustle of taffeta Cara turned with the others toward a radiant Lea, who was moving carefully down the aisle toward her husband-to-be.

Lea had described to Cara in detail the cut of her dress, but the reality was even more lovely than she could have imagined. The scooped neck, the long pointed sleeves, narrow waist and bell-shaped floor-length skirt with just the hint of a train set off Lea's small frame perfectly. The shoulder-length veil lent a sort of misty look to the lovely smile she reserved only for Tom as she approached the altar.

Cara stood there, her trembling knees so weak that she thought they could not possibly hold her upright, her hands gripping the back of the seat before her to still their trembling. A small movement at the opposite end of the pew momentarily caught her attention and, after one brief glance, a gasp was wrenched from her as she saw Sloan slip quietly between the benches.

In a kind of shock she gazed longingly at the familiar figure of the tall, dark-suited man she loved. His crisp brown hair was brushed back, shining in the dim light. She noted the way the cuff of his white shirt peeped out from his jacket sleeve. She recognized the autocratic lines of his face in the muted light of the sanctuary, the controlled features that were so achingly familiar to her, that haunted her waking and sleeping hours.

While Cara's attention had been concentrated on Sloan, the bridal couple had joined hands in preparation for binding their lives together. Suddenly, Cara knew she could stay no longer. It was all too much for her to bear. Biting her lip to stifle a sob, she slid quietly and with as much dignity as she could gather out into the aisle, escaping to the foyer. She would explain to Lea later, she promised herself. Lea would understand. As she slipped quietly through the outer door she heard the first words of the ceremony.

Early darkness was fast approaching as Cara ran toward her parked car, careless of the impression she made, escaping from the church when the wedding had barely begun. Shakily, she unlocked the car and sank gratefully into its anonymity. In a moment she was

controlled enough to start the engine and swing expertly
from the curb, escape the only thing on her mind. She
failed to see a tall figure emerge from the shadows at the
chapel door to watch her car retreat along the darkening
avenue.

Cara delayed returning to her empty apartment for as
long as possible, unwilling to encounter the loneliness
awaiting her there. As she drove, she struggled to hold
back the tears rising to her already tear-swollen eyes.
She knew that once she let go there would be no stopping
and she couldn't cope with that yet.

To forestall that moment, she drove around the city. It
seemed necessary to take familiar streets that she would
soon have to leave. She engaged in a sort of goodby to
her former life, a farewell to the hopes and dreams of the
person she had been.

By the time she turned toward home, Cara had
regained some degree of control. She noticed then that
thunderclouds had begun to make their appearance and
that flashes of lightning were beginning to flicker in the
distance. Rain, refreshing rain. She longed for it; it
would be a cleansing, a renewal. Cara found herself
rejoicing that at least Lea's wedding day had been as
beautiful as she deserved and hoping that her friend's
future life would be as lovely.

Totally worn out, Cara climbed the stairs to her
apartment. Her whole body felt bruised and beaten, her
spirits as low as they had ever been. Coming back to
what had once been a haven, a hiding place, she
suddenly saw it only as a place of torture, as she
remembered again the fierce joy she had known here in
Sloan's arms. Seeing him today had broken open the
wounds again, and she felt anew the pain of losing him.

With resignation she fit the key in the lock and swung
open the door. As she glanced around the room, her

mind was crowded with memories of the precious moments she had shared here with Sloan. In this room she had felt his arms around her. It was here that she had first known the woman in herself, discovered her needs, her desires. Here she had first experienced the specialness of the relationship a man and a woman could share.

She knew that only Sloan could give her what her mind, her body, ached for. And knowing it, the tears spilled over, running freely down her face. This time she didn't try to stop them. They were tears of sadness, but tears for healing. She remembered that phrase of her grandmother's. Oh, she hoped these were tears for healing. She needed it badly.

As the tears washed her face, deep sobs wracked her body. In total desolation she sank onto the couch, clutching a soft pillow to her body to blunt the blows her utter despair dealt her. All the frustration, the pain, the fear, the emptiness and loneliness burst forth. All the days spent rebuilding a life that was empty without the man she loved, all the while knowing that Sloan would never return her love, gushed forth in the only release available to her—tears. She cried for the compromises she had made that were not enough to hold him, for others she could not have made, even to hold him awhile longer. She cried for the hours she had spent trying to forget the excitement, the longing, the desire Sloan could arouse in her with just a touch. She knew tears for the fulfillment she had experienced in his arms that would never come again. And she cried for the sadness she felt in him for the life he had chosen, for all the love he had never experienced and might never learn to give.

Yes, tears for all the hatred, the recriminations she wished upon him for the total devastation of her career, for the ruin of her life. It all came bursting forth in wracking sobs and agony that had been bottled up for far too long.

It seemed hours later when she was finally depleted. Her body felt wrung out, dead. The darkness was complete now, but she rejected the light, needing the protection of the night's shadows. She couldn't face herself yet and she drew comfort from the cover of darkness.

At last she realized that she could not continue like this much longer. She rose then, drawn by the growing storm outside her window. Holding the small pillow to her, she stood in the windowed alcove, watching the play of lightning licking at the cloud edges and at the city settling down for a stormy evening. Cars passed in the streets below carrying their drivers home to dry comfort before the storm broke over their heads. People hurried across streets, wrapping their coats close against the rising, gusting wind.

Cara felt isolated, tower-bound. From the distant past a children's story came to mind. "Rapunzel, Rapunzel, let down your hair." But she had no lover. No one wanted to gain her ivory tower. She had rejected her lover just as surely as he had rejected her. Hopelessness enveloped her when she realized that her pain had not lessened in any meaningful way, only abated for a while.

It was not until she heard the latch click that she remembered that she hadn't locked the door after coming in. Sudden fear clutched at her and she crushed the pillow harder to her as she turned slightly, afraid of what she might see in the darkened room behind her.

It was Sloan. She knew it as surely as she knew she had been waiting for him. As surely as she would always wait for him. He stood quietly, framed in the doorway.

Unwilling to acknowledge his presence, she turned

back to look out at the unfriendly night. At least it was impersonal. It could not touch her, hurt her—not like the man who stood waiting behind her.

Out of the darkness he spoke. "Cara." Though compelling, his voice was flat with . . . what? Cold anger? Nothing had changed. She knew it, accepted it. And more of her died with the knowledge of it.

"Cara, look at me."

Finally, she turned, the window behind her framing her body in the street light's faint glow. The reflected radiance accentuated the contours of the beloved face before her. Hungrily, she reviewed the planes and hollows, the prominent cheekbones, the lines running from nose to chin, more pronounced than she had remembered them.

Carefully, she maintained the distance between them. She had learned her lesson well. But even as she stood facing him, the love she had tried to live without until she could function as a whole person again returned in full force. The familiar aching need of him had abated not at all. She could not deny that seeing him so near, so available to her hungry arms, lifted her need to fever pitch.

Sloan hadn't moved. His gaze held her even as she strove not to react to him. She struggled to maintain at least an outward control she was far from feeling. Even in the semidarkness she could not help appreciating how the cut of his dark suit molded his large frame, emphasizing the width of his shoulders, the trim span of his waist, the muscled length of his thighs, flexing as he shifted his weight.

Sliding the button of his jacket free, Sloan shoved his left hand into his pants pocket. The gesture revealed the whiteness of his evening shirt, the fabric stretching over the lean muscles of his chest. He loosened his tie slowly, as though stalling for time, stripping it off and shoving it carelessly into his jacket pocket.

Even as Cara watched him, wanted him, she remembered the cruelty of his complete rejection of her, his ruthless ruin of her career and reputation. Her resentment grew and she fed it to make it overshadow again the love for him that was still within her.

Warily, Cara stood her ground, watching him, noting each movement as if to memorize it so it would last a lifetime. Unable to maintain her calm exterior amid warring factors of the love and anger she felt toward him, she turned her back on his domineering presence to stare once more out into the night. The rain had come and the reflected lights on the wet streets reminded her of an old movie setting. The melancholy of the scene fit the unfolding emotional drama inside her. She knew she must finish with Sloan. She must cut him out of her life permanently. But doing so would be cutting away part of herself. Yet it had to be done if she was to begin living again.

In spite of her racing heart, her voice maintained a calmness she did not feel. "What are you doing here, Sloan?"

Did she only imagine the momentary hesitation before he spoke? "I came for you."

She allowed a small sigh to escape, evidence of her growing despair. No, nothing was different. He thought he could just appear and she would immediately capitulate.

"I suppose you came because your harassment campaign succeeded. You think that because I can't find a permanent job, because you've ruined me, I'll accede to your demands out of desperation."

Despair was her only feeling. "Nothing has changed.

You're still as you always were, and I'm still just myself. Though I thought I could compromise at one time, I realize I was wrong even to consider it. What I offered wasn't enough for you. You couldn't have made that more clear than it's been over the past couple of months. You wouldn't believe how successful your campaign to get rid of me has been. You're just a little early to see the complete effect. I'll be gone in a few days; you needn't have come here tonight.'' She dropped the pillow to the floor. She didn't need the shield any longer.

Again there was a silence before his rough voice came out of the darkness, nearer now. "Nothing remains the same, even if we want it to. We're all of us human, after all.''

His words were strange, disturbing, yet she could not give in to her curiosity. She watched his reflection in the window. Though his full face was somewhat obscured, the strong planes she had loved were outlined. The arrogance was softened by the misty reflection in the glass against the velvet night, occasionally blanked out by flashes of lightning.

He continued to stand close behind her, just beyond touching distance. "Is there nothing I can say? Nothing you have to say to me?''

Still, she watched his reflection. "No, it's all been said at one time or another. It's over. It's been over for a long time.''

The reflection shifted as Sloan started to turn away, then stood his ground, running his fingers through his already ruffled hair. "I'd hoped we'd just begun.''

Anger pricked her carefully constructed shell. Sarcasm was her reaction to his presumption. "How could you possibly have thought that? Do you think I enjoyed being tormented, harassed? Have your other women enjoyed being used, then thrown away like a worn-out shirt? A man like you has no concept of how degrading that can be.''

With a deep breath she controlled the anger, releasing a long breath of resignation. ''No, not a beginning. An ending. You've won, as usual. Maybe not as you'd like to have won, but you have. And now I want an end to it. An end to it all.''

The stillness of his body was reflected in the glass. She felt his searching gaze trying to pierce her armor. A strange note rang in his low voice when he spoke again. ''What do you mean, an end?''

Cara sensed, rather than saw, the sudden extra tension between them. She almost laughed in realization of what his first thoughts must have been at her words. ''No, nothing as drastic as that. Not even for you, Sloan. Not even you could drive me that far.''

Suddenly, he turned and began to pace back and forth a few steps behind her, his agitation clear. She watched him, unable to comprehend the drastic change of attitude he was exhibiting, never expecting his next words. ''Cara, you're tearing me apart!''

Anguish throbbed in his words. She was nearly unnerved by the intensity of it. It was so unlike the Sloan she knew, but she also felt there was little possibility that it was genuine emotion.

''Don't play with me, Sloan. You warned me about that and now I'm warning you. I won't allow you to manipulate me any longer.'' She closed her eyes against the image of him reflected in the rain-streaked glass.

He seemed to have regained control. ''I'm not playing games now, Cara. I've never meant anything more in my life.''

The need to see his face, to try to read the truth there, waa more than she could deny. There was something new in the tone of his voice, something that rang true.

But the pain he had caused her was a stronger voice than his pleading words.

"How can I convince you?"

His actions, his words, compelled her to open up to him, to once again make herself vulnerable. But she resisted. "Convince me? You've already done that quite effectively. You've convinced me of what a fool I've been. Convinced me I was wrong in every way to become involved with you. You showed me that I really didn't understand myself and certainly didn't understand you." She laughed derisively. "How incredibly stupid of me. I wanted so badly to know you, to learn the complexities that make you who you are. I even deluded myself into believing I had. But you fooled me every time." She bit her lips in an effort to hold back tears. "How gullible I was, and how entertained you must have been by my childish ideologies, by my virgin sacrifice." Her crossed arms hugged her own trembling body as her tightly reined emotions threatened to crumble. "Oh, yes, the mighty Sloan Montgomery. You knew exactly what you were doing. You called every play, as usual, and I lost."

He moved toward her. She sensed that and steeled herself against any reaction to his nearness. She could smell his cologne, the musky scent that was uniquely his, almost feel the warmth of his body in the closeness of the small alcove.

"Not every play, Cara. Right now I wish I could." He let out a long breath. He was so near that the released breath fanned the fine hair at her neck and she shivered in involuntary reaction. "What is that biblical phrase? 'Lo, how the mighty have fallen'? Well, it's not an original statement, but true, just the same."

Again she heard something new in his voice, some nuance she'd never heard before, and she found herself concentrating again on his reflection in the darkened glass.

He didn't meet her gaze as she searched his imperfectly mirrored face. His hand moved as though to touch her cheek, then fell to her shoulders as she hunched in a self-protective stance.

"I once told you that I didn't know how to love. Didn't know if I could learn." He hesitated before continuing, his husky voice soft in absorbed thought. It was as if he was talking more to himself than to her. "The rest of the message was, 'if anyone could teach me, it would be you.' But I never said it. I was afraid to. I didn't want the commitment that would entail."

She waited, half in fear, half in fragile hope.

"I'm not afraid anymore, Cara. I want a commitment —with you."

During those moments she'd forgotten to breathe. Now her breath came in small shudders as the meaning of his words penetrated her mind. Sensing her uncertainty, Sloan moved to stand behind her, hesitantly taking her still body into his arms, pulling her back against his strength. And with a feeling of complete naturalness, of coming home, she relaxed against him.

"I love you, Cara. I feel things for you that I never imagined were possible."

His voice caressed her, slid across her to set up familiar reactions. One part of her wanted to absorb those feelings, revel in them. Another, more practical, side knew she was asking for more heartache if she allowed herself to become involved with Sloan again. Now she was the one who was afraid, afraid he didn't know the meaning of the words he spoke.

She surrendered. Whatever the cost, she would pay it. She had to pay it. A small sigh escaped her parted lips as her head rolled back against his shoulder, revealing the soft underflesh of her throat to his questing mouth. She hungered and thirsted for him.

Unerringly, his arms enfolded her, his hands slipping possessively across her stomach, pressing her back against him to feel his shuddering need.

"Come to me, Cara. Love me again."

She absorbed his words as her body responded to his hands lifting the fullness of her breasts, their roundness filling and overflowing as he teased them to a throbbing desire for his caress. A moan of response rose from deep inside her as she turned to him in total surrender.

Ravenously, she searched his face as she raised her mouth to his. With an answering hunger he claimed her offering, drawing, giving, questing, receiving, as she gave herself over to his total domination of her. Her senses reeled with the feel of him, and when his mouth momentarily left hers she tangled her fingers in the thickness of his hair to draw him back. Boldly, now, she took his mouth, her tongue teasing, searching. And the sounds she heard were not her own. A surge of hope spurred her on, all reserve tossed aside in her need of him.

He crushed her to him as if he would absorb her total being. His hand cupped the back of her head as he cradled her face against his shoulder, his mouth against her temple, his quickened breath teasing the fine hair there. When he finally spoke, his voice was a desperate whisper. "Oh, Cara, how I've needed you."

Unable to believe she had heard him correctly, she stiffened in his arms.

"No. Don't leave me now. Please. Just listen."

There was yet another new sound in the voice of the almighty Sloan. It was a sound of desperation, of longing. In answer, she stood on tiptoe, allowing her hands to slide across his broad shoulders, probing the hollows at his collarbone, knowing his body again with a possessiveness new to her.

Turning her face to his, Cara searched the sharpened features, seeing for the first time the tortured look meeting her own. Taking that beloved face in her hands, feeling the roughness of his cheek, she softly dropped a kiss across the once arrogant and cynical mouth in a renewed promise.

"You know I won't leave you, can't leave you. Ever again. Whatever you ask, wherever you go, even when you send me away, I will still love you."

With a groan he clasped her to him, "Make me believe it, Cara. Stay with me. Whatever the reason, stay with me."

The low rumbling of thunder grew in the background as they held one another, making silent vows. The heavy spattering of rain against the window roused them both. Moving back a moment, Sloan finally spoke, his usual forcefulness coming to the fore once more.

"We have some talking to do."

Cara could only nod in agreement as she allowed him to guide her to the couch. Flashes of lightning showed the way. She lay against him, fitting into his shoulder, watching him in the dim light. Weariness was etched in every line of his face as he relaxed, his head leaning back against the cushions. Her fingers itched to smooth those lines away, but she knew that now was the time for talking.

Relaxing against him, she was still in awe of this change in him as he prepared to speak. His fingers gently caressed her shoulder; his breath was warm against her cheek. But before a word passed his lips, Cara laid a finger across his mobile mouth. "I love you, Sloan." The words held a promise, a promise she meant to keep regardless of the consequences.

A deep sigh told the depth of his feeling. "I know, now. It took me a long time to realize that."

"Yes, almost too long," she chided gently as she caressed his strong face with her fingertips. "When you kept pushing me away, I thought I couldn't bear it. And then Susan went out of her way to tell me you went straight to her when you left me. I couldn't stand thinking of that. I didn't want to believe her, but you were so cold to me after . . ." The words tumbled out as she tried to tell him how she felt.

He searched her face, as if he wanted to know for certain she believed him. "I never did that. Never went to Susan when I left you. Heaven only knows I tried everything else to get you out of my mind, but never that."

He turned away from her again, forcing himself to talk it all out. "I used her. Used her to keep you out of my mind. I'm not proud of that. She'd made it clear that she was more than willing to try her chances with me, and I took advantage of it." She could see the grim resignation on his face. "I wanted to hurt you, cut you out of my life for good."

For long moments he was quiet and she waited, knowing he needed to say it all aloud. And she needed to hear it. "When I held you, made love to you, I began to realize that that would never be enough. You responded so openly, so freely, in spite of your earlier reservations. And you asked so little of me, nothing you didn't have a right to ask. I knew that your doubts weren't just empty words. I knew you wouldn't lie to gain something from me. And holding you felt so good. Too good."

She watched a telltale muscle jerking in his jaw, showing the strain he was under. "I tried to convince myself that you were just another woman, another conquest, but I knew differently." He pulled her closer as his words made her flinch. "When I saw you at the Club that evening I didn't like how it made me feel. I wanted to retaliate in some way. Any way. Even though I was forcing you out of my life, I still couldn't stand seeing you with someone else. When you resigned, I thought that was the answer. But even not seeing you in the office didn't work. You were in my mind, imprinted on my body, and I hated it.

"That night, after seeing you at the Club, I came here prepared to force you back to me, on my terms. But you fought back. I knew then that if I couldn't live with you, I couldn't live without you, either. But I refused to face it. I'd never felt that way before. I didn't want to feel that way. I didn't want to need you."

She could hear the rain tapping in earnest against the windowpane, the thunder rumbling softly in the background as he struggled to express all the things he had felt.

"I hoped you'd leave Springfield. Then I learned that you were applying for work and I used my influence to keep you from finding anything. I hinted that if you found employment I would use any power against the company that hired you. I hated you for getting under my skin."

Wearily, he raked his fingers through his hair. The strain of saying aloud the things he'd felt was evident in his face and gestures. "Then, today, when I saw you at the church I knew defeat. I went there telling myself it was because of Lea. But I was hoping to see you. I half-hoped you wouldn't be there, though; I wanted an excuse to ignore everything I feel for you. Then, when you left so suddenly, I vindictively hoped that you were feeling a little of what I was experiencing. I've spent the last few hours coming to terms with myself. I suppose I was working up the courage to come here, half-afraid you would refuse to see me.''

A flash of lightning revealed the almost haggard look on Sloan's face as he turned to her. ''Cara, have I completely ruined what we could have had? Is it too late?''

In answer she raised her mouth to meet his, holding him and saying without words what she felt. ''I meant it when I said, 'I love you,' Sloan. I thought I could build a life without you. But it would be only half a life. I'll live by your rules. Whatever you want, for as long as I can have you, that's all I ask.''

The familiar husky voice was tense with emotion. His dark eyes searched her face as he spoke. ''I know, now, how wrong I was.'' A shudder went through him as she laid a hand against his chest, feeling the strong heartbeat against her soft palm. ''It's cost me nearly everything I am to admit that.''

He wiped a hand wearily across his face. ''What a mess I've made of things. The first day I visited the Complex I saw you. I wanted you. Just wanted you—as a woman. Another conquest. I believed my own publicity, I suppose. When we did meet, you were so aloof, so untouchable, that I was intrigued. Later, I checked up on you, read your files, talked to Quinn, watched you the few times I was at Triad, and a plan came to me. I would keep you on as my executive assistant. It was a natural. You were already there, had all the qualifications. I felt it would be just a matter of time before I had you in my bed.''

She well remembered that period in her life. She didn't want to hear the words, but she knew he needed to say them.

"Then I saw you in the cafeteria that day and heard your comments, both there and later, in Kate's office. I was annoyed that you ignored me and it was irritating that you could get to me so easily. It was a new experience and I didn't like the feeling. But I was curious, too." The sound he made was half-laugh, half-sigh. "The more you interested me, the more I pretended that it was all sexual. I convinced myself that once I had you, none of it would matter anymore. You would be like—well, like all the rest."

He turned to her and ran a finger down her cheek. "I hadn't counted on your being inexperienced, either. I didn't want the responsibility that entailed. But in the end, it didn't matter.

"Just a man wanting a woman, that's all it was. But when I held you, felt you respond to me, it didn't work out that way. You were an obsession. You kept loving me, opening yourself up to me, even when I hurt you. And every time I tried to cut you out of my mind I hurt myself more. You fought back, defending your right to independence, and that rankled, too. It all kept building until I couldn't handle any of it. I couldn't accept you at face value. I suppose it all comes down to that. I thought you must have some motive. No woman had ever given me anything without expecting a lot more in return. But you gave all of yourself without asking anything but a little of myself."

He had moved forward as he spoke and now leaned back again. "I'd never counted on the kind of commitment you needed. When I realized you'd told me the truth—when I held you and knew I was the first man you'd loved—it was more than I could cope with."

He shifted on the pillows beside her before continuing. "I arranged for you to work at Triad that day.

I wanted to see if you'd changed your mind. Maybe I realized then I couldn't let you go; I don't know. I wanted to see you, but my pride kept getting in the way, so I arranged for you to be assigned to Triad. When you ran away from me in what seemed to be total disgust, I didn't know what to do.''

So much time wasted. If only she had talked to him then, maybe they could have been together all this time.

"I'm sorry, Sloan. I was so hurt and I couldn't bear any more."

"I'm to blame. If I'd treated you with half the respect and tenderness you deserve, neither of us would have been hurt so much. I was intent on my own purposes, never giving a thought to you. What a pompous . . .'' The muscle in his jaw clenched again. "I deserved just what I got.

"As for Susan, we had one almighty row and she admitted that she was behind your problems at the second temporary agency. I had given up trying to drive you out of my life by then, but even that I have to credit to my sin. By the time I'd finished exerting my power, your reputation wasn't worth much, anyway. It was her setup, but I might have done the same. When I learned what she'd done, the situation she had placed you in, I wanted to kill her. Instead, I fired her and she's already left town."

Absently, his long fingers pleated her sleeve as he talked, regressing to an earlier time. "Cara, you'll never know what it did to me when you came to the cemetery that day. I'd never had anyone care enough to want to help me, to be a part of the bad as well as the good. You were the only one to understand that, much as I resented my father, he was all I had. I suppose I hadn't even realized that until the last time I saw him—sick, beyond reclaiming because of alcohol. I tried to see it as the fault of a woman, my mother, for leaving him as she did. But that failed.

"You were right. We are what we make of ourselves. I realized then that I had subconsciously been using my mother's actions as an excuse for my own. When you came to me that day, it was the turning point somehow, part of the reason for what I later did to you. I began to take a long look at myself and I didn't like what I saw. I wish I had done it sooner."

Her heart nearly broke at the realization of just how empty his life had been and how very much she wanted to fill it. "It's not important now, Sloan. I meant what I said. That's all past. I love you; I want us to be together."

The silence in the apartment was broken only by the growing storm outside and slowly, without words, they slid to the rug and lay together. She marveled at the feeling of togetherness, of oneness, she felt with him. It was what she had longed for.

For a moment he searched her face, reading all the love reflected there. "You said once that everything had to be according to my rules. No exceptions. I want to change the rules, Cara. It's taken me a long time to say it, but I do love you—too much to ask more than I can give in return. I want all of you. I want you there when I wake up each morning. I want to reach out and feel you beside me in the night. I want my ring on your finger. But more than that. I want to be there for you. I want to be there when you need me." He gathered her close, as if afraid that she might draw away from him even now.

"I want that lifetime commitment I thought I would never want, never need. I need it now, from you, Cara. Teach me your kind of love."

Such a welling up of hope, of total joy. Words were unnecessary. She melted willingly into his arms, into the safety of his love, and her body, her lips, told him all he needed to know. Her love for him was as sure as it had ever been.

She might never understand the how or why of it, but she knew that love was a law unto itself, a law stronger, even, than Sloan. And love had its reasons; perhaps their coming together now would be all the sweeter, all the more lasting, for the pain that had gone before. And she knew that, at last, love's sweet giving was to be hers and Sloan's, together.

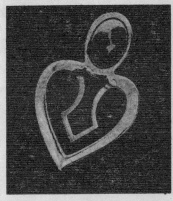

MORE ROMANCE FOR
A SPECIAL WAY TO RELAX

$1.95 each

1 ☐ TERMS OF SURRENDER Dailey

2 ☐ INTIMATE STRANGERS Hastings

3 ☐ MEXICAN RHAPSODY Dixon

4 ☐ VALAQUEZ BRIDE Vitek

5 ☐ PARADISE POSTPONED Converse

6 ☐ SEARCH FOR A NEW DAWN Douglass

7 ☐ SILVER MIST Stanford

8 ☐ KEYS TO DANIEL'S HOUSE Halston

9 ☐ ALL OUR TOMORROWS Baxter

10 ☐ TEXAS ROSE Thiels

11 ☐ LOVE IS SURRENDER Thornton

12 ☐ NEVER GIVE YOUR HEART Sinclair

13 ☐ BITTER VICTORY Beckman

14 ☐ EYE OF THE HURRICANE Keene

15 ☐ DANGEROUS MAGIC James

16 ☐ MAYAN MOON Carr

17 ☐ SO MANY TOMORROWS John

18 ☐ A WOMAN'S PLACE Hamilton

19 ☐ DECEMBER'S WINE Shaw

20 ☐ NORTHERN LIGHTS Musgrave

21 ☐ ROUGH DIAMOND Hastings

22 ☐ ALL THAT GLITTERS Howard

23 ☐ LOVE'S GOLDEN SHADOW Charles

24 ☐ GAMBLE OF DESIRE Dixon

25 ☐ TEARS AND RED ROSES Hardy

26 ☐ A FLIGHT OF SWALLOWS Scott

27 ☐ A MAN WITH DOUBTS Wisdom

28 ☐ THE FLAMING TREE Ripy

29 ☐ YEARNING OF ANGELS Bergen

30 ☐ BRIDE IN BARBADOS Stephens

31 ☐ TEARS OF YESTERDAY Baxter

32 ☐ A TIME TO LOVE Douglass

33 ☐ HEATHER'S SONG Palmer

34 ☐ MIXED BLESSING Sinclair

35 ☐ STORMY CHALLENGE James

36 ☐ FOXFIRE LIGHT Dailey

Silhouette Special Edition

MORE ROMANCE FOR
A SPECIAL WAY TO RELAX

**LOOK FOR _THE HEART'S VICTORY_
BY NORA ROBERTS AVAILABLE IN NOVEMBER
AND _TENDER DECEPTION_ BY PATTI BECKMAN
IN DECEMBER.**

Coming Next Month

A Matter Of Time by Brooke Hastings

A divorce had left Sylvie Kruger unwilling to trust. But Jordan Garner Rutledge, son of an old Kentucky family, was determined to change all that and lead her into a love that was unmatched by any passion she had ever known.

Finders Keepers by Dixie Browning

All that Hallie Parrish had found in her brief marriage was unhappiness, her only solace the child she bore. Then her late husband's brother, Trenton Northcutt, entered her life, and she found the currents flowing between them too strong to be denied.

Stormy Affair by Brenda Trent

Paige never dreamed that the Caribbean cruise would lead her from an unhappy past into a tomorrow filled with hope, but in Mac Lane's arms she found a peace and an excitement that would not let her rest!

Designed For Love by Tracy Sinclair

Merry married Jake and soon found he was a man of hidden strength; he believed in satisfied desire—and in love. Merry stood no chance against him, and soon the marriage that had begun so coolly blazed a trail to the eternal stars.

Goddess Of The Moon by Leslie Thomas

Casey Hampton had found the life she wanted, but one youthful indiscretion still haunted her. Now Brandon was back and their hearts warred once again; nothing could dim the fires that raced through their blood.

Thorne's Way by Joan Hohl

Valerie Jordan felt that her life had ended with her fiance's death. But when she met Jonas Thorne his touch lit a fire within her and with a firm determination he led her into a future brighter than any she had dreamed.

READERS' COMMENTS ON SILHOUETTE SPECIAL EDITIONS:

"I just finished reading the first six Silhouette Special Edition Books and I had to take the opportunity to write you and tell you how much I enjoyed them. I enjoyed all the authors in this series. Best wishes on your Silhouette Special Editions line and many thanks."

—B.H.*, Jackson, OH

"The Special Editions are really special and I enjoyed them very much! I am looking forward to next month's books."

—R.M.W.*, Melbourne, FL

"I've just finished reading four of your first six Special Editions and I enjoyed them very much. I like the more sensual detail and longer stories. I will look forward each month to your new Special Editions."

—L.S.*, Visalia, CA

"Silhouette Special Editions are — 1.) Superb! 2.) Great! 3.) Delicious! 4.) Fantastic! . . . Did I leave anything out? These are books that an adult woman can read . . . I love them!"

—H.C.*, Monterey Park, CA

* names available on request